THE WIFE'S REVENGE

DEIRDRE PALMER

Copyright © Deirdre Palmer, 2023

The moral right of the author has been asserted.

Ebook ISBN: 978-1-80508-069-5
Paperback ISBN: 978-1-80508-071-8

Cover design: Lisa Horton
Cover images: Trevillion, Shutterstock

Published by Storm Publishing.
For further information, visit:
www.stormpublishing.co

To Michael, Christopher and Luke

PROLOGUE

OCTOBER 2015

If this was a film or television drama, this is the moment when there would be a blood-freezing scream, or an air-splitting yell. At the very least, a short, jagged cry. The sound, whichever form it takes, would collide with the rockface and fling its echo around the valley.

But there is no echo, because there is no sound.

Mildly surprised by this silent departure – her voice had split the skies only moments before – I move closer to the bitten-off edge and peer down into the inky chasm of the chalk pit. Tree-tops shimmy in the darkness; a branch pops. Then all is still, the silence complete.

I spend a few minutes standing on the cliff edge, gazing out. It's fully dark now, the horizon mashed into invisibility. The lights of a plane flash white as it passes overhead, heading into London Gatwick, reminding me of summer and holidays. *We should go somewhere next year...*

Turning away from the rising shelf of turf, I cut across the grass, through the scrub of gorse and walk back down the path. On the cinder patch that serves as a car park, there are two cars:

mine and hers. Hers has one of those scented things dangling from the rear-view mirror. I can see its bottle-shaped silhouette.

I never doubted she'd come tonight, that she wouldn't be able to resist. Her car was already here when I arrived, and I found her standing on the crest of the clifftop. Her back was to me as she waited, and I held back for a moment, watching, enjoying the delay. Then, when she turned and saw me, the look on her face was almost reward enough.

It didn't have to end like that. Had she seen sense, accepted who was in charge here and that it wasn't her – it never had been – there might have been a different outcome.

But there, it's done now.

I get into my car and start the engine. At the bottom of the hill where the track meets the main road, I don't pull out immediately. I'm tempted to take the left-hand turn onto the road which winds around the foot of the hill and passes the floor of the chalk pit, but with the darkness and thickness of the undergrowth, I doubt there'd be anything to see. And I'm not sure I want to. Besides, it's well out of my way and I need to be home. I said I wouldn't be long.

I turn right and head back towards the village, filling the silence in the car with a phone-in programme on Radio Sussex.

ONE

FRAN, MAY 2018

The front door opens violently, colliding with the coat stand, and I tumble into the hallway, cartoon-style. In my hurry to be indoors I must have leant too heavily on it as I put the key in the lock. Righting myself, I paste on a send-up grin in case anyone's watching, but the hallway is empty and nobody comes out to see what the noise was.

I take a few moments to gather myself. My face in the mirror looks heated from the warmth of the day, but otherwise normal. I often take the short cut home, leaving the vets' practice where I'm a receptionist by the back way and following the public footpath. It zigzags between the houses behind the high street, then cuts across the point of the V-shaped woods, emerging conveniently at the end of our road, Woodside Villas, which is a dead-end to traffic. The footpath is well used by the locals, and I have never felt unsafe, even in winter when the woods are dark.

It was different today. A strapping, gum-chewing teenage boy walking an incongruously tiny dog swaggered towards me on the path through the woods. He lives down our road and gave me a nod as he passed. I saw no one else, but sensed a presence from behind, as if somebody was on my heels and wanting to pass in a hurry. When I glanced around there was nobody there, but my pace quickened anyway. After what happened earlier today, it's not surprising that my imagination had pitched into overdrive, and I'm glad to be safely home.

For once, the girls are all in the same place at the same time, lined up on the living room sofa in front of their favourite film. Kitty and Hazel are elbow-to-elbow, Caitlin a studious nine inches away from Hazel, with Miss T, our tortoiseshell-and-white cat, doing duty as a furry barrier between them.

A few more minutes' respite in mind, I sidle past to the kitchen-diner and lump the bag of shopping I picked up at lunchtime onto the table littered with abandoned homework and jam-smeared plates. My laptop is open on the counter-top, the screen stamped with fingerprints.

'Mum? Here!'

Obediently, I trot back to the living room. There's no use asking if Kitty could not have dragged herself up and come to me.

'You missed Nan. She Skyped.' Her eyes remain glued to the TV screen.

'Did she? But it's five o'clock in the morning in New Zealand. Are they okay? Has something happened?'

'Yes,' Caitlin says, looking up at me. 'The birds were singing so loudly in the garden they woke her up.'

'That's not what Mum means.' Kitty lifts her eyes theatrically. 'She means, has anything *bad* happened.'

Caitlin removes her glasses, polishes them with the hem of her school dress and puts them on again. 'That isn't what Mum said. She said has something happened and it has.'

'Birds don't count as something happening,' Kitty says.

Hazel looks from one of her sisters to the other. 'Caitlin

knows what *she* means, and *we* know what Mum means. End of. I am trying to watch this film.'

These roundabout conversations are commonplace when Caitlin's involved. They've become so much a part of the way my family communicates that it's useless trying to change it now.

'Nan Skyped for a chat then. That's nice.' I smile despite feeling disappointed that I missed my mother's call. 'Did you give her all your news?'

'We would have done if there was any,' Kitty says.

'The everyday stuff, I mean. Nan likes to know how you're all getting on at school and what you've been up to.'

'I showed her my chart.' Caitlin's eyes are bright behind their lenses. 'It tells me what sweets I ate on each day going right back to Christmas. Every kind of sweet has got a different-coloured square. There's a key on the back.'

'You eat too many sweets. You don't need a chart to tell you that. It's pointless,' Hazel says.

Caitlin pouts. 'It's *not* pointless. Nan thought it was very organised of me.'

'Nan would say that because she's Nan.'

'That doesn't make sense...'

Kitty springs up from the sofa. 'That's it. I'm gone.' At fifteen, there's only so much verbal sparring she can take from twelve and nine-year-old sisters, even if she was the one to kick it off in the first place. 'Unless you need me to help with the dinner, Mum?'

'No thanks, love. I'll do it. Where's Dad, by the way?'

Kitty follows me to the kitchen, slip-slapping along the hallway in her scuffed, half-on, half-off, ballerinas. 'He went back out. He's gone to somebody's house to measure up for a staircase or something. He said he won't be long.'

Hector is a bespoke carpenter; it's his own business and he

has a workshop ten miles away from our village. Working for himself means he's fairly flexible and, traffic allowing, he can get home in good time. As I work just along the road, it means at least one of us is on hand to deal with any family crisis.

Kitty is about to leave the kitchen when she pauses in the doorway.

'Tessa rang for you, by the way. I asked if there was a message, but she said no, she'd ring back later.'

The bottle of orange juice I'd unpacked almost slips from my grasp.

'Tessa Grammaticus?' I ask.

'Is there another one?' Kitty says, and then she's gone.

'You don't like Tessa, do you?' Hector says, as we're getting ready for bed.

I take some clean pyjamas out of the drawer. 'I didn't say that.'

If Hector knew how my heart rises to my throat each time Tessa's name is mentioned, even two years on, he might be asking a different question.

'You didn't seem keen to get involved with her latest charity project.'

'That doesn't mean I don't like her.'

Hector flings back the duvet and gets into bed. 'No, but it was more the cagey way you spoke to her.'

'Cagey.'

'Yep.' Hector thumbs his Bernard Cornwell until the till receipt he uses as a bookmark reveals itself.

'I was surprised she asked me, that was all,' I say.

A half-truth. Quarter, even.

Setting aside the link between us of which, fortunately, Tessa is entirely ignorant, she and I would never be close friends. With some people, you just know, don't you? Naturally, we come into contact through her daughter, Zoe, being friends with Hazel, and the various school and village activities, but that's as far as it goes.

Tessa has a measured way of speaking, as if she's rehearsed what she has to say beforehand, which makes me slightly fearful of what I say in reply in case I get it wrong. Grace knew exactly what I meant when I mentioned it to her. Knowing it's not just me makes my constant wariness of Tessa slightly less exhausting.

As far as Tessa's social circle is concerned, I sit somewhere on the outer perimeter, so, yes, I was surprised that she'd phoned. Most of my information from that quarter arrives second- or even third-hand. Hazel and Zoe make their own social arrangements, checking in with one or other parent that whatever they want to do is okay, and cadging lifts if necessary. I was therefore not expecting Tessa's call to be about anything of that nature, and I'd been on pins all evening wondering if she would phone back and, if so, what for. The fear never leaves me. It's part of who I am, and no more than I deserve.

She rang just after nine, sounding as if she'd raced up two flights of stairs. Her normal voice slides like chilled cream from a spoon, and again I felt the barbs of anxiety at this small difference.

'It's about my coffee morning in aid of the hospice. I'm short of volunteers and I wondered if you would join my executive team?'

Only Tessa could label a group of mostly willing volunteers as her executive team. It was a good job she couldn't see my smirk, which arose from relief as much as mild amusement. But the charity events she runs always raise buckets of money for whatever cause is flavour of the month, and I can't help but admire her flair and organisational skills. Tessa, of course, has plenty of time for these things; she stopped working when they moved to Oakheart – whatever sort of work it was. Ben never said, and I never asked him. The less I knew about Tessa, the better.

'Me?' I wondered for a second whether she'd meant to ring me or whether she'd mixed up the numbers.

'Yes. It would be good to have you on board, Fran.'

I must have agreed to help, despite my apparently cagey tone, because Tessa went on to give me details of the 'inaugural meeting' of her team.

After the call, needing something to do with my hands, I texted Grace: *Did Tessa contact you?*

Her reply flew back: *God, yes. More terribly good causes. Wasn't fast enough to think up an excuse.*

That made me feel better, knowing I hadn't been singled out. Tessa's executive team will consist of the usual suspects and I'll be corralled like a nervous pony.

It's not until I've made a last check on the girls, the lights are out, and Hector's breathing slows in sleep, that my thoughts reel back to this morning at work. I'd been chatting to the worried elderly owner of an equally elderly spaniel in the full waiting room and hadn't noticed a delivery arriving at the reception desk. A curvy basket, handle as big as a skipping rope, spilling with pink roses and white gypsophila, was sitting in front of my keyboard.

'Somebody's popular.' Evelyn lowered her glasses on their pearl-studded chain and shone a meaningful smile at me.

'Yes, right. Who are they really for? Rowena?'

Apart from the occasional locum, Rowena is our only female vet, and therefore the most likely recipient. I picked up the basket by its handle and plonked it on the table behind me.

Grateful animal-owners often leave presents for the vets. Chocolates and tins of biscuits are favourite, which we don't mind at all, as most of them end up behind reception. Flowers are taking things a bit far, in my opinion.

'Nope. The florists' girl definitely had your name on her clipboard.'

I swung round on my chair and frowned at the flowers. 'I can't see a card.'

'Let me look.' Evelyn wheeled her own chair across the space, picked up the basket by the handle, and rotated it full circle. 'You're right. No card. I expect whoever sent them forgot to put one in, or the girl managed to lose it on the way.' Evelyn lifted her shoulders and grinned. 'Hubby getting all romantic, is he?'

I laughed at that. Hector is loving and considerate, but expensive romantic gestures are not his style. 'Shouldn't think so.'

'Well, then.' Evelyn wheeled herself backwards to her computer and resumed work on the invoices, interest in my mystery gift forgotten.

Envisaging the shrill reaction of three daughters and Hector's placid grin, I left the basket of flowers at the surgery, wedged on the narrow sill of the high window behind reception.

The flowers are not the first anonymous gift I've received, although the previous one was hellishly sinister in its nature. A month ago, there was a cake – a single red velvet cupcake topped with soft white icing and sprinkles. The discreet white box – no shop name – had found its way onto the reception desk when I came back from lunch. It had my name in pencil written in tight little letters on the lid.

I was alone at the time and Evelyn said nothing later, so presumably she hadn't noticed its arrival. It seemed odd, but not so odd as to stretch my brain cells to any great extent. We were busy, with nearly every chair in the waiting room occupied, and it was only when I was about to go home that I remembered the cake, which I'd transferred to the shelf below the counter. I popped it in my bag and took it home, feeling somewhat as if I'd taken possession of stolen goods. But it had my name on it, so clearly it wasn't meant for sharing.

Arriving home, I had twenty minutes spare before I needed to leave to collect Caitlin – just time for a cup of tea, and the cake. The first few bites set my taste buds alight. Expensive chocolate, meltingly soft, sweet sponge – delicious. Then, with half the cake left, my tongue encountered pure fire.

I spat the mouthful out in the sink, but my lips, the inside of my mouth and back of my throat were already tainted with the unmistakable searing heat of chilli. As my throat closed around a fire-pit of pain, I reached for a glass and filled it with water before I remembered that milk was required, not water. I went to the fridge, poured myself half a glass of ice-cold milk and downed it in one. I sat at the table until I'd recovered. Then I examined the remains of the cupcake. I found a minuscule piece of red matter that could have been chilli, although with the cake being red in colour, I couldn't be sure.

At least it was me, and not one of the girls who'd tried to eat the cake. How dreadful that would have been.

As I drove to fetch Caitlin, I rounded up the possibilities. Chocolate was sometimes combined with chilli, I knew, although it's not something I'd ever want to eat, and in any case I imagine it would be a lot more subtle than the throat-searing taste I'd just experienced. A mistake in the manufacturing seemed remotely possible. Or could the chilli have been added to the cake on purpose before it was delivered to me? This idea was so far-fetched I almost laughed out loud.

By the time I arrived home with Caitlin, via a lengthy visit to the supermarket and then the dry cleaner's, I'd forgotten about the cake. I remembered it the day after, but for some reason known only to the machinations of my mind, I said nothing to Hector. It didn't seem important enough to begin a conversation about it, and I let it slide.

It was around a week later when I answered a call to the surgery phone from somebody who said she was a lunch assistant at Oakheart Academy. She told me Hazel had fallen over and badly cut herself on a piece of glass. I raced round to the school, but when I arrived at the school office in a sweat, nobody knew of any such accident. On my way out along the corridor, I cupped my hands to peer through the glass door of Hazel's form room and saw her in a huddle with Zoe, sitting on a table, legs swinging, oblivious to my presence and clearly in one piece.

Later that day, I told Hector about it, while the girls were out of earshot.

'Some sort of mix-up, obviously,' he said. 'Right hand not knowing what the left hand's doing. Could be some other child got a little nick from somewhere and the dinner ladies dealt with it. It wasn't Hazel, that's the important thing.' My husband has always been a straightforward kind of guy. He sees the good in everyone, finds a rational explanation for everything; that was one of the qualities that drew me to him in the first place. Even so, I felt I'd been dismissed a little too readily.

'I know,' I said, 'but it makes you think, doesn't it?'

'Think about what? Some well-meaning person getting their wires crossed?' He kissed me, briefly, on the mouth. 'You worry too much, overthink things.'

Hector is probably right about that, and I was glad then that I hadn't told him about the chilli-laced cupcake, imagining his reaction if I'd said somebody was trying to poison me.

But I can't stop the feeling that the cake 'gift' and the strange phone call are somehow related. Both incidents are hopelessly chained together in my head, one set of thoughts refusing to exist without the other.

As I drift into sleep, the familiar click-tick of the house settling down for the night becomes the sound of chasing footsteps tapping against tree-roots on the path through the wood. This time, when I turn, I see a pair of hands outstretched towards me, holding a basket of roses.

TWO

FRAN

The next morning is the usual tumble of rushed breakfasts, mislaid homework, and slammed doors. Hazel's skirt hem has come unstitched at the back, and I am threatened with Childline when I suggest she staples it up until tonight, since her other skirt is in the laundry basket.

'I'll take a picture of the staple marks on the backs of my thighs, shall I?' she says.

I hold back my retort that if she wore longer skirts, or the despised trousers they're allowed, then staple marks on thighs would not be an issue.

Finally, Kitty, her blouse tied in a knot, showing her midriff, and Hazel, her skirt angrily stapled, set out for Oakheart Academy together and there's only Caitlin left. She stands in the kitchen doorway in her grey striped uniform dress and dark green bomber jacket – a contemporary take on the traditional blazer – and waits for me to drive her to school.

Honeybee Hall caters well for Caitlin's needs. The year group classes are small, the teaching groups even smaller, and the staff foster a culture whereby children who are a little bit different are integrated, understood and nurtured. Caitlin can stay there until she's sixteen, with no stressful change of school at eleven. Honeybee is worth every penny. This, by the way, is my opinion – not necessarily Hector's. It's twenty minutes by car on a good day. Hector would happily drive her, but at the moment, for reasons unknown, Caitlin insists I take her, and that's fine by me. I bring the car home afterwards then walk to work – parking down the high street after nine is nigh on impossible.

Caitlin stands perfectly still and straight, rucksack hitched over biscuit-coloured plaits, hands loosely linked in front of her. But her eyes behind her glasses are watchful, swivelling surreptitiously between me and her father in case there's the slightest clue that she has displeased us in some way, or displeased each other – just as bad in her book.

Hector's loose schedule means he leaves any time between seven and nine thirty, depending on his workload. This morning, he's in no hurry. As I follow Caitlin out of the front door, I feel the pressure of his hand on my bottom. It makes me giggle. Caitlin whirls round to check on me, and I straighten my face.

'I'll be done by lunch,' Hector says in a low voice. 'Can you get away early this afternoon?'

I can, as it happens. As receptionists we work flexible hours, within the bounds of the surgery opening times, and I have some time owing. I widen my eyes at Hector in a silent promise, and he responds with a comedic lascivious grin.

As I see Caitlin into the car and hop round to the driver's seat, I think again how lucky I am and how close I came to losing it all.

It's Saturday morning. After a week of squally showers and a spiteful east wind that lands on our backs like physical punches as we walk, we wake to porcelain-blue skies and mild, still air. Hector is up at eight and gone by half-past. He doesn't always work at weekends, but sometimes, as today, his potential clients are working themselves all week. He's calling on a couple in Oakheart who want him to construct a tree house for their three children. Tree houses are fine with Hector. He doesn't get many commissions for those, but when he does I see the small-boy glint in his eye and it makes me glad all over again that he swapped the pressure and edgy uncertainty of the financial world, and the deadly commute to London that went with it, to follow his dream.

I tell him I hope he enjoys his morning.

'Yes, well, a tree house beats fitted wardrobes and kitchen cupboard doors.' His voice betrays the inner guilt, still there after almost three years, that he doesn't earn a fraction of his city salary. I wish I could make the guilt go away, but I can't; it has to come from Hector himself. I know because guilt has become my specialist subject.

I hang a wash out on the line – a chore that always conjures an image of my mother battling with snow-white sheets in our windy garden, a row of coloured plastic clothes pegs clamped between her lips like the instruments of some weird form of torture.

Caitlin bursts out of the back door to remind me we're going to the shops. I assure her I haven't forgotten.

'I am ready,' she says, pointedly running her gaze from my unbrushed hair down to my worn leopard-print slippers.

'Give me five minutes.'

She looks doubtfully at me. 'Okay.' She skips off, back indoors.

Twenty minutes later, Caitlin says, 'I *knew* you wouldn't be ready in five minutes!' as we set off, leaving Kitty doing physics homework in her room. Hazel is watching TV downstairs in her pyjamas with Miss T on her lap, having assured me, a shade too forcefully to be convincing, that all her homework was done, like, ages ago.

Caitlin bounces along beside me, pin-neat in spotless blue jeans and Breton top, her favourite bag slung crosswise over her slender little figure. She smiles up at me. 'Shall we have drinks after, at the café?'

'If you like,' I say.

The main purpose of this trip is a visit to the art and craft shop which faces onto the square. It's an Aladdin's cave of art equipment, craft kits, cards and stationery – Caitlin would live in it if she could. She collects stationery like a squirrel collects nuts, and spends much of her free time drawing and painting. At school she does well, but it's in art that she shines like the star she is.

She also spends time writing painstakingly in her collection of notebooks. What she writes in them, the rest of us have no idea; we are threatened with the greatest punishment if we dare to peek.

The stand with the notebooks is where Caitlin heads first. I doubt her other notebooks are full, but that is not, apparently, the point.

'Look, they've got new ones with birds on!' Caitlin holds up a pretty pale blue A5 notebook with a pair of thrushes on the cover. 'The pages have got birds at the top. *Every* page.' Reverently, she replaces the thrush notebook and picks up another. 'Oh, magpies! Is that what they are, Mum?'

'They're jays, I think. Look at the blue flash in its feathers.'

'Yes, I think you're right.' Caitlin's pale forehead draws together in a frown. She looks at me with serious eyes.

While Caitlin focuses hard on making the right choice, I walk my fingers through the birthday cards and find the perfect one for my father whose birthday is coming up soon. I pick a typically English seaside scene to remind him of home.

When I turn round, Caitlin has chosen a notebook with a fairground carousel on the front, not birds, and has moved on to a rack containing pencil crayons.

'Caitlin, you've got about a hundred coloured pencils already.'

Her shoulders tighten in response to my tone which, too late, I realise carries a smidgeon of criticism. I smile to balance it out.

'It's fine. Take as long as you want but don't buy too many.'

She smiles back, relaxed again. 'I only need one. It's for my sweet chart. Dad bought new sweets and I haven't got a colour for them. The round black ones.'

'Pontefract cakes.'

'They weren't even cakes, though. They were liquorice pennies. It's stupid to call them cakes when they aren't.'

'Isn't it just.' I exchange a smile with the man behind the counter, the owner of the shop.

'You do have a black pencil crayon,' I point out.

'Yes, but I've already used it for blackcurrant pastilles.'

I rub the side of my face as the seed of a headache threatens to germinate. I'd like to be out of this shop now but Caitlin won't be rushed. Being her mother can be exhausting, which is not her fault, of course. I plunder my inner store of patience and stand aside while I wait for her to decide. Eventually, she chooses a dark plum-coloured crayon. I take it from her before she changes her mind and add it to our purchases on the counter.

Caitlin loops her bag over her head, undoes the zip, and produces some of her pocket money. I tell her she only needs to pay for the crayon, and the notebook is my treat. Her little face lights up and she says she loves me.

'I love you, too, darling,' I say, and finally we leave the shop, Caitlin gripping the handles of the small brown paper bag as if she's expecting it to be snatched away.

'Mum! Mummy!'

I'm on my knees on the grass, trowel in hand, when I hear the yell from above. I look up, and there's Caitlin leaning across her bedroom window sill. She only calls us Mummy or Daddy when there's a problem.

I get to my feet. 'What is it, darling?'

The window next to Caitlin's opens sharply and Kitty's head appears. 'Mum, tell her to shut up. I'm trying to concentrate!'

Kitty's window bangs shut. Caitlin has vanished, and moments later she appears in the garden. 'I've lost my bag. The one I took to the shops.' She hops from one foot to the other, eyes wide as if she's witnessed some horror.

'You couldn't have lost it. You had it across you.'

'No, Mummy. You're not listening. It *was* across me when we were out, but it wasn't when we got home. I remember now, I only had the bag from the art shop. It's not in my room or in the hall or anywhere, so I have *definitely* lost it.'

She straightens her back and folds her arms, waiting for me to solve the problem.

'Did you have much money left?'

'One pound and five pence. That's not the point. It's my favourite bag and it had my notebook in it.'

'Your new notebook was in the art shop bag, Caitlin.' I try to counteract the sharpness of my tone, probably unsuccessfully.

'No, not my *new* notebook, Mummy. Another one. My pink one, with writing already in it.'

'Okay, I'll ring the shop, and if it's there I'll pop back and fetch it,' I say, knowing I won't hear the end of this until it's sorted.

She did take the bag off when she took her money out, so it seems the most likely place. But she has to learn that we won't all jump to her command. So I add, 'But not right now, Caitlin. I've got other things to do, and so have you. You're going to Maisie's after lunch. That'll be nice, won't it?'

Caitlin's friend Maisie lives a few minutes away. Caitlin doesn't make many playdates because she finds them over-whelming and after an hour she's itching to come home, but Maisie is a bright, thoughtful little girl, an only child. She attends the primary school in the village. Her elegant Ghanaian mother is a GP at the medical centre in the village, her English father is Head of Science at Oakheart Academy. Their house is an oasis of calm, and Caitlin loves spending time there. Hazel will walk Caitlin to Maisie's; her sisters are very good with her, despite their complaining.

'It will be nice but not as nice as it usually is because I'll be worried all the time.'

'About your bag?'

'Yes, and the notebook. It's important that I have it. *Very* important.'

'I know, darling, and as soon as I've got time I'll see if I can track down your bag and your notebook.'

Caitlin looks hopefully at me, not entirely pacified but she knows not to push this any further.

'Okay. But, Mummy, when you find my bag, please promise me you won't read what's in the notebook, because it's private. Promise you won't read it.'

'I promise.' I raise the trowel as if it's a symbol of an oath. A clag of soil falls from it and drops onto my sandalled foot.

Hector arrives home in time for lunch. Kitty has already left to catch the train to Worthing with her friends, and while the rest of us have tomato soup and rolls at the kitchen table, Hector hears Hazel's and Caitlin's ideas for the perfect tree house. I've quietly tipped him off about Caitlin's missing bag, and he does a good job of distracting her.

Lunch over, Hazel says she's going to the café in the park, where her gang of friends tends to congregate, and she'll drop

Caitlin at Maisie's house on the way. Hector asks me if I want to go for a drive or a walk as it's such a lovely day. But I can tell he really wants to crack on with his plans for the tree house, so I tell him I'm going in search of Caitlin's bag and that we can do something when I come back.

Before I go out, I look around the house, eventually agreeing with Caitlin that the bag didn't make it home with us. So, I retrace our steps, starting with the art shop and ending with the café, via the post office, mini-supermarket and the bakery where I bought the rolls for lunch. If she dropped it in one of those places, surely somebody would have picked it up and handed it in. A small denim shoulder bag, appliquéd with cats and dangling with charms, obviously belonging to a child. Considering, too, that it contained only a tiny amount of money and a notebook, it would hold no appeal to a thief.

But it's a strange old world, and the bag seems to be gone for good. It's a shame as Caitlin really liked that bag but I'll take her to the shops to choose another one soon. That'll keep her happy.

Caitlin's many anxieties are often unexplainable to the rest of us, but her emphasis on the missing notebook and her firm instructions to me not to read what was in it are playing on my mind, and later on I find myself in her bedroom. Telling myself I'm being protective, not nosy, I open one or two drawers and ferret about beneath the piles of clothes. Nothing. And then, as I'm about to leave, feeling like the lowest form of life, I open the wardrobe, rifle around among the shoes and other stuff at the bottom and come up with an old shoe bag, clearly containing something other than shoes. I open it up, and find what I'm looking for.

When I go back downstairs. Hector is at his desk in the conservatory, which as well as being Hector's office doubles as a games-room and general dumping ground. He sketches rapidly, the pencil making swishing sounds on the paper as planks, ladders, ropes and hidey-holes appear, only looking up when he realises I'm standing beside him.

'What've you got there?' He frowns at my fistful of Caitlin's notebooks, then gives a little laugh. 'Fran, you haven't! She'll put a spell on you, you know that, don't you?'

'I only promised not to read the one she's lost, not these. Anyway, she won't know. I'll put them back where I found them.' I look down at the notebooks, the top one out of line where my thumb is slid under it. 'I've read some of this. I'm not sure I like it much.'

Hector's pencil presses over a line on the paper, strengthening it. 'It's not for us to like, is it?' He puts the pencil down. 'Fran, if it was Kitty or Hazel, you wouldn't be going through their stuff, would you?'

A whisker below the surface of this comment lies the inference that we – I – treat Caitlin differently from our other daughters, and it isn't right. This is Hector's take on the matter and I've learned to live with it although, at the beginning, his attitude made me feel as if I was being pushed away and my opinion didn't count.

'I would if it was for their well-being and my peace of mind, yes.' I put the notebooks down on the desk, keeping one in my hand. It's small, like the others, its hardback cover sprinkled with white stars on a bright blue background. I flick through the pages. 'Listen to this: "Today Kitty said something rude and horrible to Hazel about a boy in her class. I don't think it's fair but she didn't take any notice when I said that to her." And this: "Dad and Mum had an argument at breakfast. Dad had let his car run out of petrol and had not told Mum when she went out in it because hers would not start."'

Hector smiles. 'She's got our number all right.'

I smile, too. 'Yeah. There's more like that. Little things we all do and say, things she's noticed and not been happy with.

We do have to watch ourselves, Hec. You know how she takes the smallest thing to heart.'

'Fran, Fran...' Hector always repeats my name when he wants to get his point over. 'We can't not be ourselves, not live our lives, because we've got a little mole in our midst.'

'I know. Perhaps it's her way of dealing with life, and writing things down stops her from getting upset.'

'So...?' *Why are you worrying?* Hector's eyes say.

Why indeed? Because I do the worrying over Caitlin for both of us. Okay, that's not strictly fair; Hector and I mostly agree over the girls, Caitlin in particular. Though it wasn't always so.

'Perhaps I should talk to her.' I gaze past Hector to the garden.

'And say what? That you've gone through her notebooks, invaded her privacy? Fran, she'll never trust you again.'

He's right, of course. I give a little nod, take the notebooks upstairs, and tuck them back in their hiding place.

THREE

FRAN

Caitlin's secret writings – though probably nothing to worry about, as Hector says – only serve to add to the uneasiness in my mind. The incidents of the cupcake, the fake phone call, the basket of flowers, the sensation of being watched in the wood, are strung together like beads on a rosary. I feel my way around them at regular intervals, strengthening the link between them but unable to stop.

Why have I not told Hector about these happenings – aside from the phone call he knows about – and the way they make me feel? It's a question I ask myself. I think the answer is that I don't want him to think I'm neurotic, no more than he probably already does, anyway. But it might be time to do some sharing – not with Hector, but with a friend who has no other agenda, and who won't judge me and my wayward mind.

It's early afternoon, and there aren't many appointments in the book, so Evelyn is happy to cover. There is only one other car on the cinder patch that serves as a car park, and it isn't Grace's. I'm glad of a few more moments to gather myself. Out of the car, I roll my shoulders to loosen them, then walk up the steep, short path, the turf springy beneath my sandals. The path, no more than a balding stony strip flattened by decades of feet, pushes through a miniature forest of stubby, wind-deformed trees and delivers me to the summit where a bumpy stretch of grass rises towards the sky, hiding the shock of the sheer drop below the edge to the long-abandoned chalk pit below.

High Heaven, as it's known locally – its official name is High Hovington – has dropped off the council's radar, and the protective fence has long ago stopped serving any useful purpose, its posts sagging, the broken wires in between poking the sky like cats' whiskers. The origins of the name High Heaven have been sandpapered away by time, but its dual reputation as a meeting place for illicit lovers and a suicide spot probably have something to do with it. High Heaven is a place of secrets.

I don't mind heights; I quite like them, in fact. They don't frighten me, as other things do. I stand not far from the edge, sandals planted securely between tussocks of grass, and gaze out across swatches of green embroidered with woodland and threaded with tarmac ribbons, the fringes of Oakheart emerging from the trees, the shy glint of the river. Turning my back on the view, my gaze rests on the middle distance where sheep graze perilously on the high slopes of the South Downs. I sense movement and see the red roof of Grace's car as it bumps up the hill.

'This is a bit cloak and dagger,' she says, smiling as she traipses towards me a few minutes later. She's carrying two takeout cups. She passes me one. 'I thought we might need coffee, so I stopped off in Lower Hovington and nipped in the petrol station.'

'Nice thought. Thanks.' I hadn't explained what it was I wanted to talk about when I texted Grace. 'I didn't mean to sound secretive. I just needed some air. Plus, I wanted to talk freely without being overheard.'

Now I'm here, I feel a bit silly, as if I've magnified the whole business way out of proportion. But that's what this is about, to get Grace's take on things, which will be a lot more rational than my own.

'Sorry,' I say. 'I'm taking you away from work, aren't I?'

Grace laughs drily. 'I'm glad you did. I was about to ring a client and give her the benefit of my experience, so to speak. She's driving me nuts, wanting me to put the price of her house up by another three thousand when there are hardly any viewers as it is.' Grace is an estate agent and works from home. I'm always wary of taking advantage of her relative freedom. 'I'll leave it till tomorrow now,' she says, 'by which time I'll be the epitome of calm.'

We stumble across to a lopsided wooden bench set back amongst the gorse bushes, and I recount the incidents and how they occurred: the chilli-laced cake, the anonymous basket of flowers, and the call about Hazel having injured herself, supposedly from school. I gloss over the bit about being watched in the woods, mentioning it only as an aside.

'So, what do you think? I've gone crazy? It's okay. It's what I think, too.'

'Except you don't think that.' Grace eyes me over the top of her cup. 'Or you wouldn't be here, telling me all this.'

'You can see why I'm a teeny bit freaked out?'

'Yes, of course I can. I would be too.' Grace's smile is kind and encouraging.

My shoulder blades settle against the wooden slats of the bench. I hadn't realised I'd been holding myself so rigidly.

'The cupcake with the chilli in it... my God, Fran, you could have given it to one of the girls. Think how that would have been.'

'Oh, I've thought, lots of times. My greed saved them.' I laugh without humour.

Grace and I spend a moment in pensive, lip-biting silence.

'I suppose the cake could have been an accident,' Grace says. 'It could have come from a grateful animal-owner who had no idea what was in it.'

'Yep. Except it isn't me who makes the animals better, is it?'

'But you play a part in their care, don't you?'

'A small part, yes.' Grace has a point. 'Okay, there could be some doubt over the gift of the cake being malicious,' I continue. 'But what about the flowers? Everyone likes to be given flowers and maybe I shouldn't complain. But when they're anonymous, it puts a whole different complexion on it, and added to everything else, they gave me a bad feeling.' I think for a moment. 'It isn't the flowers themselves that bother me, it's whoever sent them.'

I have only just realised the truth of this.

'Perhaps you've got a secret admirer.' Grace grins, and nudges me.

'Don't be silly.' It's all I can do to restrain the blush that threatens. I flap a hand in front of my face, as if I'm hot.

'You really think there's a connection between these... happenings?' Grace asks, clearly not convinced.

'I know, I told you I'd gone crazy.' I raise my eyes. 'But I can't seem to detach one thing from another.'

Grace nods. 'Okay. Well then, let's see.' She stands her cup on the grass and taps a forefinger against the palm of her other hand, counting. 'Your name was on the cake box so, whatever the intentions, it was meant for you. Evelyn said she saw your name on the flower delivery sheet. The phone call was obviously for you...'

'I might have dreamed the watching in the woods part,' I say hopefully. I want that to be true, I really do. My daughters use that footpath.

'You might have,' Grace concedes, 'but if you did imagine it, it's only because you were already stressed out by the other stuff, so it's the same result, at the end of the day.'

I smile, blessing Grace for understanding.

'Fran, are you okay otherwise?' she asks. 'No problems at home or anything?'

'No, no, everything's rosy. I can't tell Hector, though. Well, I could but he'd send for the men in white coats.'

Grace laughs. 'He wouldn't.'

I let a beat of silence land. 'Hector thinks Asperger's is something dreamed up by the psychologists to explain away behaviour that's outside the norm, and to rake in a few pounds in the process.'

Grace shows no surprise at my veering off-topic; we do it all the time. 'Oh Fran, surely not.'

'Okay, I'm exaggerating. But he does think I pander to Caitlin too much and I invent problems where there aren't any. Imagine what he'd say if I told him I got upset by a gift of flowers! He wouldn't understand how confusing it was. I felt almost violated, Grace. A basket of expensive roses with no clue as to who sent them, well, it's creepy, and kind of...'

'Stalkerish?' Grace says softly, and the way she says it comforts me because I know it's not just me overreacting.

'Stalkerish, yes, exactly. Anyway, Hector would think I was making something out of nothing. It's one of my many failings, apparently.'

I temper this with a little laugh, aware that I'm starting to sound sorry for myself, as well as slightly unhinged.

'No one is perfect,' Grace says, laughing too. 'I wouldn't worry.'

I bring us back to the subject in hand. 'I do have one theory. It's a bit far-fetched but it's all I've come up with.' I tell Grace about Mirabelle Hayward: the cat lady.

Mirabelle lives in a beautiful but dilapidated Georgian house called Graylings, guarded by chipped lions on either side of the grand front door and a spike of black railings along the garden wall. I pass the house on my walk to work and can never resist glancing up at its murky windows, the lower ones partly obliterated by an indoor garden of herby-looking things growing densely in terracotta pots.

Mirabelle is well-known at our end of Oakheart as 'a character', which is one way of describing her. Apparently, she's a retired schoolteacher, retired not on age grounds – she can't be more than early sixties now – but because of her tendency to reinvent herself as old film stars and entertainers, mostly dead, at the drop of a board marker. Mainly, when she wasn't being Mrs Hayward – legend has it there was a Mr Hayward back in the mists of time – she was Audrey Hepburn reincarnated, but it could have been anybody. Whether this tale is true or not, I have no more idea than have the people I've heard it from.

It's mostly at the surgery where tales about Mirabelle are hatched and fostered, since she's a regular client. Mirabelle has cats, five at the last estimation. They're well fed and cared for; in fact they probably receive more care and attention than their owner gives herself. As Evelyn says, cats don't care about a bit of dust as long as they know where their next meal is coming from.

We have no idea if the house is dusty, but judging by the state of the outside and the grime on the windows, it's a fair assumption. Mirabelle herself looks clean enough, if not particularly tidy with her wild, brick-brown hair fizzing around her head like a halo and an old pea-green coat thrown over something floral with a hem that dips up and down. She always wears make-up, with bright red lipstick, perhaps in homage to the Hollywood stars whose souls she inhabits.

Mirabelle never bothers with trivialities like appointments. She just turns up at the surgery with one, sometimes two, cats tucked into a fraying wicker cat basket along with an assortment of blankets, and the vets always see her. The receptionists have long since learned there's no point in arguing the case and getting Mirabelle to come back at a more convenient time. We simply alert the vets on duty, Evelyn with a lot of eye-rolling and tutting.

Grace is no stranger to the status of Mirabelle Hayward in our community, so I cut straight to the chase.

'A couple of months ago, Mirabelle turned up one morning with Humphrey – her tabby cat, named after Bogart, apparently – and plonked him in the middle of the counter in his basket.'

I wasn't in the best of moods at the time. I'd refereed a futile argument between Kitty and Hazel at breakfast, which had spun way out of control, ended in tears from Hazel, and put our whole schedule out. Hector was so fed up with it all he said he didn't have time to drive Caitlin to school and left me to it, and anyway she'd kicked off, saying it had to be me. By the time I'd dropped an angry and tearful Caitlin off eight minutes late, and got myself back home and to work, I was hot and cross... as well as late.

'God, I hate that, being late when it's not your fault,' Grace says. 'So, what happened with Humphrey?'

'He died, that's what happened.'

'Oh dear. Poor thing.'

'So, David, the vet who saw him, said Humphrey had probably passed away on the way to the surgery, and if he hadn't, he was in such a poor state he wouldn't have lasted much longer. Old age, basically. Mirabelle had brought him in the week before, got the vet to sort out some tablets and what have you, but really, they were giving her false hope. Poor old Humphrey had reached the end of his days; he was at least twenty-one and his body just said, "no more".'

'And Mirabelle?'

'She wasn't having it. She insisted he'd been fine when they left home and moving about in the basket when they got to the surgery. She'd only brought him in for a check-up, she said. But here's the thing: she said it was *my* fault.'

'*Your* fault? How?'

'She said I made them wait too long, and that I was "care-less" with Humphrey. That's what she said, then she made a holy fuss in front of a full waiting room. Honestly, all I did was put the basket down on the floor beside the counter because it was in the way. Okay, I got caught up with other clients and it was a while before I could slip in and tell David the cat was there, but she never said it was urgent because as far as she was concerned, it wasn't. Anyway, you know the way she swans in and expects to be seen right away, ahead of the queue. I wasn't in the mood for her. Not that it would have made any difference what time the cat was seen. He'd passed on to the great cattery in the sky, and that was that. She said I'd mishandled him, and he'd been left sitting in a draught from the door and it must have affected his breathing.'

'She didn't blame the vet then?'

'Not at all. It's those who stand guard out front she has an issue with. Me in particular.'

'So, you think she's behind all of this?'

I pause, gazing out at the view. A pair of hang-gliders appears in the distance, brilliant arcs of colour cutting into the blue. 'Maybe. It's a possibility.' I turn to Grace. 'Mirabelle isn't exactly level-headed. I wouldn't put it past her. Do you remember those slogans she painted on the pub wall that time, about the evils of drink?'

'That was her?' Grace frowns. 'Oh yes, it was, wasn't it? She owned up, as I remember. The next thing we knew she was back in the bar herself, downing a pint!'

'That's what I mean. She's not right up here.' I tap my temple. 'It's not her fault, poor soul, and I do feel sorry for her. But if she's got it in for somebody, who knows what she could do?' I shrug, appealing to Grace to support this theory because it's all I've got, and goodness knows I need something.

Grace takes another moment to consider this. 'She's wacky enough to play those sorts of tricks, I suppose. Is she that devious, though? Sending flowers anonymously when the other things – if they were down to her – were plain awful?'

'She might be delusional but she's not stupid. She might have thought about it and decided she'd make more impact if she confused me. If so, she got it spot on.'

'Unless...' Grace's eyes widen, 'unless she regretted her complaint against you and the flowers were meant as an apology.'

'I suppose it could be that, although what would be the point if I didn't know they were from her? We could sit here all night and come up with all sorts of wild explanations, if we put our minds to it.'

Grace laughs. 'Let's not, though.' She sees my face, which must display the hotchpotch of emotions that make my gut churn, and reaches for my hand. 'Fran, you can't let this upset you. If it is Mirabelle, and I can see how you'd think it might be, then she'll soon get tired of playing silly games. If it's not her, there's probably some perfectly innocent explanation, and then...'

'Then I need to forget all about it. Blame my hormones or something.' I place both hands firmly on my knees. 'You're right. I just needed somebody to say it. Thanks.'

We leave soon after – Grace for home while I fetch Caitlin from school. I can tell Grace isn't convinced that these weird happenings are even linked, let alone down to Mirabelle Hayward, no more than I am myself. But talking things through with her has definitely brought my stress levels down and convinced me – almost – that I'm not paranoid to have worried about it all in the first place.

As I head for Honeybee Hall, I put music on in the car, a compilation of eighties hits. After I've collected Caitlin, I play another CD, and Caitlin jogs about happily in time to the music, the traumas of our rushed morning forgotten.

FOUR

TESSA

It's three months now since I discovered the truth. Not that I didn't know it already, in my mind, in my heart, in every cell of me, but that shred of hard evidence gave me the leverage I needed. Before that, I'd fed my suspicion by watching and learning. I observed her movements, absorbed the pattern of her days, her working life, the dynamics of her family. This is Oakheart – it wasn't difficult. I was never sure how I was going to use the information I gathered. I only knew that one day I would. Sometimes, playing the long game is the best way. The only way. Two years since it ended. For them. For me, it never ends. At least, it hasn't yet.

I'd been searching the drawers of Ben's desk in his study under the eaves, not to pry – that's not my way – but to ferret out the paperwork from the time we had the beams treated for woodworm. Something the new insurance company wanted; I can't remember exactly why now, only if I leave these things to Ben they tend not to get done at all.

Amongst the detritus at the bottom of the drawer, I found a photo, slightly out of focus, printed on ordinary paper and roughly cut out to size. Her. Francesca Oliver. Standing on a ridge that could only be High Heaven, her hair whipped across her face by the wind. The lower part of her face was hidden by her hand, and behind that hand I sensed a laugh, a non-serious protest against the camera phone.

I never caught them in the act, her and Ben, certainly nothing so blatant as that. I could have, if I'd been so inclined. Other women in my situation would confront and blame and scream and shout, all the way to the divorce courts. I'm cleverer than that. Ben is my life, Zoe too. My marriage, my family, my beautiful home – nobody in their right mind would jeopardise all of that because of the occasional worthless slut. They get what they deserve, in the end. Maria did. Besides, Ben needs protecting from himself; that has always been my job.

Eight weeks? Nine at most. That's how long it lasted with Fran. Illicit lovers believe they're invincible – Ben did, anyway. But it's there if you care to look; the body language, the studious keeping away from one another whenever their paths meet by necessity or accident. Minimal direct speech. No eye contact. No touching. Definitely no touching.

Even now, all still there, so incredibly obvious. Laughable, really, their naivety. As for her husband, Hector the carpenter, either he's an idiot or as shrewd as I am. My money's on the first, although he may yet surprise me.

Once you begin to find your way into somebody's head, the path becomes clearer and straighter, as if it's signposted. Inspiration and opportunity strike when you're least expecting them. Fran wasn't on my mind at all when I was shopping in the high street the other day and saw her and her smallest daughter – Caitlin, I think her name is – going into the art shop on the square.

I sat on the bench beneath the oak tree and watched; I was in shadow, so unnoticeable at a distance. They were in the shop a long time and I'd begun to lose interest when out they came, the child practically dancing, changing a small carrier bag from hand to hand. She stopped and bent down to do something to her shoe, and another bag, one of those kiddy ones, slipped off her shoulder and landed right there on the pavement. She didn't notice. Neither did her mother.

It's a pretty little bag, denim with appliquéd cats, and those dangly charms attached to the zip tab – Zoe's got quite a collection herself, although she mainly keeps them in her bedroom now as if she still likes them but feels she's getting that bit too old for them. But it's what I found inside the bag that's of interest. There was a little money – shame about that – but it was the notebook that caught my attention: pink, satisfyingly chunky to hold, though not so easily replaced as the money and bag, considering what's written in it. How extraordinary that it came into my hands at just the right time.

It's here, in the bottom drawer of my bedside cabinet. Ben has no cause to look in there, nor Zoe. She has all she needs; nothing I have is of any use to her. The small change I dropped into Zoe's money box, and the bag itself I put out in the wheelie bin on collection day, wrapped in newspaper.

I check my watch; Zoe will be home in ten minutes. But it's enough time for my daily fix. The writing has become familiar now – small, round letters, carefully spaced. She writes well for a child of her age. I've turned down the corner of the page of my favourite part:

We went to London today and in the big shop the escalator was broken and we wanted to go upstairs. Kitty and Hazel went in the lift but Mum went all funny and squashed my hand really hard so I went up the stairs with her. There were hundreds of stairs to the top but I didn't mind because Mum has something called clostofobia which means she gets really scared in small places like lifts. I wish she did not have that thing. I don't like it when Mummy is scared.

The key turns in the front door lock, and I hear chatter. Zoe's home, and it sounds as if Hazel is with her. I shove the notebook back in the drawer and I'm still in the bedroom when Zoe calls out.

'Mum? You there? I'm giving Hazel some mags. Is it okay if she comes up?'

'Of course!'

I hear Zoe coming upstairs, Hazel clumping behind. The child has a heavy tread – how she ever did ballet I'll never know. Her elder sister is as lithe as a show pony, and the little one's shaping up to be the same.

I come out onto the landing and say hello to the Olivers' middle daughter.

'How's your mother?' I smile at Hazel.

'Fine, thanks.' She smiles back with a touch of shyness, her eyes sliding past mine.

Zoe gives me an exasperated look and the two girls vanish into her bedroom and shut the door.

A fountain of girly chatter erupts now that I'm out of their hearing. I can't help but smile as a wave of love for my daughter pitches to shore and curls itself around my heart. I would never put her through the trauma of separation from her beloved daddy, no more than I could be apart from her myself.

When I was Zoe's age, I lost everybody I loved, and everybody who loved me – if they did love me; that was never a given. My father had a string of other women going back years, and my mother, at the end of her tether and sick of pretending everything was fine, eventually stopped protecting me and my sister, Amelia, from the truth. She would make pointed remarks to us behind his back, and in front of him, too, sometimes, which he would brush off as a joke. But it was more what was not said than what was: our father's absences, the loaded silences. Not that Amelia and I hadn't already worked out for ourselves what was going on. Why she hadn't divorced him years before was a mystery to me.

And yet, perhaps it wasn't so strange. My parents had

married when my mother was twenty-one, my father thirty-two. He was the manager of a small scaffolding firm. My mother was a nurse but hated it, and instantly gave it up when she married my father. Thoroughly immersed in domesticity, she would have found it hard to return to the world of work, had she been willing. And with the two of us to care for, she needed my father for financial security which, although limited – there never seemed to be much spare money – was the only thing he had to offer, as far as I could see.

He left us several times, sometimes on my mother's insistence, occasionally of his own volition. Then, one day, he left and never came back. A cautious peace settled over the house, and I began to think that life with just the three of us may not be such a bad thing. But before long, my mother retreated, as surely as if she'd found herself a cave and dragged a boulder to its mouth, shutting herself inside and everyone else out. Amelia and I looked after ourselves, went to school each day, and kept our small terraced house in a scruffy Plymouth street in reasonable order. And we looked after our mother, when she let us.

Amelia was – is – two years older than me. As time went on, I began to notice how like our father she was, in looks and in mannerisms, whereas I didn't seem to be like either of them. Somehow, she made contact with Dad – I never knew how; she kept it secret from me, but perhaps he wrote to her – and she went to live with him, somewhere up north, I understood. I never heard from either of them again.

Everyone's gone. I include my mother in that because living inside her own little bubble, she might as well have been. She did eventually stir herself sufficiently to move from Plymouth to a tumbledown cottage in the Devon countryside, a place I managed to visit only once because I didn't feel welcome. She's dead now, in any case, killed in a horse-riding accident five years ago. Nobody was more surprised than me that she'd taken up riding. It was her escape, she said, in a rare moment when she said anything at all.

Ben is nothing like my father. Too handsome for his own good, he's tempted by a pretty face, a willing victim in the games these women play; women like Maria and Fran. He doesn't have feelings for them. They're his entertainment, his little sideline – Ben has the lowest boredom threshold of anyone I've ever met.

Ben loves me, would do anything for me. I wanted Rose Cottage from the moment I saw it. I deserved that house. It was a stretch even with Ben's salary – he worked then, as he does now, in television advertising, braving the daily commute to London – yet he bid more than the asking price to make me happy.

So, I love our house, and the village is quaint and has plenty to offer, but I've never felt completely a part of it. I don't have friends, not real friends. I'm just not good at making them. I can be sociable when the need arises but I'm not the sort of woman other women are drawn to, not with any measure of closeness. I wonder sometimes if I'm like my mother and I put up barriers, preferring to inhabit my own private world. I hate to think I'm like her in any way, but I guess it was always a possibility. If so, I can live with that. I keep busy and I'm never lonely.

Our lifestyle, our family, is all I've ever wanted, all I need. The Grammaticus family unit, with all its flaws, is for ever. Others must pay the price.

FIVE

FRAN

As instructed, we gather at seven p.m. in the small back room of the Crown, conveniently opposite Tessa's house, which is a Grade II listed affair: leaded light windows, dark beams splicing dirty-cream walls, thatch as heavy as a frown. Its name – Rose Cottage – is engraved on a bit of slate that purports to be rough-cut, attached to the wall beside the door, around which the eponymous pink roses gallivant in supreme artistic formation.

Okay, I'm being catty. It is a beautiful house, much admired, too big to be called a cottage. Hector would love to live in it, or something like it, instead of our practical box with no kerb appeal. He would move in an instant if he found something like the Grammaticus's house that we could actually afford. But I like our house. I've grown fond of its angular ugliness. One day, I may have to face Hector's hankering for wonky walls, impractical rooms and an inglenook, but not yet.

There are eight of us around the table in the pub, squashed onto an L-shaped banquette or perched on stools. Like Grace and me, the other women – they are all women – are mostly Oakheart Academy mothers. The school is Tessa's favoured hunting ground when lassoing her volunteers. It makes things easier, I suppose. Grace nudges me and makes a face as Tessa, in a chair with arms, set a foot or so apart from the rest of us, sips her iced-and-sliced tonic water as if it's finest Champagne, which it wouldn't be as Tessa doesn't drink. The rest of us sink into our glasses of wine or halves of cider and wait for our leader to begin.

The red-brick Victorian building that houses Oakheart's public library and small museum has a function room with a kitchen on an upper floor, and this is apparently where the coffee morning will be held. Tessa looks around us all for approval – a rubber-stamping exercise since she's already booked it, but we all agree it fits the bill. Obviously, we can't hold the event at the hospice itself, and anyway, it's too far out of the village. We go on to discuss ideas for publicity, ticket prices, what food to serve with the teas and coffees, the practicalities, logistics and economics of the event. Tessa taps efficiently into her tablet before closing the lid with a snap. The rest of us scribble on bits of paper, doodle into phones, or simply will our brains to remember what's been decided.

Being face to face with Tessa, knowing I'm going to be spending time with her, is easier than fielding an unexpected phone call, running into her at school or in the village with no prior warning. I'm never completely relaxed – my penance never ends – but I am prepared, as much as I can be, and tonight is fine. Usually, her gaze slides over my face as if she'd rather not be looking at me at all. She doesn't single me out for this treatment, it's the same with everyone. If she did, I would be truly alarmed, even after all this time. But tonight, something is different. Her steel-blue eyes flick constantly in my direction and it's all I can do not to look away in order to avoid them. I notice, too, that Tessa's chin-length, pale-blonde hair is less razor-edged than normal, her complexion less even. Infinitesimal changes that nobody but me would notice.

The faint discomfort in my gut makes me fidget, and Grace

slides along the seat an inch, thinking I haven't got enough space.

'Naturally, the venue will need to be checked out beforehand, assessed for any possible hitches, and our use of the space planned out. We don't want any hiccups on the day.' Tessa lets out a brittle laugh. 'Wendy, perhaps you'll come with me to do that. And... Fran?'

I double-take, hopefully not obviously. 'Of course, yes. Whenever.' I smile brightly, too brightly. 'Text me a time.'

Tessa leaves the pub first. Through the open door of the back room where we're gathered, I can just see her through the pub window, walking purposefully across the street – every movement she makes is purposeful – towards Rose Cottage where Ben will be waiting. This thought, coupled with my slight discomfort at being around Tessa, brings a peculiar taste to my tongue. I go to pick up my wine to wash it away, but my glass is empty.

The others trickle out of the pub, leaving me and Grace.

'Well, you're the favoured one, being chosen to check out the venue.' She laughs. 'Another drink?'

'No thanks, better not. Or actually, yes, just a small one.' I could do with the soothing effect of a drop more alcohol. 'I thought she'd choose one of her cronies. Anne, or Cherie, maybe.'

'I'm not sure she's got any cronies.'

I don't reply. I know what Grace means. Tessa doesn't seem to have any close friends, which is surprising as most people seem to like her, even if they do find her a touch bossy. Not that we follow her life that closely, it's just our impression. I never quizzed Ben about his wife; I didn't seek out information about her that I didn't already have. I had no need – I never felt jealous of her, and I figured that the less I knew, the better. It was as if Ben's wife and family were connected to us, but separate, like different carriages at opposite ends of the same train. He felt the same about Hector and the girls. It had to be that way, otherwise our... whatever it was, would have been tainted from the start, and what would have been the point of that?

This, by the way, is how I felt at the time. Now, viewed from a distance, the whole thing is a regretful muddle and nothing more.

A few days later, I arrange a late start at work and dutifully turn up at the library where Tessa is waiting in the foyer. She's wearing a loose-fitting yellow shell top over cropped jeans, with spotless white trainers. Even in casual clothes, she exudes a businesslike air. Wendy joins us a minute later. Tessa has acquired the keys to the room, and we puff up three flights of stairs behind her.

The high-ceilinged room, the size of a small hall, feels chilly, even though it's a warm day. I rub at the goosebumps on my bare arms and regret my decision to leave my cardigan at home. I'm about to mention it when I realise it might be me, and not the room. But again, I was prepared to meet Tessa today, and I tell myself it's fine.

I'm glad of Wendy's friendly company as we follow Tessa about, agreeing with her suggestions as to how to arrange the tables, where to put the raffle prizes, how much circulation space to leave, agreeing with everything. Wendy looks at me; we are of the same mind. Tessa has already decided how it's all going to be, and we have no idea what we're doing here.

'Fran,' Tessa says, 'I wonder if you'd be in charge of the meet-and-greet on the day? If you're in the foyer, you can direct those who need it to the lift. For example, if that nice man from Church Close comes, he uses a wheelchair, so there'll be no option. Although...' she stops to think for a moment, 'I don't imagine it's his sort of thing. Anyway, there are bound to be a number of older people. They love the chance of coffee, cake and a natter while they support a good cause,' she adds, quite patronisingly, I think.

Her smile flashes across the room like the dusty sunbeams that pour in through the high windows and lands on me. I glance down at the treacly floorboards.

'There's a lift?'

Wendy interjects. 'Yes, if you go right to the back of the foyer past the library, it's by the door to the museum. There are rather a lot of stairs. For some, I mean.'

I remember now bringing Caitlin to the library one day and seeing the clamped double steel doors of the lift at the end of the dark corridor, an image I would have frogmarched out of my head right away.

'A little encouragement might be needed, Fran,' Tessa says brightly. 'People don't like to admit they can't walk up the stairs. You could pop in the lift with them and see them out on the right floor.'

I don't bother to point out that there is only one floor they could get out on. Tessa is looking at me, waiting for me to concur, like it's something of mammoth importance. She's making heavy weather of this stairs-and-lift business. But I guess it is all important to her, every detail catered for, every box checked. Again, I can't fault her efficiency in ensuring everything runs smoothly on the day, which it will. The coffee morning will be a roaring success and the hospice will benefit from our efforts.

'Fine,' I say, smiling. 'I can do that, no problem.'

Wendy and I are released soon after, and ten minutes later, I'm at work. The surgery is quiet, thank goodness – my head isn't precisely where it ought to be. Whether this is due to my recent dealings with Tessa, I have no idea. All I know is I feel raw and exposed, and have an irrational sense of impending doom.

Sally, the other receptionist on duty, tilts her head and taps a fingernail at an appointment on the screen for later this morning: a dog to be euthanised. It's commonplace, but there's always a ring of sadness about it. I know the dog's owner, Giles – a sweet widower in his seventies. He's lived in Oakheart all his life, as has Samson, his lumbering old golden Labrador, whom he's had since he was a pup. Samson's time has come, as it comes to us all in the end. This gloomy thought follows me through the morning until Giles leaves the surgery alone, bravely waving us goodbye, the dog's lead clutched tightly in his fist like a lifeline.

I amble through the rest of my shift, part of my brain giving the job the attention it warrants while another part spits out random thoughts and snatches of memory, like sparks from a Catherine wheel. As I walk home later – the long way, through the village, not via the woods – my mind latches onto Ben and refuses to be sidetracked. This gives me a clue that it was indeed being with Tessa twice in one week which put me at sixes and sevens today.

Two years on, and I'm no nearer to understanding how I could have let it happen. At Hazel's ballet class, of all places! What kind of a woman – one with a husband and three children, at that – makes a date with her daughter's friend's father right there among the jetés and the brisés and the wobbly arabesques? What sort of a mother does that make me?

More accurately, we didn't actually make a date then. We exchanged mobile numbers, that was all. But all was everything. After the way he'd been looking at me, and the way I'd been looking at him – mesmerised, intoxicated, appalled, thrilled, all those things – the rest was a given.

I walked into that hall a perfectly sane woman, and at some point between the twisting of soft hair into buns, the adjusting of Lycra straps, the re-tying of shoe ribbons, and the last triumphant chord from the tinny piano, I became quite the opposite.

A kind of madness – that's the only way I can describe it. I was gripped by it, held in its power for the two months it lasted. And beyond, of course. That kind of crazy obsessiveness leaves a mark, a big fat stain. It grows fainter with time but never disappears completely, like indelible pen on a white gym shirt.

A kind of madness. Sounds like an excuse, doesn't it? But that is, truly, the way it was. I may be many things but I'm not so blind to my own flaws that I go around making up excuses for being unfaithful. Hector is not a wife-beater or a serial adulterer or a compulsive liar or a controller, or anything like that.

I'd been facing a few challenges at the time – who doesn't? I'd just lost my parents in one hit – though not in a tragic way; they'd sold up the family home in Essex and moved to New Zealand to join my sister, Natalie, and her family. But it did feel like a tragedy and caused me many sleepless nights while I raged internally with resentment and sadness that my parents had chosen to live with my sister on the other side of the world and not here, with me.

On top of that, my beautiful, clever Caitlin had at the age of seven been diagnosed with a high-functioning form of autism – Asperger's, we learned, after many rounds of tests and consultations. I thought we were lucky that she'd been diagnosed at such a young age, but Hector shocked me by refusing to accept that Caitlin was anything but a sensitive, quirky little girl going through a difficult phase.

Rather than having my husband irrefutably in my corner, my struggle to understand Caitlin and her condition was magnified by my dismay at his head-in-the-sand attitude. During one conversation when I expressed my fear at what the future might hold for our little girl, he cheerfully told me not to worry. I felt patronised, angry and deeply frustrated.

I needed Hector then, more than at any other time, and he just wasn't there.

As time has gone on, Hector has come to accept that Caitlin is different, but he still believes she'll come through it, and that the best way of handling the situation is to parent her in exactly the same way as our other daughters.

So, life wasn't easy at the time. I felt isolated and so alone. I could see no hope, no brightness, as if a blind had been drawn across the sun. I knew I shouldn't have felt that way, that I should have fought off the negative feelings, picked myself up and concentrated on all the good things I did have. Instead, I ran away inside my head, and let myself be beguiled and stupidly flattered by the attentions of a handsome man with whom I felt a distinct connection, other than the purely physical. Or, thought I did.

I can't claim that Ben led me astray; I would never say that. I walked into the affair with my eyes not exactly wide open, but certainly focused on the answer to my low mood.

Except, of course, it wasn't the answer. A diversion, yes, for a while, but not the answer. Infidelity solves nothing. It's like diving headfirst into a black, bottomless pit.

Hindsight is a wonderful thing.

I was a disgrace, there was no other word for it. I'll never forgive myself for what I did to Hector, the girls, and to Ben's wife and child. And ultimately, to myself, though I don't deserve any sympathy, and I don't seek it.

It began, on the face of it, quite innocently.

During the ballet class at the village community hall, my gaze had slid constantly between Hazel, and Zoe's father, who'd been sitting sideways on from me on the hard seats around the edge. I couldn't help it; he'd kept looking at me, drawing me in. And then, as our gazes locked momentarily together, he'd smiled, and widened his eyes, just perceptibly. I managed not to return the smile, just, although it was there, on the inside, clamouring to be let out. Nobody had flirted with me in ages, unless you counted the rather handsome medical sales rep who came to the surgery every week, but he flirted with all of us. This – Ben, as I later learned he was called – was different. I sensed that immediately.

When the class ended, I tried not to notice the brush of his sleeve against mine as we readied our daughters for the journey home in the cramped confines of the cloakroom area. We made for the exit at the same time, which was when Ben offered us a lift home.

Our house is no more than a ten-minute walk from the hall, but he politely insisted, and I politely refused, fearful of what came next. Fearful of myself.

The two girls had never met before that day. I learned later that Ben's family had not long moved to Oakheart from Brighton, and although his daughter had joined Hazel's school, she was in a different class. It was obvious they'd taken to one another straight away. I hid a smile when I noticed Hazel, at nine and a half, giving her bossy nature an airing as she explained to Zoe the whereabouts of the toilets and exactly how her hair must be done. No plaits, no partings, just a plain bun with a net over it. I sensed a budding friendship; it may have been better if they'd hated each other on sight.

The girls disregarded my protests that a lift was not needed and clambered happily into the back of Ben's silver Peugeot, leaving me to give in gracefully and climb into the front passenger seat. It was then that Ben formally introduced himself and his daughter as Ben and Zoe Grammaticus, and told me his wife's name was Tessa.

'Francesca Oliver. And that's Hazel,' I said, nodding towards the back seat as the engine purred into life. 'But you already know that.'

I wondered later if Ben had been testing me by mentioning his wife, checking whether I knew her – I didn't – and making his status clear, so there were no misunderstandings. I hadn't mentioned Hector; it didn't even occur to me.

'I couldn't stop looking at you, back there,' he said quietly, once the jabbering in the back seat filled the car. 'And you were looking at me, so, I wondered if we'd met before?'

I pretended to be thinking about this, while pushing from my mind every bad romantic film I'd ever seen. 'Nope, pretty sure we haven't. Unless I've seen you around the village, in the minimart, maybe...?' I shrugged.

'I don't do a lot of shopping. Unless I'm under orders.' He chuckled.

'Nor me. Usually.' What was I talking about? I was always popping in there for this and that. My mouth seemed to be working without referencing my brain first.

'Maybe at the school gate?' Ben continued.

He was playing games. He knew as well as I did that we hadn't clapped eyes on each other before today. This was dangerous territory, and I was ploughing right into it.

'Don't think so,' I said.

'You'd have remembered, right?'

Of course I would.

'That's a bit presumptuous.'

'I know. I'm out of practice.'

'So I should hope.' My grin escaped before I could capture it. What was wrong with me? I willed myself to get a grip.

Finally, we were almost home, and I felt nothing but relief. I asked him to drop us at the corner of our road, by the British Legion club, but he took no notice and bumped right on down the uneven stretch of private road which forms Woodside Villas.

I wordlessly pointed out our house. A seventies picture-windowed box, erected in somebody's garden and nothing like the characterful older properties in the rest of the road, it sticks out like the proverbial sore thumb.

Ben and I got out of the car, and Ben opened the back door to let Hazel out. Zoe followed her. Reluctant to part, they hopped about on the pavement, still chattering nineteen to the dozen.

'Well, then,' I said, turning towards our gate. 'Thanks for the lift.'

'You're very welcome, Francesca.' Ben stood very still, looking at me the same way as he had inside the hall.

'It's Fran,' I said. Only my mother calls me Francesca. Nevertheless, that was apparently the name I'd given him, only I couldn't remember saying it.

'Give me your phone, Fran.' His voice was gently commanding.

He held out his hand. I took my phone from my bag and gave it to him.

'Thank you,' he said, fishing in his pocket and handing me his.

The warring factions inside my brain drew swords. The side I wanted to win – needed desperately to win – was losing its grip faster than snow sliding off a sun-struck roof. But we were only exchanging numbers, as fellow parents. Where was the harm? I reasoned. As if reason came into it. Not even a whisper.

'Now you've got Zoe's dad's number, Mum, we can ring and ask Zoe round to our house,' Hazel said, performing a jeté beside the car. 'Yay!'

Hector never knew about Ben and me, and the girls certainly didn't. I was never found out in that way. In every other way, I'm found out every minute of every day. My mind plays tricks, making me believe that Ben was no more than a crazy moment of physical longing, a dangerous dance of my imagination. Then I have to pull back sharply to the truth in case in some obscure way my manner gives away the secret.

Oakheart calls itself a village but has the footprint of a small town. Its core of ancient, picture-perfect architecture, the sleepy square with its massive oak tree at the centre, remains intact, a draw for the tourists, a meeting place for the locals. But beyond the original village, ribboning developments from all decades unroll through fields and woodland to the foothills of the South Downs in one direction and the plains of the River Adur in another. Because of its unruly sprawl, Oakheart is not, therefore, a village where everybody knows everybody else and gossip is its lifeblood. We felt safe, Ben and I. Safe from the eyes of the village, if not from ourselves.

SIX

FRAN

'Where are we going on holiday?'

Hector and I exchange a look as Caitlin throws this question across the dinner table.

'New Zealand?' I say, with a laugh to show I'm not serious, although actually I'm very serious indeed.

'One day.' Hector smiles, his brown eyes full of warmth and sympathy finding mine. 'One day.'

'Yes.' I nod and smile back.

Hector has suggested several times that I make the trip on my own to see my parents and sister, but I couldn't do that. Aside from the cost, I don't want to go on a dream trip and leave my family behind, even though none of them would raise the slightest objection and I'm sure they'd be perfectly fine without me.

'I've been looking at the Maldives,' Kitty says, following this with a long, wistful sigh. 'The beaches are to die for.'

'Again, one day,' Hector says brightly.

Caitlin's carefully constructed forkful of spaghetti unwinds itself and slides back onto her plate. She frowns at Kitty. 'How can you have been looking at the Maldives? It's miles away, isn't it, Mum? Where is the Maldives?'

'Online, of course. On the screen. Why must you take everything so literally?' Kitty puts down her fork and throws her head back, raking her fingers through the sides of her pale gold hair, the same colour as Hector's and Caitlin's, before letting it fall forward again.

'Don't do that over the table, please,' I say. 'Yes, Caitlin, the Maldives are miles away. Hundreds of miles. They're a group of islands in the Indian Ocean.'

'Sounds good to me,' Hazel says. 'I bet it'll be the same old, same old, though.'

'Yeah.' Kitty lifts her eyes dramatically. 'With the same old rain.'

'There's nothing wrong with a fortnight in a cottage by the sea,' Hector says. 'And it didn't rain once in Cornwall last year, as you well know. It was a glorious summer. When I was a kid, we didn't go on holiday at all, so count yourselves lucky.'

It isn't true that Hector's childhood didn't feature holidays, but they were modest ones; the girls know that, but it fits the tone of the conversation and Hazel and Kitty immediately lift virtual violins to their chins and la-la a plaintive tune, making Caitlin giggle.

'We should sort something out, though,' I say. 'It's already May. Everywhere will be booked up soon.' I stand up to clear away the dinner plates and fetch the strawberry cheesecake from the fridge. 'Perhaps we could stretch to a hotel this year, a package holiday in Spain or somewhere.'

Hazel and Kitty exclaim in delight at the idea of *abroad*, while Caitlin weighs it up in her head and stays silent. Hotels are not her ideal environment, there's too much risk of sensory overload with all those people and activity. She would manage, with our help, and she would never complain, but Caitlin is happiest where she can be guaranteed her own quiet space whenever she needs it.

A hotel, wherever it is, would make a nice change for me, though, and for Hector – he does his share of the shopping and food preparation. But hotels are expensive, wherever they are. The house needs some attention too, and Caitlin's school fees are going up again in September. I wish I hadn't said anything now.

'I only said *perhaps*.' I dole out wedges of cheesecake and put the tub of ice cream on the table with a spoon.

'We'll have to see,' Hector says, eliciting told-you-so groans from our eldest daughters. He's probably thinking about school fees as well, though he will refrain from saying so, at least in front of the girls.

'Zoe's going to Italy,' Hazel says, conversationally. 'She's not looking forward to it because she'll be dragged round art galleries and old ruins, and only get to go to the beach if her mum can sit in the shade.'

I give a little start at the oblique mention of Tessa. She seems to be invading my life just now, in ways I don't like.

Hector laughs. 'That doesn't surprise me. It would never do to spoil her porcelain skin with anything as common as a suntan.'

'Ha, you're right there.' I grin, feigning a casualness I don't feel.

'I could put up with a couple of old ruins,' muses Kitty, 'if I could be at the pool or the beach most of the time.'

My mind arrows straight to Ben, and I realise I have no idea if art galleries and historic buildings form part of his holiday wishlist, or whether he does it to please Tessa – assuming Zoe has not made that up for effect. Ben and I talked, when we gave ourselves the chance, but that kind of basic information, his likes and dislikes, eludes me, which seems odd, looking back. I told him plenty about me, though; that I do remember. He asked a lot of questions which I answered readily, happy to have somebody take a fresh interest.

I'm mulling over this imbalance, in a distant sort of way, when Hazel changes the subject to one which I find no less disturbing than the conversation involving the Grammaticus family.

'The mad cat lady spoke to me, when I came past her house on the way home,' she says, retrieving a shard of cheesecake that's shot off her plate as she's chiselled into it.

I put down my spoon and sit up straight. '*Did* she?' Everyone turns to look at me, as if I've overreacted. I temper it with a little laugh. We all know who Hazel means. 'You shouldn't call her that, Hazel. It's unkind.'

'She is, though,' Kitty chips in. 'She's got cats and she's not right, up here.' She taps her temple, like I did with Grace.

'Your mother's right,' Hector says. 'You mustn't go around calling people mad. What did she say to you, Hazel?'

Hazel shrugs. 'Nothing much. She was by her gate with a cat in her arms. I stopped to stroke it and she asked me if I'd had a nice day at school.'

'Is that all?' I ask.

'Yep. Oh, she asked me if I had ever seen some old film with somebody called Doris Day in it, and I said I didn't think so. Then as I was going, she said something about me not having far to walk to Woodside Villas.'

Mirabelle Hayward knows where we live. Of course she does.

'I wouldn't get too involved in conversation with her, Hazel,' I say. 'We see enough of her at the vets' surgery, nice as pie one minute then saying all sorts the next. You never know where you are with her.'

Hector raises an eyebrow but says nothing. I never told the girls about Humphrey's demise and Mirabelle's complaint against me, mostly for Caitlin's sake. I did mention the incident in passing to Hector, making light of it, but he's clearly remembering now.

I'm almost tempted to blurt out my suspicions about Mirabelle playing 'tricks' on me, but I don't because Hector would want to know why I've not said anything before. He might even march along to Graylings, knock on her door, and demand to know what she thinks she's playing at, which would be awful if it wasn't her at all.

'Doris *Day*? Who's she?' Kitty nods forcefully. 'I rest my case. She's as mad as cheese.'

This time we don't pick her up on it.

'You don't know where you are with someone like that, that's all,' I say.

'I expect she felt lonely and wanted somebody to talk to. That's why she was standing by her gate with the cat,' Caitlin says, displaying one of her flashes of insight that always delight and surprise us.

'Well done, love.' Hector smiles. 'I think you've hit the nail on the head.'

Caitlin frowns. 'This is not about a nail. Dad, you can't say that because...'

Kitty and Hazel exchange a here-we-go-again look, and immediately scrape back their chairs and vanish. Hector steers Caitlin away from the subject by asking if she'd like to share the last piece of cheesecake with him, and I take the opportunity to leave the table too. Upstairs, I stand at our bedroom window, looking out at the rosy evening sky between the chimneys opposite and wondering if I will ever feel normal again.

I can hear Caitlin chatting away to her father as they clear up after the meal, and I know I can stay up here for a while. On the wall above the chest of drawers is a group of framed photos which Hector calls the 'rogues' gallery'. It's all family photos, of us and the girls at various stages of our lives. My gaze alights on a picture taken at our wedding reception in October 2001 – a cobbled-together, jolly affair held in the back room of a pub in Hammersmith after a civil ceremony. Hector is wearing a white shirt and red silk tie with a grey suit he borrowed from a mate – the first time I'd seen him in anything approaching formal dress – his smile a mixture of elation and resignation at being asked to pose yet again for my father's camera. I'm pressed against Hector, a proprietorial hand draped across his shoulder. I'm wearing a sunset pink dress with lace inserts, from the Monsoon sale; my long, cinnamon-brown hair is loose, brushed shiny, with a flower pinned to one side. My face is mobile with the effort of restraining an outbreak of giggles.

A rushed wedding, for no other reason than we were desperate to be shackled together for life as fast as possible.

My mother stalwartly held her tongue, after her hopeful suggestion that we marry in church in my home town in Essex was quashed by my insistence that the only thing we cared about was getting hitched, with the minimum of fuss and frills. Hector's mother had died two years earlier, and his sweet, easy-going father was only too happy to run with our plans and turn up as instructed, whenever and wherever.

Our relationship had been on fast-forward from our first date; it stood to reason that the wedding would go the same way. Many people say that their wedding day was the happiest day of their life. For me, it was the day I watched Hector deftly changing places with a woman in the coffee shop queue so that he would be the next customer I served.

Having recently given up teaching English in a comprehensive, through sheer disillusionment and the blatant knowledge that teaching and me were never going to gel, I was working as a barista while I took stock of my life and worked out where it went next. Hector was a postgrad student at the London School of Economics. The coffee shop was near his campus, and enjoyed a steady trade of students and academics.

According to Hector, the very first words I spoke to him

were, 'Are you having it in or out?' His reply – 'Oh, definitely *in*' – made me blush. This is Hector's version, and whether true or not, it has become fact by being absorbed into our history.

I was twenty-seven when we met and Hector was twenty-five. We were 'getting on', we told each other, with rueful grins, in which case we'd better speed things up. And so we were married within ten months of that first meeting, while we were still in the heady throes of world-conquering, forever love.

I appraise the image of myself in the photo now and try to see beyond the love-struck, triumphant girl beginning the most exciting adventure of her life. I try to see that girl – woman – reach the point where the desire to run her finger along the sharp edges of life and taste the blood of exquisite danger triumphs over loyalty and honesty and real, lasting love. But I can't; I'm blinded by the dazzle.

The head-rush I experienced when I first set eyes on Ben mirrored the sensation that doubled my heart rate in the coffee shop on that long-ago day. Was my brain – or, more pertinently, my body – urging me to reignite that feeling without my conscious input? Was my life so flat that I craved a high, at whatever cost? I don't think so. I mentioned excuses before; this sounds like another, and as such it must be ignored. I am not a good person. It's that simple.

I didn't use the mobile number Ben gave me. Not that I didn't think about it, dream about it, my mind leapfrogging to a fantasy world where we were both young, free and single. But of course, we weren't. I took up running, the soles of my ancient Nikes slapping the pavements of Oakheart every morning before breakfast, as if I believed that forcing the air out of my body would also expel my treacherous thoughts about Ben. Hector and the girls found my apparent attempt at staying in shape hilarious, and after a fortnight or so, I gave in, none too graciously, and consigned the trainers to the bin.

Refusing to be defeated in my attempt at distraction, and still leaning towards the physical, I joined an evening yoga class at the community centre. It turned out to be held in the same room as the ballet classes, and instead of being alarmed at the coincidence, I decided it must work in my favour.

It wasn't the resonant tang of stale milk, cheap floor polish and feet that had me retreating after only two sessions, nor even the discovery that my body refused to bend in the ways the tutor expected it to. It was the shock I felt when, at the end of my second session, I queued to tick my name in the book and pay my six pounds and saw the tall, lithe blonde in front of me place a tick against her name – 'Tessa Grammaticus'. I'd observed her cool, perfect performance on the yoga mat from my chosen position in the back row, but once I knew who she was, it was impossible for me to carry on, even if I'd wanted to.

'It wasn't my cup of tea,' I told Hector and the girls, and nobody questioned me further.

The ballet classes themselves weren't a problem. The week after the Ben incident, Hazel had a cold and didn't go. The classes broke for Easter after that, and I embraced the respite, feeling in some way that I'd been let off the hook, while I knew I didn't deserve that kind of luck.

Of course, I had no idea whether it would always be Ben accompanying Zoe to ballet or if her mother would take over but I didn't want to risk it. When the time came for the class to resume, I had a mild headache but pretended it was worse than it was, and Hector took Hazel, Kitty going along with them. They didn't stay throughout the lesson, as I usually did, but nipped home in between before fetching her two hours later. I had no intention of quizzing Hazel as to whether Zoe had been at the class; I didn't want to know.

I was told anyway.

'Guess what, Mum? Zoe said could I go to her house on Saturday morning. Isn't that fab? I can, can't I?'

'Fab,' I muttered.

'Zoe's got loads of great stuff.' Hazel sighed, eyeing the both of us.

'And you haven't?' I asked.

'Er, no?'

Neither Hector or I rose to that.

'Zoe seems a nice child,' Hector said, handing me Hazel's bag containing her ballet clothes, which were all screwed up, I noticed. 'Her mother's a pleasant sort, too. You'll meet up some time, I expect.'

I said nothing about Tessa being at the yoga class; I hadn't actually met her anyway.

It was out of my hands. Hazel needed to be dropped at Zoe's house – the delectable Rose Cottage, as I found out then – and it would be me doing the dropping off as Hector had other plans for Saturday.

We stood at the gate of Rose Cottage at the appointed time, Hazel virtually airborne with the excitement of spending time with her new friend, and me scanning the windows of the house and praying to any higher deity who would listen that Zoe's mother would come to the door and I could wave my daughter off and hurry away to some fictitious commitment.

My prayers were not answered. Or perhaps they were, depending on how you look at it. The front door of Rose Cottage was flung wide before we were halfway along the path, Zoe darted out, grabbed Hazel by the arm and pulled her inside. I was left facing Ben, as the girly giggles died away.

We looked at each other for what seemed an extraordinary length of time, and then he invited me in for coffee. I should have refused. For one thing, I wasn't prepared to come face to face with Tessa and have to go through the motions of making her acquaintance in front of Ben. The whole thing would have felt forced, as well as embarrassing. For another, well, there were too many reasons to count as to why I should run away as fast as I could.

But somehow he made it impossible to do anything other than accept with thanks, and I found myself sitting on a trendily battered-looking leather sofa in a country-style kitchen, watching Ben as he made coffee – instant, I was pleased to note, nothing fancy from a machine – and wondering if the rub of dark stubble on his chin that suited him so very well was permanent or if he hadn't shaved because it was the weekend.

Then, of course, I remembered he'd looked exactly like that when I'd first met him at the ballet class, which brought me to thinking that sporting just the right amount of stubble, exquisitely shaped, was a high maintenance way of carrying on.

It was a diversion, focusing on Ben's shaving habits. An attempt to manoeuvre my head into some kind of sense and touch base with reality. Because this was not reality, the way he passed my coffee to me whilst his eyes never left my face, the way he stood for a long moment, cradling his own mug, before he seemingly made a decision and sat down on the sofa next to me.

We chatted. Don't ask me what about – I couldn't have told you even straight after. I know he mentioned Tessa without going into detail, and I mentioned Hector and the girls in a general kind of way, but that was all. While we chatted, we listened to bumps and squeals coming from above, and exchanged indulgent-parent smiles. I had begun to think I was safe, that whatever had taken place between us could be written off as one of those silly moments following a mutual flash of attraction.

Then Ben stood his mug down on the flagstone floor and his hand crept along the ridges of the leather seat and touched mine. A brush of fingertips, a ghost of a touch. That was all it took.

I sighed. I remember that. A long, deep sigh that seemed to come from somewhere, or someone, else. I stood my own mug down, keeping my eyes averted.

'What is it the locals call that hill, the one above the old chalk pit?' Ben said, his tone conversational, nearly fooling me into thinking we were back to the small talk, which had not felt small at all.

'High Heaven?' I studied my hands in my lap, twisting my wedding ring twice around my finger. I sensed Ben's searching gaze, the question it contained.

'That's the one. High Heaven. Very appropriate.'

His words fell into the quiet room, soft, burning with meaning. I had to look at him then, and once I had, I felt as if I would never look away.

It's Saturday, the day of the coffee morning in aid of the hospice, and I'm not looking forward to it. But it's for a good cause, I'll have Grace, Wendy and the others to have a laugh with behind the scenes, and it will be fine. I'm telling myself this as I stand at the bathroom mirror, applying an extra coating of mascara and gathering my hair into a ponytail in case Tessa has any hygiene issues with it being loose.

I check my appearance again in our bedroom's full-length mirror, and decide I look more than presentable in my blue-and-white cotton dress, worn with flat sandals in case I fall over with the plates or something. Grace would snigger with delight if she saw me going to all this trouble – she'll probably be in faded jeans and a slogan T-shirt – but the last thing I want is to give Tessa any cause for criticism.

Voices float up to the open window, and my stomach jolts as if I've driven fast over a speed bump. I look down to see Ben's car at the gate and Hector talking to him in our front garden. Somewhere from the direction of the woods comes the sound of a chainsaw, splitting the air with a squeal and whine, and Hector steps nearer to Ben, tilting his head in order to hear better what he is saying. The stairs creak and bump as Zoe and Hazel descend from Hazel's room before appearing on the front path. Hazel's rucksack hangs loosely from her shoulder; there's a bottle of water in her hand.

I hadn't forgotten that Hazel is going with Zoe to the trampoline park, and that Ben is driving them – Tessa being otherwise engaged – but somehow I'd missed the part where it was arranged for Ben to pick up my daughter. I'd assumed that she would walk along to Rose Cottage and they'd leave from there. I watch the two men: Hector's compactness and fair, slightly tousled hair contrasts with Ben's lean strength, his sculpted darkness. Two dads on Saturday morning child duty, making small talk. An ordinary, everyday scene, yet it steals my breath and heats the back of my neck.

Ben turns towards his car, raising a farewell hand to Hector. The girls climb into the back seat and as the car pulls away, Ben glances through the windscreen, upwards at the window where I'm standing. This is how it appears, although the sun was on the windscreen and I might have imagined it.

As Tessa predicted, the charity event is a sell-out; the room is packed predominantly with the over-sixties, and well beyond, judging by the undulation of grey hair and pink pates. Having flogged up the stairs to secrete my handbag in the kitchen area and touch base with Grace and the others, I scurry down again before Tessa feels the need to remind me of my meet-and-greet duties. There's an A-board propped up inside the front entrance telling people which room to head for, with a huge green arrow pointing to the staircase, so I have no need to give directions. Instead, I nod at the paper tickets as they're held out, smile and exchange a greeting with people I recognise, which, this being a village, is quite a number.

I only remember the lift, having studiously not thought

about it since my last visit, when two elderly women, both leaning heavily on walking sticks, doubtfully eye the staircase. My stomach quakes as I shepherd them along the Victorian tiled corridor towards the steel doors, which, surprisingly, are already standing open. *It's only one floor up* repeats itself like a mantra inside my head. *Just do it.*

Okay. Telling the new arrivals hovering in the entrance to go on up and not to wait – I don't care if they've got tickets or not – I step into the lift as if I'm entering a shark's jaws. The women follow me in, and my voice takes on a ridiculous jollity as I press the button and say, 'Up we go!' as if I'm talking to a couple of three-year-olds.

The lift is small, confined, with no room for more than six people, and has a mirrored wall at the back designed to give the illusion of space. It's not the newest bit of kit you've ever seen, but there's no earthly reason why it shouldn't take us to our destination and, more to the point, release us when we get there. But since when did phobias have reason? That would defy their definition.

I fight the urge to hang onto the sleeve of one of the women as I press the button again, thinking I'd been too hesitant the first time. Nothing happens. The doors don't close. The lift goes nowhere. I pat my clammy palms against the cotton of my skirt, and then the doors grind, slowly and apologetically, towards each other but don't quite meet in the middle. The lift moves, hardly noticeably, but to me the tremor beneath my feet might as well herald an earthquake as the floor rises about six inches then shudders to a stop. I stare at the blank, unlit face of the button panel and think I might very well be sick.

'It's busted,' says one of the women. 'Typical council building.'

The other woman tuts in sympathy and they both look at me. But I've lost all concern for their welfare, if I ever had any. All I want to do – *need* to do – is get out of this box, and I twist both hands sideways, sliding them into the gap between the doors, and use all my strength to lever them apart. It works, the doors open almost to their fullest extent and I leap through them shamelessly, landing heavily on both feet. Turning back to the lift, I help my companions down one by one, taking their weight against me as they calmly negotiate the gap. We head for the stairs, the walking sticks tapping a resigned symphony on the tiled floor.

A uniformed caretaker with a florid complexion marches towards us. He holds up a hand as if he's directing traffic.

'No, no, you can't use the lift. It's out of order,' he says, leaving me to wonder where he was when we were heading in the other direction.

'We know, dear,' says one of the women. 'This kind lady took us in, but it didn't go.' She gives me a crinkly smile and pats my hand. I feel grateful to her for recognising my discomfort in the lift, if not my sheer panic.

'It might have been an idea to put an "out of order" sign on it,' I say, sounding rather haughty as I gather my scattered wits.

'There is a sign. I stuck it on myself, personally, first thing.'

'I think you'll find there isn't,' I say, and the two women echo me in agreement.

'Ah-ha!' Our uniformed friend wheels round and points to a darkened alcove beside the lift.

We look, too, and see what looks like a large white card-board sign slung to the rear of the alcove.

'Kids! I don't know. They come for the museum and get up to all sorts.'

We leave the caretaker to retrieve his sign, and I plod up the stairs behind the women, watching their slow progress as they grip the polished banisters, ready to leap into action should one of them stumble.

As if the last fifteen minutes hasn't been enough, Tessa is there to meet us at the top, peering over the banisters with a concerned smile on her lips while her eyes say something quite different.

'Before you ask,' I hiss, not needing any of her nonsense, 'the lift is out of order.'

'Oh dear, I'm *so* sorry, ladies,' Tessa gushes to the two women, leading them away and ignoring me completely.

Quietly fuming, I sidle through the buzzing crowd to the back of the room and stalk into the kitchen.

'The stragglers can find their own way up,' I say, in answer to Grace's enquiring look. 'Effing meet-and-greet.'

Grace laughs, and together we plate up more shortbread fingers, cheese straws and miniature scones, to replenish the tables out in the hall while Wendy controls the ferocious steam-belching urn. Anne and Cherie circulate the hall with pots of coffee and tea, and the other helpers ferry dirty china to the kitchen and wash up in the inadequate sink.

The two hours we've allowed for the event whizz by. The raffle has been drawn by a senior member of the hospice staff who then gives a little speech, to much applause, and I've long forgotten about the lift incident by the time Tessa exerts her authority, with a bonhomie so fake it might have been cut out of cardboard, and ushers everyone out of the door. At least she doesn't ask me to go downstairs and see them all safely off the premises, and I wonder if she's feeling guilty about stationing me down there in the first place.

The coffee morning has been a rousing success. Everyone seemed to have a good time, and apart from Tessa perhaps needing something to do with her time, she has to be admired for taking on these things.

Admired? Okay, not quite the right word, coming from me, but I try my best to be dispassionate about her and, most of the time, I manage it. I've had plenty of practice, after all, and I'm the one in the wrong, not Tessa.

· · ·

'Such a nuisance about the lift,' Tessa says, when she and I are the only ones left and I'm stacking the last of the china in the cupboards. Her voice cutting through the silence makes me start; I thought she was still downstairs talking to the caretaker and hadn't heard her approach. 'I do hope it wasn't too much of a bother for you, Fran.'

'No, it was fine,' I say. 'There were only those two women with the sticks, and they made it up here as good as gold.'

As Tessa well knows.

She smiles. 'You were all right, though?'

Puzzled as to why she's labouring the point, I turn fully towards her and see her eyes searching my face, which heats up under her gaze.

'Yes, as I said, it was fine.'

Tessa nods, moves towards the kitchen door and then turns back, as if she's just remembered something. 'Fran?'

'Mm?' I go to the cupboard where I stashed my handbag, take it out and close the cupboard door, the noise of it loud in the echoey kitchen. I want to be out of here now. My duties are done, I've no reason to be closeted with Ben's wife any longer and I'm beginning to feel uncomfortable. I pray it doesn't show.

Tessa leans against the ledge of the closed serving hatch, and I have the impression she's aiming for a casual stance when in fact it looks anything but. I take a long breath in and put on what I hope is a friendly, enquiring expression. Now she's got me cornered, she's probably going to ask me to help with her next charity shindig. What else would it be?

'I think there's something you should know.' Tessa bows her head in that way people do when they want to seem unwilling to say something but actually can't wait to say it.

'Oh?' I loop my bag across me and glance at my watch.

'I ran into Mrs Hayward – Mirabelle – that woman who lives at Graylings. She was in the square, outside the art shop. I'd popped in to buy a card and she waylaid me when I came out.' Tessa gives a forced little smile. 'She can chatter for England, that one.'

'I know.' I hadn't realised Tessa knew Mirabelle. No reason why she shouldn't, of course. 'She does go on a bit if you get caught.'

'She was talking about you, Fran. In fact, she made rather a serious allegation, and I thought you should know. You know how gossip runs around the village like wildfire through heather. If she told me – and I hardly know the woman – then who else is she telling?'

I feel hot all over, scared of what might follow. 'What's she saying about me?'

'That you killed her cat.' Tessa flaps a dismissive hand. 'I expect it's complete nonsense, but I thought it best to warn you.' Tessa's face is serious but, tuned in to every nuance as I am, I don't miss the spangle of delight in her eyes.

'Ha, that's old news and, for the record, totally untrue,' I say, relief pounding through me. It's not great that Mirabelle is still spreading her poison, but it reinforces my theory that she is responsible for the strange things that have been happening to me.

Although I really don't need to, I explain to Tessa exactly what happened that day at the surgery. 'Mirabelle won't be swayed from her version, but the important people know the truth, the vets included.'

I emphasise the word 'important', implying that the description does not apply to Tessa. A whisper of disappointment crosses her face and she brushes it away and pastes on a smile.

'That's okay then, as long as you're happy.'

I frown at her odd choice of phrase. 'Yep, it's all good. And now I've got to get home.'

I tap across the empty hall and down the stairs. I hear Tessa locking the kitchen door and following me down, but I don't stop or look back. I can't wait to get away from her.

But Tessa hasn't finished with me, and I'm compelled to turn round as she catches up with me at the front entrance.

'I'm pleased you've managed to put the cat business into perspective,' she says, in an annoyingly patronising voice. 'But you know, you can never truly leave the past behind.'

She smiles, while I freeze, one foot on the second step down. I almost break into a run as I hit the pavement and head for home.

EIGHT

FRAN

When I reach home there's nobody in.

Hazel will still be at the trampoline park with Zoe and Ben. They were having lunch in the café there; I remember Hector mentioning it after Ben and the girls had left. There's a scribbled note by the kettle from Kitty to say she's gone to meet friends, and not to make dinner for her.

Hector has left a message on my phone to say he's taken Caitlin with him to his workshop. She loves going to work with her dad. He lets her use the simplest, safest of tools on odd pieces of wood, which she enjoys. Hector's workshop is part of a courtyard development of converted stables housing other businesses, including, to Caitlin's delight, a sweet and ice cream shop.

It's almost two o'clock but I'm not hungry, so I make myself a mug of tea and sit with my hands curled round it at the kitchen table. Miss T is slumped on the table in a patch of sun, her furry, tortoiseshell bulk steadily rising and falling in sleep. The clock on the wall ticks loudly into the silence. I don't want to sit here; I'm wired with nervous energy, and the house's emptiness is too conducive to the chain of disconcerting thoughts that wind through my head.

Taking a rational slant on it – not easy in my current frame of mind – I concede that Tessa probably thought she was being friendly and helpful by passing on Mirabelle's gossip. But why add the bit about not being able to leave the past behind? What was that supposed to mean? It sounded almost like a warning, and too heavy to be a reference to Mirabelle's accusation.

My mind refuses to contemplate the awful possibility that Tessa knows about my affair with her husband. It can't be that – it just can't. Tessa wouldn't waste time passing on trivial gossip if that was on her mind and, in any case, Ben would have found some way to warn me.

My mind trips on, regardless. Is Tessa lonely? The idea induces a pang of guilt. Does she over-dramatise ordinary things to induce an intimacy that would not otherwise be there? I pull my phone towards me, thinking I might call Grace and ask her what she thinks, until I realise I can't do that without making her wonder why I find anything Tessa says important, or interesting.

Five minutes later, I leave the house, intending to clear my head with a walk, but as I reach the gate, I change my mind and take the car instead. I have no particular destination in mind, yet somehow I'm not surprised to find myself driving through the hamlet of Lower Hovington and past the petrol station, to where the public footpath sign points a finger up the narrow track leading to High Heaven.

It's a fine day, and there are three other cars parked. Two whippets cavort on long leads near the crest of the hill; dogs are not usually let off their leads up here because of the drop. Their owner is a middle-aged woman I've seen around the village, and we exchange nods and smiles as we pass. A thirtyish couple hold the hands of two small children as they amble along, staying well back from the edge. They all have rucksacks, the children's shaped like animals. The third car must belong to two walkers I can see in the near distance.

It is possible to walk a fair way along the tops of the hills in a westerly direction before you meet fenced-off farmland where sheep graze. The east offers no more than a sharp descent into impossibly tangled bushes bordered by beds of nettles. Ben and I almost got stuck down there once as we wandered on, our heads in the clouds, our minds on nothing but each other and being alone. Footholds were few and far between, as we discovered when we made our way up again, after we'd perched, kissing hungrily, on an uncomfortably sharp, chalky ledge.

Not our first time together. Third or fourth, perhaps. The first time, I'd sat self-consciously in my car while Ben had sat, with no visible trace of self-consciousness, alongside in his. I would even go so far as to say his expression held a touch of arrogance, but if that was true, in my heightened emotional state, I would have found it appealing and sexy.

I had arrived a few minutes before him, my feet hardly able to operate the pedals, my hands sweat-glued to the steering wheel, while I alternately prayed that he would or wouldn't turn up. When I saw his car, I switched on the engine again and turned the wheel, intent on getting out of there as fast as possible, asking myself what on earth I thought I was doing. Then, seeing my car, he raised a lean, tanned forearm out of his window in laconic greeting, his expression solemn, and my car straightened as if of its own accord as he pulled in.

It was ten o'clock in the morning – a ridiculous time for a date, if you could call it that. Ben and I had skived off work, me by arrangement, him, well, I don't remember now, but he always seemed to be able to do what he liked with his time, work notwithstanding. High Heaven doesn't have many visitors – apart from the view, it's not a beauty spot that draws the crowds. Even so, we could have bumped into anybody; friends, neighbours, clients from the vets' surgery with their dogs, anybody.

Had we considered that? I don't remember that either, but ten in the morning seemed a time of innocence, of ordinariness, and I suppose we just ran with that.

Natalie had Skyped just before I left to meet Ben; it was nine thirty in the evening in New Zealand and my parents were already sleeping.

'Their heads are all over the place from the flight,' she'd laughed. 'I won't tell them I've spoken to you or I'll be in trouble for letting them miss out. Fran...' Her pixellated frown reached me from the other side of the world.

'What?'

'Mum and Dad love both of us the same, you know that.'

'Yes, I know.' I felt the familiar sadness that claimed me whenever I remembered Mum and Dad were no longer an hour and a half's drive away.

'Mum's worried you'd think she was favouring me and my kids.'

'Nat,' I'd sighed, 'Mum and I talked about all that before they went, and I do understand, I honestly do.' *Did I?* 'Once they'd gone out for a holiday and Dad's emphysema was so much better, they couldn't stop rattling on about how much they'd loved New Zealand. I could tell then how it was going to go. It took them a while to tell me what I already knew.'

I could only think that my sister was dragging me over old ground because she felt guilty about having persuaded our parents to take up residence in the bungalow at the end of their garden. But we both knew it was the right thing for them; an opportunity to enjoy endless sunshine and more comfort in their later years than they'd have had in Harlow. Naturally, I missed my big sister like crazy when she and her husband Jonny emigrated with their two boys, but that was ten years ago, and I've got used to not having her around. I've had no choice. With Mum and Dad, it was different.

The rest of the Skype conversation was fairly brief, mainly

due to my inability to focus on anything other than what I was about to do. I didn't even tell Natalie about Caitlin's suspected – by then almost certain – autism. The appointment with the child psychologist, although only five days previously, had seemed unimaginably distant, as if it belonged in another lifetime. But we ended the call on a happy, sisterly note and I finished getting ready to meet Ben while kidding myself I was simply going to meet a friend for coffee.

The woman with the whippets has gone. The walkers have disappeared. I can see the family way ahead, the children clinging to the rungs of the dividing fence, watching the sheep. I move away from the cliff edge where I've been deep breathing the invigorating air and trying to order my brain into some sort of calm. I succeed, almost, and as I step onto the grassy scar of the path, I slot Tessa and her weirdness back where she belongs, inside my mind-box of slightly irritating incidentals that don't deserve any more attention.

As I stroll on, my thoughts return to that first meeting with Ben. He got out of his car and waited while I fiddled with this and that and eventually got out of mine, and then we stepped towards one another and hugged in a perfunctory way, like friends.

Friends. Was this how it was going to begin – and end? I admit, at that point I had no idea. Then I remembered the way we'd looked at each other, the touch of his hand, and I was gripped with fear. But still I felt compelled to say 'Yes, fine' when he asked me if we should walk for a while. There was no other answer. We were on the path I'm on now when Ben reached for my hand, and we strolled along the crest of High Heaven, not talking, wrestling with the novelty of being together. At least, I was wrestling. Ben's face, when I dared to glance, showed none of the tightness I felt in mine.

We hunkered down in the grass amongst the rabbit-holed hillocks, and I managed to relax as we chatted about nothing in particular – at least, nothing I remembered later. When we lapsed into silence, Ben reached for my hand and I thought he was going to help me up. Instead, he pulled me towards him, and we kissed. The whole thing felt unreal, as if I had fallen down one of those rabbit-holes.

Ben is still on my mind, but only in a ruminative kind of way, when I arrive home to find the man himself on my doorstep. I spend some moments composing my face into a neutral expression as I walk up to the front door, where Hector is seeing Hazel in and thanking Ben. He swings round as I approach, and I add my thanks to Hector's and hurry indoors without a backward glance. Ben takes the hint and, seconds later, he drives off with Zoe.

Hector follows me to the kitchen. He asks me how the coffee morning went, and I tell him it was one of Tessa's undeniable successes.

'Ah,' he says. 'Well, that's great. Maybe we should invite Ben, Tessa and Zoe over here for a barbecue or something, one day?'

'Maybe.' I shrug, while inwardly something quietly gives way. Casual encounters with the pair of them I can handle, but being sociable for hours on end is another matter. Caitlin is sitting on top of the table, swinging her legs. She holds her arms out to me and I oblige with a hug and a kiss on top of her head, inhaling the scent of her at the same time. She shies away from physical contact and doesn't often invite it, so that when it happens, it feels like a gift.

'I had a *lovely* time,' she says, sliding down from the table. 'I planed some wood and I put all the shavings in a bag and brought them home. They're like little curls and they smell nice.'

'More mess.' Hazel lifts her eyes theatrically, as if she is the tidiest person ever. 'There's already shavings all up the stairs.'

Caitlin pouts. 'I couldn't help it. There was a hole in the bag.' She looks at me. 'Shall I hoover them up for you, Mum?'

'No, it's fine. A few wood shavings won't hurt.'

'You're too lax with her,' Hazel scolds. 'If that was me, I'd be made to clear it up right away!'

Hector, washing out mugs at the sink while the kettle boils, gives me a sideways grin. He agrees with Hazel, but also knows it's something too trivial to worry about. I look at the four of them and feel a rush of love for my family cascade over me, like a warm shower.

'Caitlin was a great help today,' Hector says, flicking the wet dishcloth playfully at our youngest daughter. 'Now I have some perfect pieces of wood, ready for when I need them.'

Caitlin ducks the cloth, and giggles.

I turn to Hazel. 'How was the trampolining?' I venture.

'Fine. Natch.'

'Natch.' I smile. 'And Zoe's dad, what did he do while you were on the trampolines?'

Hazel shrugs. 'I don't know. Whatever you would do, I suppose. Went for a drive, whatever. We met him in the café at lunch and he got us burgers and fries. Why d'you want to know?'

Good question. 'I don't really. I was just asking.'

Hazel shakes her head at my complete hopelessness and slopes off to watch TV.

Hector pushes a mug of tea across the counter towards me. I plant a kiss on his cheek.

He smiles. 'It's only tea.'

'Just what I needed,' I say.

I'm so sorry, my love, whispers my inner voice.

NINE

TESSA

That little comment I made about never being able to leave the past behind was a fitting end to the morning, I thought. Just a little warning, that's all it was. I don't know what she made of it, but she didn't like it, that was obvious.

I hadn't been there to witness her brief entrapment in the lift – there was no way I could have been – but when I saw the look on her face as she came up the stairs behind the two oldies, I knew it had worked. Grim-faced, clearly annoyed – she threw a cross remark at me – she was also a little shaken. Not as much as I'd have liked, but it was something.

The caretaker had told me about the lift being out of action when I arrived. Once his back was turned, all I had to do was remove the notice. Such a useful coincidence after I'd read Caitlin's jottings – as if it was meant to be.

Meeting Mirabelle Hayward was another bit of good fortune. I wouldn't normally have stopped for someone like her – I'd have exchanged a few words out of politeness and moved on. I don't know why I didn't do that. Perhaps it was because I bumped into her at the art shop, and my brain made the connection with Fran and her daughter, and the lost bag.

I'd barely spoken to Mirabelle before that day. I knew of her – who in this part of Oakheart doesn't? – and had witnessed her waylaying passers-by with her ramblings. She had never targeted me before, but she needed to talk, and apparently I would do.

She spoke about the traffic to begin with, her voice well-modulated and cultured, which made me wonder about her background. Didn't I think the council should do something to stop the lorries using the village as a shortcut? Wasn't it dreadful how they thundered by with no regard for man nor beast?

Actually, Oakheart doesn't suffer in that way, and most of the time it's an oasis of calm; too calm, Ben once said. He is a city boy; he likes bright lights, not endless swathes of green. Moving to a rural village was my dream. Ben went along with it, pretending it was his dream, too – I'm under no illusions about that. Sometimes I think I know Ben better than he knows himself. If he didn't have his other life in the capital to look forward to each day, he'd go out of his mind.

I agreed with Mirabelle about the traffic; it would have been pointless not to.

And then she changed the subject, and through my half-listening and wanting to get away, I heard Fran's name. I tuned in fast at that point.

'Do you know her, the woman who killed my Humphrey?' Mirabelle began. 'Oliver, that's her name. Francesca or something – I saw it on her badge. She's a receptionist at the vets'.' Mirabelle leaned close to me, too close, wafting something that smelled surprisingly like Dior. 'She denied it, of course. I made a formal complaint but got nowhere. The vets believed her, you see.' She snorted. 'Although why they took her word over mine when I'm such a good client of theirs is a mystery.'

'Quite,' I said, not certain of what I was hearing. I asked Mirabelle to tell me exactly what happened with Humphrey, in detail, and she obliged. Well, I was a sympathetic ear, and I doubt she encounters many of those.

But when I passed this nugget of information on to Fran, it didn't quite achieve the desired effect. Oh, I could see she was rattled, but not enough. That was why I pursued her down the stairs and flung my parting shot.

She won't get off scot-free. Nobody who is evil enough to have an affair with my husband gets away with it. It's time I upped my game, took it a step further on from simply using whatever falls into my hands to stick pins in her. I could confront her, force her to admit to me what she did, but what would it achieve? A little satisfaction for me, but nothing much would change for her.

It will take more than that to finish this once and for all.

Much more.

TEN

FRAN

On Monday, Caitlin's school is closed for a staff training day. I've taken the day off work, and last night I asked her if she would like to do something special.

'She gets all the treats,' Hazel complained. 'Her school's always shutting for something, *plus* she gets longer hols than we do.'

'Yeah. Spoilt little madam with her posh school,' Kitty said, then she'd grinned at Caitlin and poked her tongue out to show she didn't mean it.

If Caitlin's in the right mood, she takes her sisters' ribbing in good part, which she did last night.

'No, *you're* spoilt,' she said, pointing a finger at each of her sisters in turn. '*You* are and *you* are.' Then more playful teasing and laughter broke out all round, and Hector and I grinned at each other.

Unusually, we were all together, playing a favourite board game involving 'driving' little coloured plastic taxis around in a race to reach certain destination points. We'd not seen much of the girls during the day. Hazel went to a friend's house – not Zoe's, I was pleased to note – and Kitty had gone swimming with a group of friends, including boys, whom I am, under no circumstances, permitted to question her about. I try to oblige whilst keeping everything crossed that there's nothing going on that I wouldn't like. Fifteen is a tricky age, for those who are fifteen and for those who care for them. I try not to think too hard about that.

Caitlin had been having one of her quiet days, when all she wants is to stay in her room, playing with the Edwardian-style dolls' house Hector originally made for Kitty, or simply sitting on her bed surrounded by books and those infernal notebooks. She doesn't want to talk or be sociable with anyone at those times, and that's fine; it's what she needs.

Hector and I had been for a walk in the morning, then he'd gravitated to his drawing board where the tree house is taking magnificent shape, and I'd done the usual Sunday things like recolouring my hair – which came out a shade too red, like a conker, but Hector said he liked it – finished the ironing, and read a book in the garden until the sky clouded over and it got chilly.

When Kitty and Hazel came home, I coaxed Caitlin from her room for dinner, and then, her quiet time having done its work, she asked to play the taxi game. For the millionth time I blessed my luck, luck I don't deserve, at having family time to enjoy. After two rounds of the game, Hazel and Kitty went to watch TV and I reopened the conversation with Caitlin about our day out.

'We could go to London, on the train,' I suggested. 'Go to a museum, or a boat trip on the river?'

'We would get the bus, in London, though?' Caitlin frowned at me. 'Not the Tube thingy. Because, Mummy, you're scared in the Tube thingy, aren't you?'

'No, I'm not scared in the Tube, Caitlin,' I said, with a little laugh. It's true that I'd rather not use it, and if there's a lift and not an escalator, I'm stuffed, but it's fine as long as the train keeps moving and I don't have to spend too long below ground.

I smiled at my youngest daughter, whose caring nature has the power to reduce me to a tearful wreck in moments, as nearly happened then, until Hector rescued me.

'Mummy *can* go on the Tube,' he said, 'but if it was me, I'd rather go by bus because you get to see everything, especially if you sit on the top deck.'

But Caitlin decided in the end that she'd rather not go to London, and did I mind? Of course I didn't mind, I assured her, and we settled on Worthing.

So, here we are now, strolling along Worthing pier, having been round the shops. I bought some shorts and a cute flowered dress for Caitlin, and a white linen shirt I found in a charity shop for me. We've just had lunch at a coffee shop facing onto a square. It's a fine day, still spring but with the promise of summer so close you can touch it. Being a Monday and term-time, there aren't many people about, which suits both of us very well. The springy feel of the boards under my feet, the expansive views along the coast, the soft breeze on my face and the gently lapping sea work their magic on my nerves which have been more frayed than I'd realised. Caitlin was right; we didn't need the hustle and roar of the capital today.

As we reach the gallery of painted glass panels depicting local life, Caitlin darts from one side of the pier to the other on a tour of inspection. The colours and designs appeal to her artistic nature. It's the simple things, the small things, that make her happiest. Isn't that the same for all of us? We pass the attractive art-deco buildings housing the amusements and café, and arrive at the end of the pier. Caitlin had skipped ahead of me, but now she holds back, staying close to my side, as one of the fishermen looks up from the lower deck and grins at her.

'It's okay,' I say. 'Watch.' She watches as the man casts his line in a great loop against the blue-green sea and settles into a chasm of patience to wait for a bite.

Other fishermen do the same, ranged along the deck, surrounded by the clutter of fishing gear, discarded outer garments, flasks and lunch boxes. Caitlin, her shyness gone, sits down on the higher deck, legs dangling over the edge, and observes with fascination the scene below. When a young bearded man lands a fish, she tenses with delight as the squiggling silver creature is reeled in. It's a tiny one and is thrown back into the sea to live another day. Caitlin nods in silent satisfaction and then says she really, really would like to have an ice cream now.

Back at the café, I buy Caitlin's ice cream, and coffee and ginger cake for me, and we take it to an outside table. Apart from an elderly couple, their faces upturned contentedly towards the sun, the tables are deserted. But then I swivel round on my seat and there's a man sitting alone at the end table, gazing out to sea, a drink in front of him.

Caitlin realises at precisely the same second as I do.

'Mum, I can see Zoe's dad over there. It is him, isn't it?'

I can only nod in response, as at that precise second, Ben turns away from the sea view and looks directly at me.

'Hey, Fran.' His voice is faint on the breeze, but I see his mouth form the shapes of the words.

Okay, I see Ben plenty of times around Oakheart, and only the other day he was troubling our front step. This is different. Anxiety swills around inside me.

'Hi,' I mouth back.

He stays right where he is, and I can't not go over. He makes it impossible. I get up from my seat and walk across, Caitlin following, clutching her ice-cream cone. Having my daughter with me keeps me grounded in normality as I approach Ben's table and give him what I hope is a neighbourly smile.

'Day off?' I ask.

'Yes, but don't tell the missus.' He laughs, flashing his eyes. I must look confused, because he adds, 'I needed time out, didn't realise until I was at the station, so I came here instead of getting the London train.' He laughs again softly. 'It was so early when I got here, way too early.'

I nod to say it's fine. 'You'll tell her when you get home, though, that you played hooky today?'

I have no idea why I care. Well, I don't, but I have to say something. This is feeling pretty weird as it is.

'I might.' The eyes again. 'Okay, yes, of course I will. I'll head home soon, anyway.'

'Well, my coffee's over there, so...'

'Fetch it over.' Ben indicates an empty seat at his table and drags another across. It sounds like a command, a command I obey. It would seem strange to Caitlin otherwise.

'I wouldn't have thought this was your sort of place,' I say, sitting down in the seat furthest from Ben while Caitlin wriggles onto the other one and concentrates on licking her ice cream.

'Worthing, or the pier?'

'Both.'

'You know me so well,' Ben says quietly, and immediately I regret my words. 'I just fancied the peace and quiet for a change, and the sea. I like the sea. It doesn't have that remote feel, like the rural setting we happen to inhabit. In any case, it was where the next train was going, so...'

He looks at me in a way I remember all too well, a look that at one time would have set my pulse racing. Now I simply feel annoyed to have my day encroached upon. As if my recent dealings with Tessa weren't enough. I wonder wildly if some kind of spell has been cast that is designed to glue me and the Grammaticus family together for ever.

Caitlin slides off the seat and crosses to the railing to look at the sea.

'How are you, Fran?' Ben asks. He tilts his shoulders back, links his hands behind his head, and gazes up at the sky, as if the answer is of no consequence.

Which it isn't, of course. It's just small talk. He's an Oakheart parent, an acquaintance, the status he was relegated to, long ago. I answer just as casually.

'Oh, fine, thanks. You?'

He waits before he replies, brings his hands back and rests them on the table, his eyes scanning my face. 'I miss you. I really do.'

'No.' I shake my head. 'Just *no*, Ben.'

He should know we don't have that kind of conversation. It's as much against the unwritten rules as you can get.

He shrugs. 'I speak only the truth. It's okay if you don't feel the same. I can live with that. If I must.'

I don't favour this with a reply. I'm shaking inside with shock and anger.

I get up from my seat and call Caitlin. 'Come on, love, time we were going.'

She comes, and we leave.

I can feel Ben's eyes on my back all the way along the pier.

ELEVEN

FRAN

Since that day, I see Ben all the time – or it certainly seems that way. He leaves Rose Cottage before seven on weekdays and doesn't return until seven in the evening. I'm not often around the village in the evenings, but the other night we ran out of fillings for the girls' sandwiches, so I walked to the other end of Oakheart where there's a shop that stays open late. On the way back, I saw Ben in the high street ahead of me, walking towards Rose Cottage. He didn't see me. He may have been for a drink in the Crown, although he's not a regular; I know that from before. Unless his habits have changed.

Other reasons threaded through my mind as to why he might be out and about at nine p.m., of which there could be several, none of them interesting or extraordinary. Which led me to wonder why I was even thinking about it.

He's home at weekends, of course, but it's not as if we live that close. And yet I've seen him on both the weekends since Worthing. A Saturday trip to the high street had me ducking into the bookshop as Ben swung past on the other side of the road. A week later, on the Sunday, the five us were driving along the road out of Oakheart to have lunch at a favourite restaurant as a treat, when we passed him coming in the opposite direction, alone in his car. He glanced at us – at me – but gave no sign of recognition.

I even saw him striding along the perimeter path of the park when I was on my way to meet Grace for coffee at the park café. It was four o'clock in the afternoon, on a weekday. I couldn't be a hundred per cent certain it was him – he was some distance away and the tree shadows provided cover – but in my head it was definitely him.

Ben is suddenly everywhere, and it isn't helping my state of mind.

I am overthinking this, I know. He's probably not around any more than he was before; my brain has somehow retuned itself to spot him. This takes me back to how it was in the weeks after we broke up, if 'breaking up' is the right term. I virtually went into hiding, creeping along the streets to work or the shops, putting my foot down in the car whenever I passed his house. But Ben was conspicuous by his absence then and I need not have bothered. When Hazel and Zoe had social arrangements, it was Tessa who did the running about, if any was needed.

Had he kept a low profile during that time for my sake, to save any awkwardness should we accidentally meet? I don't know the answer to that. I was the one who ended the affair. Ben, the arrogance I'd previously found so attractive in full force, refused to believe me when I said we had to stop seeing each other. All this said, I couldn't imagine him creeping anywhere, so it may have been pure coincidence – with a dash of luck – that our paths didn't cross during those after-weeks.

Whatever, none of this helps now, and I resolve to put what happened in Worthing down to a moment's impulsiveness on Ben's part and forget it. And while I'm about it, I'll try to forget about Tessa, too, with her crazy comment about the past catching up with you. Not so crazy, of course, because it does, and it has, all the time. But again, I tell myself I'm safe and she knows nothing. If she did, something else would have happened by now.

Sometimes, in the still, small hours, I wonder if we should move, indulge Hector's dream and buy a rambling, timbered house in another village or down a lane in the middle of nowhere. But rambling, timbered houses are beyond our means, unless they're riddled with woodworm and need a new roof. Besides, how would I get to work and the elder girls to school if we moved away from Oakheart? In any case, I'm not the type to run away, and have no intention of doing so now.

Looking back to that crazy time with Ben, I'm amazed at my daring. It wasn't as if I had a friend to give me an alibi, because I told no one. This was my mess, my doing, I told myself, and it would be unfair to involve anyone else. Unfair? Yes, okay, nothing about it was fair to anyone. But that is what I thought, at the time.

I lied. I'm so ashamed about that, not just of the whole thing with Ben, but the lies I told to Hector as to my whereabouts when I was with my lover. That first afternoon, up on High Heaven, we talked and we kissed, once. That was all. We didn't make another date. Ben just said, 'See you,' when we parted in the car park, and I said the same back. But we knew. We knew we were already at the stage where we couldn't keep away from one another.

I didn't lie directly all the time; it was more by omission. I had time owing at the surgery, as I'd been filling in on Saturday mornings for Sally who had been on holiday, and Ben would skive off work – something he seemed to find easy to do and, apparently, still does – and pick me up in his car around twelve thirty. He would park in a side street, near the back entrance to the vets'. We spent a lot of time in that car, trolling around the countryside, smiling at each other, touching hands, before we settled on a distant park or riverbank where we would lie in the grass and kiss until our lips were swollen. Just kissing, a little more, that was all. I refused to go any further in a potentially public place.

The result of all this holding back was that by the time we did have sex – in a small country hotel miles away, where we knew nobody and nobody knew us – we fell on each other like wild animals. I was shameless, I admit that. The feeling of being wanted, desired, to that extent, the sensations Ben awakened in me that had been missing for a long time, the frisson of a secret relationship... it was heady stuff and I was hooked. I was hurting nobody, I reasoned, because nobody knew.

I truly believed that, at the time. It seems incomprehensible now.

That little hotel – I do remember its name, but I never say it now, not even inside my head – became our love-nest. Love? I use the word loosely. It was never love like the feeling I have for Hector. Yet it was still love. Ben and I talked about that. He said he had fallen in love with me, and I challenged him over it. Did he not love his wife? Yes, he loved her. But this was different, another brand of love. There are many forms of love, and all of them real in their way, he said. I couldn't disagree. How very convenient.

Afternoons with Ben were easy to get away with. Hector assumed I was either at work or at home, and I never failed to respond to a call or text from him, whatever state I was in at the time. I was never once late collecting Caitlin, and I was always there when Kitty and Hazel arrived home from school. I say these things now as if I'm proud of them. I am not. Far from it, believe me.

One day while I was at work, I received a text from Ben asking if I could get away for an evening, ideally a whole night. Using our regular mobile phones was always a risk, but what other way was there? We both took to hiding our phones when we were at home, either on our persons or secreted in a drawer. On the rare occasion I forgot, I would suddenly spring up from my chair and dash off to retrieve my phone from the bathroom or hall table.

Ben never forgot, or so he said. At least one of us stayed relatively sane.

I lied outright and invented a girls' night out in Worthing. Ben and I actually went to Brighton, to a smart hotel overlooking the sea. Not for the whole night – I wasn't crazy enough to risk that, although Ben seemed remarkably cool about the whole thing – but I didn't get home until half past one in the morning. He dropped me at the station, and I got a taxi home from there.

We'd had a memorable night, with dinner amongst other diners like a proper couple. We took the last of the Champagne up to our room, time being of the essence. I ended up drinking most of it because Ben was driving.

During those frantic weeks, Ben was my drug of choice, my go-to in my head whenever I felt worried, anxious or sad, about Mum and Dad, about Caitlin, about anything. Not only did I find Ben achingly attractive in a physical sense, I saw something in him that was never made crystal clear, something in his eyes that spoke of inner secrets which, should they be released, would spoil the effect. Ben made me feel more alive than life itself.

It couldn't go on, though. Not only did I begin to panic that the longer it continued, the more likely it was that we'd be found out but, more pressingly, I didn't want to betray my husband and children any more. I'd been living in a dream world, convinced I wasn't harming them, or Ben's wife, until one day I woke up in a maelstrom of self-hate.

I texted Ben and asked to meet him. We would talk, and Ben would agree I was right. We would share a goodbye kiss and it would be over. Damage limitation.

It wasn't an easy conversation. How did I ever imagine it would be?

TWELVE

TESSA

Zoe is not seeing so much of Hazel these days, not outside of school anyway. She prefers to hang out with a girl called Tayler – skinny little thing, I do hope she's not anorexic. Zoe isn't easily influenced by her peers, but you never know quite who you're dealing with.

Zoe and Hazel haven't fallen out as such, not according to Zoe, anyway. Friendships when you're twelve are fluid things, allegiances easily switching around. But it does mean my access to the Oliver family's movements, Fran's in particular, are more limited.

Keep your friends close and your enemies closer. That's how the saying goes, isn't it? Well, it works for me.

I saw Fran briefly the other day, when I'd made a snap decision to walk to the school and meet Zoe. My daughter doesn't particularly like me meeting her, but on the odd occasion that I do, she accepts it with indulgent resignation. I was waiting by the main gates when I saw Fran pass by in her car. She slowed as she passed the school, scanning the entrance, and then she must have found a parking space because five minutes later, she appeared on foot. Caitlin wasn't with her, being picked up her father, perhaps. The entrance was thronging by then, but I waved across and she saw me. She hesitated for a moment, seemingly unsure as to what to do, and then she started towards me and ran into a testosterone barrier of large, loud boys in rugby kit.

'Meeting Kitty with her science project,' she half-mimed at me, and I sensed a relief in her that she couldn't actually reach me.

I nodded and smiled, then Zoe sidled up to me, Tayler peeling off and disappearing into the mêlée.

'I didn't know you were coming,' my daughter said.

'I didn't plan to. I fancied a walk and it was time so... Not a problem, is it?'

'Course not.' She shrugged and tried to look pleased, and I felt glad she's still young enough to make the effort.

'Look, there's Hazel over there, with her mum,' I said.

Zoe shrugged, as if to say, *what of it?*

Hazel was standing beside Fran, looking impatient. Seconds later, I saw Kitty come through the gates and push her way towards her mother, her arms wrapped protectively around some kind of model.

It seemed like an omen that as Zoe and I wove a path along the crowded pavement, we passed Fran's car, parked in a tight space with two wheels up on the kerb. The girls were in the back, Kitty's model wedged in front of their knees. Fran's window was halfway down. I gave her a knowing smile.

'Yeah, it's going to take an age to get out of here.' She nodded towards the stream of traffic, then remembered her manners. 'Would you like a lift? That's assuming we ever get on the road. Zoe can squash in the back.'

'Oh, no, we're fine, thanks,' I said. 'I came out for the walk. We don't have as far to go as you.'

'Right.' Fran smiled. 'Well, see you around.' She scanned the traffic for a gap, drumming her fingers on the steering wheel.

'Actually,' I said, leaning towards her window, 'I was wondering if you, Hector and the girls would like to come to dinner at ours one night next week, say, Friday? Nothing formal.'

'Oh.' Fran's face was a portrait of surprise and uncertainty. 'That's very kind of you, Tessa. Friday? I'm not exactly sure what we're doing then...'

'That's fine. Let me know.'

'I will. Thank you.' She edged the car out, and Zoe and I walked on.

'What did you do that for?' Zoe scowled at me.

'We're too insular, the three of us. Not social enough. It'll be fun, don't you think? Hazel's your friend, Fran is a friend of mine, Dad has met Hector a number of times, so why not invite them?'

I knew I was sounding too enthusiastic, and probably defensive. But I need to keep an eye on Fran, and putting her and Ben together, in the same space, for a few hours at least, well, that was a masterstroke. I know the invitation will be accepted; Fran won't want to seem impolite. And I will be watching.

It's the day after I invited Fran and her brood to dinner. As I expected, she texted last night to say they would love to come. Deal done.

It's no surprise when another opportunity to further my campaign arrives in the form of Mirabelle Hayward, gesticulating at me across the high street, indicating that I should go over. Perhaps she remembers telling me about Fran killing her cat, perhaps she doesn't, and thinks I'm a complete stranger. Whichever, I cross the road with alacrity and say hello.

'I saw you outside the art shop, didn't I?' She points a scarlet fingernail at me, a smile opening up her pinched face.

She does remember. 'So you did,' I say. 'How are you, Mirabelle?'

She thinks for a moment. 'I'm very well, thank you. I'm sorry, I can't think what your name is.'

'It's Tessa. Tessa Grammaticus.'

'Grammaticus.' She pronounces the name slowly, spacing out the syllables. 'My, that's a mouthful.'

'Was it something particular?' I ask. She looks puzzled. 'You waved me over just now.'

Her small grey eyes emerge from deep sockets, gleaming like marbles. 'Ah yes. I know what it was. I wondered if you knew what that film was called, the one with Greer Garson and Walter Pidgeon? It was set in the Second World War and there was a Nazi pilot in it. The title escapes me, and I thought you might know.'

Momentarily fazed by the random question, I half-regret my decision to cross the road and engage with this silly old hag, until I think about how useful she could be.

'I'm sorry, I don't. I'm not very up on old movies.'

Mirabelle studies her brown brogues, then looks up again. 'It had a woman's name in the title, I'm sure of that... *Mrs somebody?*'

'*Mrs Miniver?*' The answer spirals up from the depths of my memory. After my father left for the last time, my mother would watch old films in the afternoons, sitting prim and upright on the sofa with the curtains closed. Our curtains were often closed during those days, as if summer belonged to everyone apart from us.

'Yes, *yes!*' Mirabelle's brogues hammer the pavement in a little jig. 'How clever of you!' She taps the side of her head and speaks in a half-whisper I have to lean in to catch. 'Mind you, I should have known, even though it was a long time ago. I had a lot of fun playing that role. A *lot* of fun! They were all in love with me, you know, all the men on set.'

'Right...' I glance along the row of shops. 'I was just going to have coffee in that café, just there. Would you like to join me? My treat.'

Mirabelle clutches her throat. A string of seed pearls catches around her thin fingers and she has to disentangle them. 'I would *love* that. Thank you, Tessa.'

The café has a main area inside the door where the service counter is, and a cluster of smaller, cosier rooms leading off. I lead my companion to a room with a shallow glass conservatory filling one wall. The only other occupant is a smartly dressed man thumbing through a set of documents, pen in hand, and I figure that the peace and quiet and the view of the garden with its stumpy apple trees and dangling bird feeders will help Mirabelle feel settled. After all, she and I are almost strangers, although Mirabelle doesn't seem to make any distinction between people she knows – if she knows anyone – and the population of the village in general. We're all fair game for her nonsensical ramblings.

The waitress takes our order for coffees – flat white with soya milk for me, black for Mirabelle – and toasted teacakes.

'This is nice,' Mirabelle says, looking around. 'Do you often come in here? I don't think I've ever been.'

'Sometimes. It is nice, isn't it?' In truth, I've never been here before, but it doesn't fit the occasion to say so.

I make small talk about the weather and so on until our order arrives. I slide half of my teacake onto Mirabelle's plate to offload some of the carbs, and she twinkles a child-like smile.

'I've been thinking about what you told me,' I say, 'about Francesca Oliver having something to do with your poor cat dying. It was on my mind, after I left you. What a tragic thing to happen.'

Mirabelle looks up from buttering her teacake, her eyes darting lizard-like to mine, not in surprise that I've raised the subject but with gratitude that she has an ally.

'Poor Humphrey. It *was* tragic, and *wicked*, the way she handled him. Mishandled him, rather. Do you know her, that woman? Do you know her, Tessa?'

'I know *of* her, that's all. Her children go to the same school as my daughter. I don't have any dealings with her otherwise.'

Mirabelle pats my wrist with a buttery hand and it's all I can do not to flinch. 'Good. She isn't the sort of person you should be having dealings with. I'd keep it that way, if I were you.'

I nod. 'Mirabelle...?'

'Yes?'

'I wondered if you'd thought about exacting a little revenge on her?' I give a little laugh, put a hand to my throat. 'I don't know where that came from, I'm not the revengeful type. Take no notice of me.'

I sip my coffee, gazing out to the garden, as if the subject has flown from my mind.

'Revenge, you say? Really, she should get her comeuppance. I'm the only one who knows what really happened. That other woman on the desk at the surgery was busy doing goodness knows what and taking no notice at all, and the vets sided with Mrs Oliver because that's what they do. I stood no chance of a fair hearing, no chance at all.'

I stay silent, waiting while the seed I planted swells and bursts and sends out a tiny shoot.

'You've made me think, Tessa,' Mirabelle says, eventually. 'You certainly have.'

I hold up a hand. 'No, no, forget what I said. It was silly of me.'

The shoot develops leaves. 'Something to alarm her, something a little bit nasty to make her all twitchety...'

'Twitchety?'

'Yes. Like I felt when I realised poor Humphrey had stopped breathing and his dear little heart had stopped beating. Like I've felt ever since.'

Mirabelle's grey eyes are moist and I pray she isn't going to cry, not here in public – not anywhere if she's with me. But if it serves a purpose...

I reach for her hand but stop just short of touching it. 'I'm sorry. Don't get upset.'

Mirabelle takes a deep, huffy breath, and smiles. 'I'm fine, dear. It's not your fault.' A pause, and then, 'She wouldn't need to know it was me, would she? Putting a little nuisance her way would be enough. And, do you know, I think it would help me, knowing I'd taken some *action* against her. It's so frustrating otherwise.'

I can't help smiling. Batty or not, Mirabelle Hayward is a woman after my own heart.

'You have a point there,' I say. Then, when we've sat in pensive silence for a while, 'She has children, three girls, I think.'

Mirabelle flaps a hand. 'Oh, I can't worry about them. I expect they're as hard-hearted as their mother. Although the brown-haired one seems quite a nice girl.'

'I expect they are,' I say, ignoring her last comment as I'm thinking how easy it is to influence somebody if you catch them in the right frame of mind, at the right time. Timing is all – I'm thinking of Fran again.

'I believe,' I begin, gazing out of the window again, 'they live in that private road, the one with the British Legion club on the corner. But I could be wrong.' It's not a good idea to admit I know too much about Fran.

'Oh no, you're absolutely right, dear. Woodside Villas. I

followed her home, when I was still all of a dither over poor Humphrey. She went through the wood, the public footpath. It's a shortcut. And then I saw her come out the other side and go into that modern house halfway down. Oh yes.' Mirabelle clatters her cup into her saucer and nods firmly. She looks almost triumphant. 'I know where she lives all right.'

THIRTEEN

FRAN

'We can't not go. I've accepted the invitation now.'

It's Thursday evening, and everyone but me has 'forgotten' that we're going to Rose Cottage for dinner tomorrow, until I reminded them just now and was met with a barrage of moans from the girls. My own private wish that we do not have to do this could not be more fervent than theirs. The impending occasion feels like a physical thing, an industrial-sized wheel with lethal, jagged teeth, rolling unrelentingly towards me. But what could I do? If I'd said we were busy on Friday, Tessa would have proposed another night. She wouldn't have let it drop. Once she's made up her mind about something, it happens, no matter what. That much I have learned about her.

'It'll be fine,' Hector says, rubbing his hands together in the same jolly-father way he did when the girls were small. 'We all get on, don't we? And Mum helps Tessa with her charity stuff. In fact,' he turns to me, 'I suggested we invite them here for a barbecue, didn't I?'

He did indeed. I'd forgotten about that, or rather, I'd deliberately wiped it from my mind. Hector's reminder somehow makes the prospect of spending an evening with my secret ex-lover who seems to have lost the plot, and his wife, ten times worse.

We're expected at seven for dinner at seven thirty, Tessa having first checked with me that it's not too late for Caitlin to eat. This consideration helps soothe my anxiety a little, reminding me that Tessa's intentions are sound, if a little off the mark at times.

We're on the cusp of leaving the house when Hazel decides she detests what she's wearing, vanishes upstairs to change again, and my carefully planned timetable goes awry.

'She's got a point,' Kitty says, sinking down on the stairs and automatically reaching into her pocket for her phone. 'That top is miles too tight across the bust for her. It has been for ages. I told her that when she put it on.'

In my wired state, the idea of my twelve-year-old having a bust in the first place is enough to send my nerves flying in all directions.

'Kitty, go up and tell her to get a shift on, will you?'

'Fran...' Hector gives me a smile that means *stop stressing*. 'We're fine. It only takes ten minutes to walk to theirs. Did anyone feed the cat, by the way?'

I screw up my face as if I'm trying to remember.

'I'll take that as a no, then.' Hector disappears to the kitchen.

Caitlin plucks at my sleeve. 'Are we going soon? Because if we're not, there's something *really important* I have to do that I didn't have time for.'

'*No*, Caitlin, you stay right where you are.'

'How can it be important?' Kitty says, from the top of the stairs. 'Nothing you do is important.'

'*Kitty!*' If she upsets Caitlin now, the whole evening is doomed. Like it wasn't already. 'Where *is* Hazel?'

'I'm here. There's no need to panic, Mother.' Hazel flounces down the stairs. She's changed from tight jeans and a top into a pink and grey striped mini dress and her denim jacket. She looks fresh and pretty, as do her sisters, and I'm proud to show off my daughters.

Hector returns and, finally, we leave.

'So sorry we're late. The girls and their outfits...' I gabble at Tessa as she opens the door of Rose Cottage and ushers us inside.

'You're not late at all, Fran.' Tessa beams round at all of us. 'Anyway, it wouldn't matter if you were.'

She has more make-up on than I've seen her wear before, and I wish I'd put on eyeshadow as well as mascara, except when I do it makes me look like a clown. She's wearing navy-blue wide-leg culottes with a belt tied in a bow at the waist – which only someone as slim as her can get away with – and a mango-coloured Bardot top revealing creamy-smooth shoulders. Her inverted bob hairstyle has recently been trimmed.

Yes, Tessa looks perfect; stylish but the right side of casual for such an evening. I look fine, too. I may be a seething mass of anxieties, but I've learned enough to feel reasonably confident in the way I look. Tonight, I'm wearing narrow, ankle-grazer trousers the colour of summer sea, and the white linen shirt I bought in Worthing worn loose, the sleeves rolled back neatly to elbow length. I also put on a simple pendant and matching earrings. My hair has behaved itself for once and falls in shiny waves to skim my shoulders.

'You scrub up well,' had been Hector's comment before we left home, but his eyes spoke of deeper compliments. The things that remain unsaid are often the most telling, don't you think?

Hector and Ben greet one another in an effusive all-guys-together manner, which comes across as slightly fake on Hector's side – for all his so-called enthusiasm for socialising, he's actually on the shy side. Of course, it's totally fake on Ben's, but he hides it well. I can't help wondering what he's making of all this. I decide I don't care. Now we're here in the same room, my anger towards him for that stupid thing he said on Worthing pier glows hot inside me, as if a dying fire has been rekindled. It's not a pleasant feeling, and I avoid looking at him directly in case I give him a clue that he's ruffled me. I won't give him the satisfaction.

I move to Hector's side and link my arm through his as we stand about beneath grey-painted beams in the plaster-pink dining room, drinks in hand. I need the support, both mentally and physically. Or perhaps it's to show Ben that my marriage is solid, I honestly don't know.

This is already worse than I'd envisaged, and the evening's barely begun. Hector glances at me quizzically, and I smile, giving his arm a squeeze before detaching myself. I stand at the window, feeling stranded like a non-swimmer in the middle of a pool, and admire aloud the back garden of Rose Cottage. My admiration is genuine; it's not a huge garden but it's a controlled riot of cottage garden flowers, with two rose-covered arbours, honeysuckle climbing the fence, and the brightest of emerald lawns, free-form in shape and clipped to perfection.

'Thank you, Fran.' Tessa is beside me. 'I have to say it has come on well this year.'

'We do have help with the garden,' Ben says, almost crossly. 'Be honest, Tessa.' He fastens her with a glacial look that Hector and I don't miss. Hector widens his eyes at me, just perceptibly.

'I never said I did it all myself, nor that you did,' Tessa says, through a brittle smile. She turns back to me, while her eyes flick to Ben. 'We managed to track down a gardener when we first moved here. He's a bit creaky but worth his weight in mushroom compost. The garden's a work in progress, though.' She chuckles. 'A bit like me.'

I laugh, too. 'Aren't we all?'

I'm starting to believe I can get through this. Tessa's sense of humour has been hiding itself away, but this glimmer gives me hope, and again I wonder if I've been too hard on her in the past. Which is not surprising, under the circumstances, but I owe this woman. I owe her normality, peace and security, and if I could give her that on a plate, I would. I sense a coolness between Tessa and Ben that scares and saddens me, in case I am partly to blame. I made things right between me and Hector, hopefully before he noticed anything was wrong, but perhaps Ben did not achieve that so easily.

On the other hand, perhaps it's nothing to do with me at all. They could have had a row just before we arrived, as simple as that. I go to finish my gin spritzer and realise the glass is empty. Ben notices.

'Top-up?' He gives me a secret kind of smile that makes me want to kick furniture.

'No, I won't, thanks.' There are wine glasses on the table. The last thing I will do tonight is drink too much.

The girls, Caitlin included, have understandably ducked the adult chit-chat and taken themselves off to the living room where I hear the jangly opening tune of an American teen drama from the TV.

'You must be very creative, Hector.' He's been telling Ben about his latest projects, including the tree house, and Tessa moves to join them. 'I admire anyone who has the vision to make something wonderful and unique. And the skill, of course.' She gushes a bit, which may be the product of the shyness I've attributed to her.

'I enjoy the work, that's the main thing, don't you think?' Hector says. 'Advertising's creative, too, though. That's what you do, Ben, isn't it?'

'I work for an ad company but I'm more on the accounts

side,' Ben says, with a reluctance that suggests the last thing he wants to do is talk about himself. As if he ever did.

Tessa calls the girls, and she and Ben ferry dishes to the table. Caitlin suddenly turns shy and wants to sit between me and Hector rather than with Zoe, Hazel, and Kitty.

Tessa smiles. 'Sit wherever you like, sweetheart.'

'Yes, I will,' Caitlin says, causing Kitty to harrumph at her across the table. I send my eldest daughter a warning look.

Every taste has been catered for. There are vegetarian quiches, cold roast chicken breasts, a platter of ham, a steaming bowl of cheesy pasta, and a pyramid of dainty filo parcels with a variety of fillings.

'The ones this side have chilli in them,' warns Tessa. Accompanying the main dishes are bowls of salad, French beans, garlic and plain bread, and, to the girls' delight, a huge dish of golden chunky chips.

'Tessa, this looks wonderful,' I say. 'What a lot of trouble you've gone to!' *Now who's gushing?*

She looks pleased. 'No trouble really, it's all easy stuff. Anyway, I enjoy entertaining, when I get the chance.' She throws Ben a loaded look which I can't interpret. He responds, if you can call it a response, with a blank stare, and I'm thinking, don't spoil this now. Let's just get on and have a nice evening.

And we do. The talk flows easily, Ben the most taciturn of us all but I can't say he's unfriendly. The girls chatter away to each other, and by the time Tessa brings puddings – three types plus ice cream – Caitlin has moved herself to be next to Zoe, whom she has taken a liking to, and we've all shuffled good-naturedly round to accommodate her.

Tessa, her pale complexion turning faintly pink, raises her glass of sparkling water. 'To family and friends.'

The adults raise their glasses in response, but for some reason, nobody repeats the sentiment.

· · ·

'That went well, didn't it?' Hector says, as we trail home in the semi-darkness.

There's a smidgeon of relief in his voice that tells me he wasn't looking forward to the evening any more than I was. My own sense of relief centres around Ben having behaved himself, which he more or less did, and Tessa being the perfect hostess and not letting her superior side slink through the cracks.

'It was fine.' I link my arm through Hector's. 'I shan't want any more to eat for a fortnight, though.'

'Or drink.' Hector pulls a face.

'God, I didn't drink too much, did I?'

'Of course not. Why do you say that?'

'I only wondered.' I'd not had any difficulty controlling my expression and body language, but that's only my view from the inside.

'You said we mustn't say "God",' says Caitlin, breaking away from her sisters to skip back to me.

'You're quite right, love. I'm sorry.'

Kitty looks behind at us. 'One rule for them, one for us.' But she's good-natured in the way she says it, and I know she's enjoyed the evening.

'Zoe drove me *nuts*!' Hazel says, her face dark as rainclouds. 'Tayler this, Tayler that. Like Tayler's the *only* person in school who matters. La, la, la.'

'Yeah, I noticed that, too,' Kitty says casually, adding another stick to the fire.

Hector glances at me. 'Let it go,' I whisper. 'It's normal schoolgirl stuff. They were fine, Hazel and Zoe.'

Hazel overhears the last bit. She shrugs. 'Zoe's okay, I guess. She's coming over one day next week, after school, if that's all right.'

'Of course it is,' I say. 'She can stay for dinner if she likes. Just let me know which day.'

And so, our social evening with the Grammaticus family ends on a pleasant note, and I have emerged unscathed.

FOURTEEN

TESSA

I watched her the whole time she was in my house. She wouldn't have known it, but every word she spoke, every move she made, every flicker of her eyes depicting her innermost thoughts... I was there. True, I couldn't interpret every tiny thing, but what was not clear I made an educated guess at.

And Ben, I watched him, too. Watching Ben is my specialist subject. He still holds a candle for her, would get her into bed as soon as look at her. And Fran? Oh yes, Ben still holds the same appeal for her. They hardly spoke directly to one another – whether by design or whether it's a habit they can't shake off, I don't know. Whatever, the effect is the same. But it wasn't hard to miss his glances when he thought she wasn't looking, and the way he refilled her glass, almost as an afterthought. Casual, too casual. Oh, he fancies the pants off her, no doubt about it.

This, of course, was the main reason I brought them together, as a kind of test. I'll be watching Fran even more closely now, while I consider my next move. The ultimate strike, my finale, I will save. She isn't ready; her head has not yet been invaded to my satisfaction, her nerves not strung out to near breaking point, as mine once were.

If Fran knew all this, if Ben, too, realised how much I know, how much I understand, they would know that my actions are not only for my own sake but also for theirs. The pair of them need saving from themselves as much as from each other.

Ben rescued me from my life as it was, and I will always rescue him. That is the deal.

Ben is quiet after the Olivers have left. He moves silently from dining room to kitchen, washes the glasses and the best china by hand, putting the rest in the dishwasher. I watch his face reflected in the darkened glass of the kitchen window, his expression pensive. This is one time when, if I was handed a key to unlock his thoughts, I would throw it away.

'Leave that.' I wrap my arms around him from behind, pressing my face to his back, inhaling his warmth through the cotton shirt. 'I'll finish it in the morning.'

He swivels round and smiles. 'Nearly done. You go on up and I'll follow you.'

It's still early, not even half past ten. Zoe is in bed and she always falls asleep wearing earbuds.

The message is clear.

We make love with indolent passion. I turn away straight afterwards so as not to witness the distant look in Ben's eyes.

FIFTEEN

FRAN

It's almost midsummer's day, although you'd never know it to look at the rain bucketing down, and I feel chilled to my bones. I pray to goodness it isn't like this when we go to Cornwall in August, otherwise we'll never hear the end of it from the girls.

Hector and I finally got round to having a proper discussion about the holiday, batted various options to and fro, examined our finances until we were squint-eyed, and then looked at one another and said, 'Cornwall it is, then.'

'We're not very adventurous, are we?' I said, as we bagged what seemed to be the last available cottage in the whole of the county, fingers crossed that it really is as close to the beach as it says on the website.

Hector gave me a wry look and slapped down the lid of the laptop. 'What do you suggest? Lug three daughters and a houseful of stuff on board a ferry to some cheapo French camp-site with smelly toilets? Interrail across the Alps with ten euros and a toothbrush between us?'

I laughed. 'Now you're being silly. I'd hate that sort of thing, we all would. At least the girls still think Cornwall's cool, despite the moans and groans.'

We will have a good time; we always do. Except this year I can't seem to summon any enthusiasm for holidays, or anything at all that doesn't involve the familiar, the tried and tested. Our village, the vets', the schools and home, are all I need right now. Despite what I said to Hector when we were looking at holidays, I don't want adventure.

Does that sound strange, coming from somebody who was clearly once in need of adventure and took the biggest risk of her life for it? I expect it does. But that's me, a kaleidoscope of contradictions. Being with Ben made me lose my focus; sometimes I think it's gone for good. A scary thought.

Mum Skypes one evening when Hazel and Caitlin are in bed and Hector has gone to collect Kitty from a friend's house. Seeing my mother beaming at me from the screen reminds me there is one adventure I would jump at – a trip to New Zealand. But actually, visiting my sister and parents would be just another way of coming home, so perhaps not so bold.

'How are you, Francesca?' she begins, her brown eyes identical to mine peering out at me. 'You look peaky. Are you looking after yourself? Are you getting enough fresh air?'

I laugh, and lower my glass of wine, out of shot. Fresh air was always Mum's answer to everything – along with nutritious, home-cooked food, of course. When Natalie and I were children, at the first sign of lethargy or a sniffle we were cocooned in woolly layers, socks pulled up, hats pulled down, and either sent out to the garden to play, with instructions not to come in within the hour, or frogmarched to the park.

We were generally healthy children, rarely succumbing to whatever ailment was doing the rounds and hardly ever off school, so I daresay our mother knew her stuff. One of my failings as a parent is that I seem incapable of following suit, preferring to cave in to the duvet-on-the-sofa scenario rather than face dejected looks and loaded sighs. I'm referring to Kitty and Hazel here; Caitlin resorts to tears, not yet having learned her sisters' more subtle pathways to the molten centre of my heart.

I hasten to reassure my mother I'm fine, and if I look peaky it's only because, apart from the essential trips, the weather has confined me to the house for days. Mum, I am pleased to note, looks positively glowing and I tell her so.

'Do I? I've not got my make-up on yet either.' She chuckles, then falls serious. 'Francesca, I do miss you, darling. I miss you *all*.'

'Oh,' I say, wrongfooted by the sudden switch in tone. 'Well, it's only natural. I miss you both as well, but you're in the right place. We are all in our rightful places.' I smile, more at my dumb response than anything. My mother smiles back and my heart judders.

This is so not what I need right now. Mum is the one who is guaranteed not to dwell on the unchangeable, nor to become over-emotional. My father has more trouble hiding his feelings, as I do. Except you learn to do that out of necessity, of course.

'Is Dad there? Natalie and the boys?'

'Natalie's at work, the boys are at school.' Of course they are; I remember it's around ten in the morning where they are. 'They'll call another time, I'm sure,' Mum says. 'Ah, hang on, here's Dad.'

My father's kind face appears on screen, behind Mum's. 'Hey there, Sunshine! What's new?'

Mum and I giggle. 'What is he like?' Mum says. She's seems to have cheered up, for which I am thankful, for both our sakes.

I ask what they've been doing, then give them a rundown of the girls' activities, Hector's boyish passion for building tree houses – he's gathered two more word-of-mouth commissions since the first one – and relate an anecdote about amusing incidents at the vets' surgery, exaggerating slightly for comic effect, as you do.

When the screen has turned black, I sit, wine glass in hand, listening to the silence in the house, my ear tuned for the welcome sound of Hector's car, and try to analyse the way I'm feeling. A little sad, partly because of what my mother said, but by no means entirely because of that. Something else, harder to pinpoint, signified by a dragging sensation in my gut; a generalised anxiety that I can't shake off, as if something bad is about to happen.

Was it an omen, that feeling? I don't believe in such things. But the very next day I have cause to ponder the outlandish possibility that I've somehow been endowed with the dubious gift of second sight.

The rain has finally cleared, and a washed-out blue sky appears through the windscreen as I drive towards Honeybee Hall. Unlike Oakheart Academy, parking is easy in this countryfied area and I slot into a nearby space and join the horde at the gate. Caitlin's little face shines a welcome as she spots me, her arms full of her rucksack, PE kit bag, lunch box, and trailing raincoat. She asks for music in the car – it seems to calm her, help her settle after her busy day. She chooses one of her favourite albums by Take That, made before she was born, which never fails to shock me – and we sing along as we go.

Parked in front of our garage, I gather up Caitlin's possessions abandoned on the back seat in her eagerness to be home, and as I follow her through the front gate, I see her stop and bend down.

'Oh look, Mummy!'

She points to a badger, a large one, lying across the lower of the two steps leading up to our front door, its nose nudging the concrete, fur parted and clumped by moisture, a glue of mud and leaves on its hind quarters.

'Is he dead?' Caitlin looks up at me, her eyes full of curiosity. Dead animals don't upset her; she's pragmatic about that kind of thing.

I put a hand on her shoulder and usher her round the badger and up to the door before she can start poking at the poor thing. Goodness knows what germs it harbours.

'Yes, he's dead.' That much is obvious. I can't see any sign of injury, and my first thought is that it's often the case when an animal has been hit by a car.

It's not unheard of for a badger to wander down from the woods, but this is a no-through-road, a dead end. We don't have passing traffic, and the residents drive slowly out of necessity because of the pitted, unmade road surface. In any case, if it had been knocked down, surely it would be at the roadside instead of coming to rest virtually on our doorstep.

The anxious feeling returns tenfold, sending my heart crashing against my chest wall. I see dead and dying animals all the time, but it's the context that's changed. I don't like this. I don't like it one bit.

'What shall we do with him?' Caitlin asks, her tone bright and conversational.

My question, too. After a moment's thought, I fetch a pair of rubber gloves and a bin liner and unceremoniously shovel the animal into it. I knot the bag at the top and take it to the garage, Caitlin in close attendance.

'There. Let's leave him for Daddy to see to, shall we?'

'Okay.' Caitlin skips back indoors. 'Mum? How did the badger die?'

'I expect he got knocked down by a car,' I say, though I still doubt this.

'In that case, why isn't there any blood on him, or any

squashy bits? I didn't see any blood, did you? Unless it was underneath him.' She sounds almost disappointed.

'I have no idea, Caitlin.' I use my motherly-but-firm voice to allay any further questions. I'm too shaken to deal with any more right now.

SIXTEEN

TESSA

'What did she want, the barmy woman?'

I'm so thankful Ben didn't stir himself to answer the door to Mirabelle Hayward. Trust her to call on a Saturday. Trust her to call at all; I hadn't factored a home visit into my dealings with her.

'Nothing. Well, *something,* obviously. Nothing I could help her with.'

'What, though?' Ben's unusual curiosity riles me, but I try not to snap.

'She cornered me in the high street the other day, asking if I thought we needed a traffic calming scheme. It wasn't just me; she was stopping everybody.'

'But she happened to find out where you lived.'

'She already knew. Everybody knows Rose Cottage. It's the prettiest house in the village. By default, they know who lives in it.'

I'm winging it now, but by the half-satisfied, half-bored expression on Ben's face, I'm convincing enough. I don't remember telling Mirabelle directly where I lived, but obviously I must have mentioned it in some form or other, during our conversation in the café. Probably while I was busily feigning intimacy in order to gain her confidence.

'My reputation goes before me. People know about the charity work I do. I expect Mirabelle interpreted that as community spirit. I told her I didn't want to get involved.'

Ben slopes off to the kitchen and I hear the makings of lunch getting under way. It'll be just the two of us. Zoe has gone to her new friend's house, Tayler, the one I don't like much. I take the opportunity to slip upstairs and have another dip into Caitlin Oliver's pink notebook.

Mummy comes to meet me from school EVERY day. When she comes out of work. I REALLY LIKE Mummy meeting me. I feel best when it is Mummy. Daddy would be at his workshop then anyway. He is very busy making his wooden things. Mummy is never too busy to come and get me.

A loyal daughter. Mother-fixated, but they are at that age. Though, come to think of it, Zoe used to like her father meeting her from junior school. Seemed to think he was more of a status symbol than me. Or perhaps it was the rarity value. Predictable mother, always at her beck and call. Charismatic dad, taking a well-earned break from an exciting job in the big city. Turning the heads of all the mums at the school gate, without even noticing. Or pretending not to. Which parent would you choose?

I stifle a rueful laugh, put the notebook back in the drawer, and turn my mind to Mirabelle. She's had an idea concerning Fran and can't wait to put it into practice. In fact, she's already made a start.

Taken aback to find her on the doorstep and afraid she'd expect to be asked in, I'd joined her outside, pulling the door to and walking her around the side of the house to the relative shelter of the weeping willow. Clearly, not before Ben had seen her from the window, but that couldn't be helped.

'She must be used to seeing dead animals, working at the vets','

I said. 'She wouldn't be upset by them, would she?' Mirabelle's face fell, and I knew I needed to bolster her up again. 'But, actually, Mirabelle, I like your thinking. You want to get her back for Humphrey's demise. Seeing an animal who has clearly suffered, right outside her front door, might make her understand how you must have felt, and how cruel she'd been to your poor little cat.'

Mirabelle brightened at this. 'That is *exactly* what I thought! I think it might *disturb* her, just a little?'

'It's certainly worth a try,' I said.

Mirabelle clutched her scrawny chest. 'And you'll help me? You said you would.'

Did I? It doesn't matter whether I did or not. In fact, if I do take part in this act of retaliation on Mirabelle's behalf, it brings me closer to the hub of the matter. One up from revenge by proxy.

'I'd be delighted,' I said. 'You have the animal... badger, you say?'

Mirabelle rubbed her hands together in glee. 'I was *so* lucky! It was on my mind what to do, after you said what you said in the café, and one evening I went for a walk. It helps the brain to function, walking, don't you think? I used to tell my pupils that, though heaven knows if it sank in!'

I glanced round at that point, hoping Ben wasn't coming out to see what was going on, and tapped my hand against my thigh, rhythmically. It's a device, to hurry up proceedings when somebody's speaking. Nine times out of ten, it works, as it did with Mirabelle.

'I walked through the woods over the back,' Mirabelle waved a vague arm, 'and it was raining so hard I nearly turned around and went home, but the trees helped to shelter me. That's when I found it, lying just off the footpath where *she* takes her shortcut, and I thought, this is meant to be. So, I scooped it up and put it in the carrier bag – I always have one in my pocket – and took it home. Poor thing. I couldn't see any sign of injury. Died of natural causes, I imagine.'

The following day, having worked out the optimum time to go ahead with the plan and shared the information with Mirabelle in a lengthy, repetitive phone conversation, I drove along to Graylings at four in the afternoon and knocked on the door. I knew what time Fran left work – I had double-checked that with a little extra surveillance – and by the same method, I knew what time she left the house and returned again with Caitlin. I also knew what time her other daughters were likely to arrive home from school. As for Hector, I had to take a chance on him, and on curtain twitchers in the neighbouring houses. To tell the truth, the element of danger added a nice little frisson.

Why didn't we do it at night? I did consider it, but it's not usual for me to go out after dark, and I didn't feel up to inventing a charity meeting or an unlikely-sounding social event, both of which would see me hanging around for ages before I could return home.

It was still a risk, going to Woodside Villas in broad daylight, but one I felt worth taking. Besides, I had started this thing with Mirabelle and I had to see it through.

I'd driven Ben to the station that morning, so his car was at home. I decided to use it in favour of my white Mini as being the less conspicuous. It took me an age to secure Mirabelle's seat belt – she seemed incapable of dealing with it herself – and the hour was fast approaching by the time we got going. It's only a few minutes' drive to Woodside Villas from Graylings. I drove slowly, firstly because a speeding car in the village is more noticeable than a leisurely one, and secondly because my passenger was clearly so wired by this uncommon bit of excitement, I wanted her to get the full benefit. I thought that was kind of me.

I was wearing dark glasses, but as we arrived at the corner of Woodside Villas and stopped outside the British Legion, I snapped the sun visor down and urged Mirabelle not to dally about. Then I sat, head down, and watched as she lugged the poor dead creature in its carrier bag along the road.

Minutes later, she was back. This time, she had no trouble fastening her seat belt. She kept the carrier bag on her lap as I drove her home. It stank dreadfully – I could still smell it in the car when I checked it later, so I went and bought one of those scented things and hung it on the rear-view mirror.

Ben has not complained about that, which surprises me. If he does, I shall make up some excuse for having placed it there. On the spot, probably. It's amazing what your brain can come up with if the situation warrants it.

Which is, of course, something my husband knows all about.

SEVENTEEN

FRAN

As I began to see Ben everywhere, now I also see Tessa frequently, too. Since the evening at Rose Cottage, my status has clearly been elevated in her eyes, and whereas previously I could expect a smile and a wave, now she doesn't hesitate to dash across the street if she sees me on the opposite side. It's only a hello-how-are-you kind of thing, and we might have a chat about school and the girls, nothing more. But I can't help feeling that Tessa would like to be closer, and that if she doesn't already have a best friend – I've seen no evidence of one – she would like to cast me in that role.

This is dismaying and comforting in equal measure. Dismaying, firstly because of the shameful way in which I've betrayed her, and also, although I am beginning to warm to her, it's not enough for me to want to spend too long in her company; comforting because it entrenches my belief that Tessa knows nothing about the affair.

She may be hoping we'll invite them to our house for the return match. If Hector has his way – he takes his social duties seriously – it will happen at some point. But please, not yet. I couldn't cope.

'Think of the do at Rose Cottage as a one-off,' Grace advises, when we escape domesticity one warm evening to share a bottle of wine in the garden of the Crown. 'Let the time go by and she'll forget about it. The moment will have passed.'

Of course, I've only told Grace about the Tessa side of things, no mention of Ben, and there never will be.

'I think she's a bit lonely,' I say, digging my own grave a little deeper.

Grace almost chokes on her drink. 'Are you surprised? Whoever wants to be bessie mates with somebody that bossy and superior? By the way, you do know she's starting up a Saturday morning art club for kids, don't you?'

My turn to choke. 'Art club? Are you joking? What's it got to do with Tessa?'

'Search me. I heard it third-hand so it may not be true. Although,' Grace drains the bottle into our glasses, 'I overheard a couple of Oakheart mums talking about it. One of them used to teach art and she was saying Tessa had asked her to help. She sounded quite keen. So, there must be something in it.'

'Well, I hope she doesn't ask me to help.'

'Nor me.' Grace pulls a face. 'Still, you know what they say. Forewarned is forearmed. Have something ready in case she asks.'

'I will,' I say. 'No worries.'

I'm not concerned about being asked to help with this so-called art club – I can say no to Tessa, if I concentrate – but if Caitlin gets wind of it, she'll be eager to join. Socialising is difficult for her, especially if it's with new people, but her love of drawing and painting supersedes her fears, if the pull is strong enough. It lifts my heart to know that Caitlin is learning to manage her condition, and it would be selfish of me to deny her any opportunity to do so. I just feel I need to protect myself, which seems to be getting harder as time goes on, not easier.

I remember the badger – not that I've truly forgotten it –

and can't decide whether to tell Grace about it or not. It seems such a trivial bit of nothingness now. Or it would, if my brain could only see it as a separate incident, and not another bead on my virtual rosary of unpleasant incidents.

I tell Grace anyway.

'Aw, poor badger. I bet it looked awful. What did you do with it?'

'Actually, it didn't look awful at all, except it was muddy and wet from the rain. It looked as if it was asleep, though it wasn't breathing. It was a shock, though, finding it on our doorstep. Hector got rid of it, took it with him when he went to work the day after. I didn't ask the details, but I suspect he chucked it in the woods or something.'

'Did the girls see it?'

'Caitlin did. We'd just got home from school. She noticed it first, as it goes. She wasn't upset, just curious as to how it got there.'

'It must have been knocked down, like you said. Either that or it wandered down from the woods and happened to die when it got to your house.'

This sounds so ridiculous, we laugh out loud, drawing amused glances from the nearby tables.

'The way my luck's been lately, I wouldn't be surprised!'

More laughter. Grace trots off to the bar and comes back with two white wine spritzers. 'Well, we can't sit here with empty glasses.'

A moment later she says, 'Seriously, though, you don't think the dead badger is sinister in any way, do you, Fran?'

'Well, yes, I do, actually. I mean, wouldn't you? Badgers are nocturnal. It was broad daylight. What was it doing out at that time? Never mind getting run over, or dropping dead, whatever happened to the poor thing.'

'I expect it was a teenage badger, stopping out at all hours just to piss off its parents.' Grace rocks back on her chair.

I splutter into my spritzer. Clearly this is one drink too many, for both of us, but it's exactly what I needed. A fun night with a good friend. One who is the voice of reason, even when she's not exactly sober.

I don't go so far as to confess my fears that the dead badger was planted by whoever dosed the cupcake with chilli, made the phone call that scared me rigid, and spooked me with an anonymous basket of flowers. But those things happened a while ago; I can't really believe there's a connection. Even so, the niggle of doubt has kept me sleepless and wondering at three in the morning, and thinking about Mirabelle Hayward.

Ben comes to collect Zoe from our house one evening, around half past eight. She had come home from school with Hazel and stayed for dinner. The two girls seem to have put aside their differences – if there ever were any – and are as close as before. I guess our visit to Rose Cottage may have something to do with it. I'm pleased for Hazel, and will have to live with any nervousness on my part.

I have armed myself mentally against the unavoidable inter-action with both Tessa and Ben, and my face doesn't change as I answer the door to him. He marches straight in without being invited, directing a smile at me of the calibre that used to spread fire in my veins. I answer with a curt nod. He exchanges a few words with Hector, who has left his desk at the sound of Ben's voice.

Ben's presence fills the small square of our hallway. As the three of us stand idly chatting while we wait for Zoe to appear, he heels a nonchalant hand against the wall, taking ownership; Ben has that about him.

Eventually, Zoe tears herself away from whatever she and Hazel have been doing and, immune or not, I feel the sag of relief. As they go out of the door, Hazel hovering, still chatting to Zoe, Ben suddenly turns, pulls a wodge of paper from the pocket of his linen jacket and thrusts it into my hand.

'I'll be in trouble if I forget to give you these. Another of my wife's village community efforts.' He raises his eyes, and I'm annoyed with him for sounding so uncharitable and demeaning Tessa in that way.

I look at the papers in my hand. They're fliers, about Tessa's proposed art club. So, it is true, then. The wording explains how it will work: every other Saturday morning; in the village hall; children aged seven to eleven; attendees to bring their own materials plus drinks and snacks; adults including a qualified art teacher on hand to supervise and give creative help. There's a clause to say that all helpers will be DBS-checked. Tessa is inviting expressions of interest before she sets this thing up, and we are to email her if we have a child or children who might attend.

'Oh,' I say, as if this is the first I've heard of it. 'Well...'

'I'll leave it with you, then,' Ben says, his face a picture of disinterest. 'Tessa asked if you could pass the fliers around amongst your friends and neighbours?'

'Of course,' I say. 'Tell her thank you.'

Hector and Hazel have gone back inside, and Zoe is swinging on the gate, waving at Hazel in the window. It's just Ben and me on the doorstep.

'See you soon, huh?' He doesn't foist that smile on me again, but what his eyes say is a hundred times worse.

'Goodbye, Ben.' I turn on my heel and go inside, shutting the door with a decisive click.

Hector is back at his desk. Caitlin is in bed, while Hazel and Kitty are watching TV. I wander to the kitchen, make myself a camomile tea, and stand with it at the sink. As I gaze out of the window, watching the evening light cast a luminous glow on the garden, the realisation hits me that, even after all this time, Ben still believes he can reel me in with a flash of those eyes.

It's only a game, the flirting, the blatant reminders of what we once were to each other. Well, I don't need reminding, thank you very much. It's a dangerous game, and I refuse to play along.

Is Ben really that bored with his life that he needs to do this, or is it that he can't stop? When we were together – I use the word 'together' in its loosest sense – he told me he'd never been unfaithful to Tessa before, never thought he was capable, and that with me it was different, special, et cetera, et cetera. I believed him; after all, the same thing was happening to me. But now I'm beginning to think there might have been other women, before me. Perhaps after me.

I truly don't care what Ben does, or with whom – setting aside my sympathy for his wife and child – but I don't like the idea that he lied to me. That's rich coming from me, I know, when my whole life at that time was based on unspoken lies, but it makes the sorry episode even more regretful than it already is, if that is possible.

My mind leaps backwards, to that final meeting at High Heaven. It wasn't my idea to meet there. I'd have preferred somewhere entirely different, a place where the scenes of my crime were not for ever stitched into the collage of the landscape. That evening was only the second time I'd lied outright about my whereabouts, the first being when Ben and I spent half the night together, and even then, there was a strong link to the truth. Not that it makes it any more palatable.

My parents' house in Harlow – my childhood home – had been left in my charge, contracts having been exchanged only a week before they left for New Zealand, and I'd made the journey into Essex the previous day to oversee the disposal of the last of the contents before completion. I'd stayed overnight, relishing my last chance to indulge in nostalgia and spend some quiet time, thinking about the happy times the house had seen. The following day, the charity van arrived bang on time and the lads in charge of it were super-efficient, so I was able to drop the keys off to the estate agent and leave for home earlier than I'd expected.

My overwrought mind had been foraging for a solution to the Ben problem – he had become a problem by then – for days, if not weeks. I wanted to end it, I *had* to end it. But my emotions swung me back and forth as if I was on the end of an out-of-control bungee wire. How could I bear to tear myself away? More to the point, how could I tell Ben it was over?

But being at the house, where the atmosphere was flavoured with new beginnings, seemed to help the process along. At six in the morning, I rose from my sleeping bag on the living room floor and, in my heightened emotional state, I texted Ben, telling him I needed to see him and it was urgent.

I had told Hector and the girls not to expect me home until well into the evening, which was when I'd imagined I'd be back. But my early departure meant I could safely lose a couple of hours. The timing was perfect, my brain up to the task; as close as it was going to get, anyway.

High Heaven, said the return text. *Meet me there. I'll get there at seven and wait if you're late.*

Just that. No questioning as to why the urgency. Knowing Ben, I expect he thought I wanted him and couldn't wait. His conceit was unbelievable, looking back. I didn't have the heart or strength to argue about the venue. It wasn't that important, as long as I stuck to my agenda.

I was a quarter of an hour early, arriving breathlessly at the top of the hill as if I'd run up it instead of driven. Ben was twenty minutes late. I'd almost given him up, imagining he'd not been able to get away. That was fine by me, I'd leave it until another day; my nerve was faltering anyway.

And then he showed, his car crunching across the cinders,

his smile on full beam. It was early September; the air smelt of autumn as we walked up to the crest of the hill. The sky had been stubbornly grey all day, and morose clouds were banked low on the horizon, muting the sunset to an unspectacular pinkish glow. We were alone, the only sign of life the sheep huddled beyond the distant fence.

'Don't say it, Fran,' Ben said, half-turning away from me as we stood facing the edge of the chalk face, then swinging back. 'Don't let me hear that. Ever.'

Too late, I'd already said it. Having decided that any prevarication would make this so much harder for both of us, I'd swerved his embrace and come right out with it, told him how much I'd loved our time together, but the longer it went on, the more likely it was that we'd be caught out. Neither of us wanted that, did we? Ben hadn't answered that. He'd just looked at me, shock and disbelief in his eyes, his mouth a cartoon downturned crescent.

I really hadn't wanted to go into detail, spell out the obvious reasons why we couldn't just carry on as we had been, as Ben seemed to think we could. But in the end I did, citing my husband and children, his wife and child, our security and theirs, our reputations, our future, our *wrongness* for having let it happen in the first place; all of it. Every single cliché that applies in that situation, and believe me, there are many.

And still Ben said 'no'. As if what happened between us was his choice, and only his.

'I won't let you do this, Fran,' he said. 'I won't allow it.'

I began to point out, gently, that I had made my decision and he had to let me go, when I noticed a change in his demeanour. He became very still, the only visible movement in his eyes which darted over me and all around us.

'I could...' he began, and I was so afraid he was going to say he could tell Tessa, or even Hector, come clean and see what happened. I was so afraid he was about to say something of that kind that I backed away from him, an involuntary reaction. I stumbled on the uneven ground and he caught me, pulling me in, his arms encircling my waist. And oh, the warm, familiar feel of his body against mine almost caused me to cave in. But I didn't. I pulled away, using as much force as I needed, and looked at him, waiting for him to speak again. I thought of walking away, getting into my car and driving off. But I had started this, and it couldn't be left unfinished.

Ben was pointing, waving wildly towards the cliff edge. 'I could do it. I could take us both over. You and me. A lovers' suicide pact.' I stared at him, stunned into silence. Then, he added in a voice that was more breath than sound, 'We'd be together for ever, our bones sinking into the earth, neither one of us distinguishable from the other.'

'Oh my God, Ben!' My voice hit a high note, almost like a shriek. 'That's a terrible thing to say! A terrible thing to *think*! You don't mean that, you know you don't. Just... *please*, Ben, stop this. Let's go back there, yes?'

I held his arm, and after a small resistance, he let me lead him away from the edge. I was so shocked. His words were scrambled in my brain and I couldn't work out if he'd threatened to jump or not, but I had to get him off the precipice. And then I did remember what he'd said about taking us both, and for a second, I feared for my life. But only a second, because I sensed the energy drain from him, energy which renewed itself with vigour when he shook me off, approached the wooden bench, and began kicking the hell out of it.

I stood aside helplessly while his boot collided with the leg of the bench, over and over, his body rigid with tension, his face a petrified mask of anger. He stopped as suddenly as he'd begun, turned and looked at me, then sank onto the sagging bench.

I sat down beside him, holding him, not speaking, feeling the tension in him ease.

'Ben, look at me.'

When he looked up, his face had altered. His eyes still glittered with tears or anger, or whatever other emotions were rampaging around inside him, I couldn't tell. But he had changed, and I sensed the meltdown I'd witnessed was over. However I'd imagined our meeting would be, it was nothing like this.

'I'm so sorry,' he said. 'I didn't mean to scare you. I didn't mean it. I'd never harm you, you must know that. I was just... *am* just... so sad. I couldn't bear it if you left me.'

I said nothing, thinking whatever I said might make things worse.

Ben sat up, detaching himself from my embrace and taking my hand instead. 'You are leaving me, Fran, aren't you? You did say that.'

'Yes. We're leaving each other. You know it had to happen some time. You always knew it couldn't last.'

He nodded. 'I know, and you're right. We've come this far, and it stops here. But I'm devastated, Fran. Can't you see?'

'Of course, and I feel the same. I'm sad, too.'

'Are you?'

'Yes, I'm very sad. I wish we'd never...'

Ben sat upright, squaring his shoulders. 'Don't say you wish we'd never started. Please. I love you, Fran. I won't stop loving you.'

I didn't say I loved him back. I couldn't. For one thing, I wanted to leave him in no doubt we were over; for another, I didn't love him. I might have thought I did for a while, fed by Ben's view that that are many variations of love, all of them valid, but I'd known for a while it wasn't love. Not on my side, not on his. But I was never going to convince him of that, so I didn't try.

We left High Heaven soon afterwards. Before I got into my car we kissed. I made him promise he would leave first, and told him I wasn't going anywhere until I'd seen him take the road.

'It's okay, I'm not going to do anything stupid,' he said. 'I'm not that brave.' He smiled then, a real smile. And for the first time since we'd arrived, I thought: This is okay. It's going to be all right.

I let Ben get a three-minute start on me, then I bumped down the track and onto the road, back to Oakheart, crying silent tears.

EIGHTEEN

TESSA

I knew Fran had put a stop to it. I knew she'd left him. For the very first time, he'd let his guard down, let his emotions sneak through the façade of breezy confidence. I saw it as soon as he walked through the door that night.

Well, truthfully, I didn't *know* – how could I? But I suspected, and after, when he stopped disappearing at a moment's notice with some vague excuse he could hardly be bothered to make sound plausible, I knew it had ended. She would have ended it, not him. Of that I was certain, because that is the way Ben operates. He takes what he wants, and he wanted her. His desire was not going to end overnight. As it didn't with Maria.

This, of course, happened long before I had my proof, in the form of that photo, that it was Fran he was seeing. But it was definitely somebody, and that night, my brain imported her name and merged it with the story. I knew that one day I would discover for certain the identity of Ben's latest lover, for want of a better word. All I had to do was wait.

We made love that night. Ben was unusually reluctant at first, but my persuasive powers soon overrode that. Why did I want to have sex with him, knowing where he'd been only hours before? Lots of reasons: to stake my claim, show him who really needed him, remind him what real love was all about. Also, probably, to punish him, make him feel guilty, if such a thing had ever been part of his emotional vocabulary.

There was nothing remarkable in the way Ben and I met. It was standard stuff; we first set eyes on each other in a pub near Oxford Circus, one of those old London pubs with dark furnishings and brass fittings that had suddenly become fashionable again and was packed to the green-tiled walls with office workers after six on a Friday – on most nights, actually. Drinking after work was a costly business, but I went along because I had nothing better to do other than return to my rented Earls Court studio flat, open a tin of spaghetti, and sit there feeling sorry for myself.

Feeling sorry for myself was not, *is* not, in my nature. It was a phase I imposed upon myself, thinking of it as a rite of passage, probably as a result of reading too many bad novels. It was with a kind of irony that I went through the motions of being a lonely single girl in the big city. I could have made more of an effort, had I chosen to.

The phase didn't last; it didn't feel right, and it wasn't authentic. I had some real living to do but had no idea where to start, so I got myself some therapy, which took a large chunk of my salary. I was sceptical, but curious as to how it worked. The therapist, a motherly fifty-something called Elizabeth with a growing-out fringe and comfortable shoes, prompted me to talk about my home background. I'd expected and prepared myself for that, even going to the lengths of forming complete sentences in my head so that I wouldn't be diverted from what I saw as the main source of my problems.

The talking helped at first – there wasn't a lot else to the therapy other than me talking and Elizabeth listening – and I'd begun to put the mess of my early life into perspective. For the price of a bottle of wine I could probably have used a friend as my sounding board instead of the therapist, but then I'd have spoiled the picture I presented to the world of the smart, middle-class girl from a boringly suburban middle-class home, coming to London in search of excitement.

I kept up the illusion when I was getting to know Ben – I'd almost convinced myself by then that the bland, commonplace background I'd invented was the real one. After we'd made eye contact across the crowded pub, he made his way over and bought me a drink. My observation of him beforehand showed several women in his thrall, over-animated in their laughing responses to whatever he was saying, surreptitiously elbowing one another to be the one by his side. I had to smile. They were beautiful women, and I could say I don't know how he came to notice me, but that would be false modesty, something else I don't do. I looked good; I'm tall and naturally blonde, both of which give me an advantage in a crowd.

When, after several months of dating, Ben opened up and told me his own story, it seemed as if it was meant to be. We were two people who had faced tremendous challenges in their lives and emerged all the stronger for it; it seemed right that we had found each other. But although the scars had faded, we still bore the imprints. There was always the possibility that the damage would erupt, burst through the surface, and poison our carefully constructed lives with its lava.

We were on the brink of moving in together, flat searching whilst spending part of our time at my place, most of it at Ben's, which was where we were when he told me his story. He was in a house share in Islington at the time, the other four occupants were never around much, which suited us well. We'd been out to a restaurant, and hadn't held back on the wine as it was Saturday night.

Back at the house, Ben opened another bottle. The alcohol must have loosened his tongue – he'd been vague and dismissive about his past until then. He told me his mother had suffered from depression almost all her adult life, and when Ben, the only child, was eight years old, she took a bottle of whisky and an accumulation of sleeping tablets to bed with her and never woke up.

'How could she *do* that? How could she just go and leave me? I was only a little kid, for Christ's sake!' Ben's face showed anger and confusion, no trace of sympathy. A twitch set up in the corner of his right eye. I tried to hold him, but he shrugged me off. 'No, let me finish.'

My heart raced as I heard how Ben's father, the CEO of a company that supplied industrial catering equipment, went straight out and hired a live-in nanny, a sullen Spanish eighteen-year-old who neglected the child in her charge and eventually took off, leaving Ben alone in the house for twelve hours.

'God knows where he dredged her up from. She must have been all he could get at short notice,' Ben said, smiling grimly. 'He didn't want to risk hiring another nanny – which I suppose I should have been grateful for – and tried to look after me himself, farming me out to other parents at school, the neighbours, anybody who was willing. It was all a bit erratic, and I never actually felt I was in a place where I was truly wanted, not even at home – mostly at home. He blamed me for my mother's death, you see. It was never going to work, him and me, living in the same house.'

'Why did he blame you? How on earth could it have been your fault?' I was incredulous, full of anger on Ben's behalf.

'The depression got worse after I was born. She couldn't cope, so neither could he.'

'But...'

'I know. That's how it was, though. Then, eighteen months after my mother's death, my father was killed in a car accident. I only found out years later, when I was old enough to ferret out the details, that there was no other vehicle involved, no person or obstacle, apart from the tree he ploughed into at the side of the road.' Ben made a sound; it was half laugh, half snort. 'He couldn't live without my mother, that was the truth. I wasn't enough for him.'

'It was suicide,' I whispered.

'Accidental death was the verdict, but yes, I reckon that was it. I went into care, got swallowed up by the system. I was unlucky and it wasn't the best experience, but I survived. You have to, don't you?'

'You do,' was all I said. Ben's face had closed down. Nothing more was required of me.

Much later, after we'd moved into our first flat together, I told him my own story. He didn't show much reaction, just scraped the surface with platitudes. But that was fine; I imagine my life, though less traumatic than Ben's, brought back memories too painful for him to handle.

Then, early one morning, I crawled off a work friend's sofa after a night's clubbing in honour of somebody's birthday, and arrived home to find Ben slumped on our own sofa, a depleted bottle of vodka tilting in his hand and several open packets of co-codamol on the floor. At first, I thought he was dead, until my shocked mind detected a shallow rise and fall of his chest. He hadn't taken enough tablets to do serious harm, and I managed to rouse him without help. Afterwards, he said he was sorry, he didn't know what made him do it. He didn't need to; I knew.

Neither of us referred to the incident again. I went on loving Ben, showing him he would never be alone again as long as I had breath in my body. And all the time I held onto my private fear that, eventually, I would lose him.

Back then, Ben and I were the broken ones.

But not any more.

NINETEEN

FRAN

Caitlin was even more keen, if that was possible, to join Tessa's art club when she found out her friend Maisie was going, too. There's no stopping this, not that I want to for her sake, and I've prepared myself for more interaction with Tessa, although avoiding her altogether is the more attractive option.

'Do you want to take Caitlin to art club?' I casually enquire of Hector after breakfast.

He looks up from the paper he's reading at the kitchen table. 'Not especially. Why?'

He knows I'm not doing anything particular at this moment. Caitlin appears, dragging an overfull rucksack.

'Oh, love, don't take too much, not on the first day. What've you got in there, anyway?'

Caitlin drops the rucksack and counts off on her fingers. 'Drawing pad, painting pad, pencils, crayons, charcoal, acrylic paints, brushes...'

'Okay. But *you* have to carry it, right?'

'Right.' She smiles.

Kitty appears. 'I'm off to Sarah's. See you laters.'

'I don't suppose you're going anywhere near the village hall?' I ask, clutching at the proverbial straw.

I feel Hector's puzzled gaze on me. 'Nowhere near, whatsoever,' Kitty says. Moments later, the front door bangs shut.

Hazel is upstairs, for once doing homework before the witching hour of six p.m. on Sunday.

'Come on, then,' I say to Caitlin.

'Have a good time, Picasso,' Hector says, giving her a kiss.

'Who is Picasso?'

'I'll tell you on the way,' I say, and we leave.

I don't know why my stomach's hitched a lift on a fairground switchback. It's an art club run by Tessa, yes, but she'll be busy. No time to spend chatting to me.

On the way, we pass Graylings, Mirabelle Hayward's house. Could those be chilli plants? I wonder, as I catch sight of the rampant greenery growing inside the downstairs windows. I'd assumed they were herbs before. Herbs seem to fit with Mirabelle, chilli peppers don't. But what do I know about her, aside from her dubious mental state?

'That's the lady with the cats,' Caitlin says conversationally.

'That's her house, yes.' I force aside my thoughts about chilli plants, only to see a mind picture of me racing into the school to 'rescue' my injured daughter, then one of the dead badger on our step. I can do without my wild imaginings this morning.

'She was at the window upstairs, looking at us,' Caitlin says. 'Perhaps she wanted us to wave.'

I don't answer, and hurry Caitlin on. We meet Maisie and her mother at the corner, and the two girls go on ahead, Caitlin struggling to keep the rucksack aloft. Afia and I are chatting as we enter the village hall, and at first, I don't notice Ben. Then I hear his voice, and I'm stupidly wrongfooted. Tessa I was prepared for, but not Ben. He doesn't normally put in an appearance at any of Tessa's events – keeps a wide berth, in fact – but this is a bit different, I suppose. He is arranging Formica tables, lifting them with ease and setting them down in a semicircle.

A woman called Cleo, whom I know vaguely as an Oakheart Academy parent and is apparently the qualified art teacher, comes to greet us. It's not long before I've signed Caitlin in and paid the rather hefty sum required, but the hall has to be paid for so it's fair enough. I see Caitlin settled, which doesn't take long, as she is sharing a table with Maisie and clearly can't wait to begin. Afia has already left to do some high street shopping and I sidle out of the door with others who have brought children.

Ben is standing on the pavement, leaning nonchalantly against the noticeboard of village information, arms folded. I hadn't noticed him leaving the hall. He rights himself as he sees me.

'Fran, hey! I'm glad you brought your daughter. Into art, is she?'

'Yes, she's quite talented.' My voice comes out more curt than I intended. Or did I intend it?

'Marvellous. Look, I was going for a coffee. Would you like to join me?'

I face him square on. 'Ben, it's not a good idea. You know that, so why ask? Anyway, I have to get home.'

'And then come back later to fetch her?'

'Well, yes, of course.' Sarcastic now. He's annoying me, and what has that got to do with anything?

'Fran, Fran...' Ben's eyes search for mine. I meet his gaze, chin held high. I won't be intimidated. 'We're friends, aren't we? All of us? What harm is a quick coffee going to do?'

I sigh. Ben smiles. The smile sends my pulse scurrying. Muscle memory, that's all it is. To tell the truth, I could do with a coffee, and the Pot and Kettle opposite, which Ben indicates with a jab of a thumb, looks busy with customers. It's not as if we'll be alone.

'It looks full,' I say, half-hoping for a last-minute reprieve. 'There might not be a table.'

Ben isn't listening. He shepherds me across the street, towards the black-painted café.

And so it is that this morning's *bête noire* is not Tessa but Ben, Tessa only having had time to call a quick 'hello' across the hall. But all is well. We squeeze ourselves onto a table among the Saturday morning crowd, Ben allowing me to pay for my coffee without demur. We chat lightly about nothing of any note, and then I leave.

No unwanted remarks, no innuendos, no meaningful looks. No apology, either, for what he said on Worthing pier, but I suppose I shouldn't have expected it. Ben, I have learned, is not big on apologies, mainly because he never believes he has anything to apologise for.

When I return later to collect Caitlin, he is nowhere to be seen. I exchange a few words with Tessa, who is clearly on a high due to a successful morning. And as I leave with my daughter, again I experience the weird sensation of having escaped, though from what I have no idea.

I have some time owing at work and take a couple of days off. Hector is busy with commissions and restocking his small display area with items for sale. An eighteen-year-old called Dillon has been taken on for six months to help out and further his carpentry training. Hector can't leave Dillon on his own at present, and he apologises for the rotten timing. But in truth, I'm looking forward to having the house entirely to myself, a rare occurrence.

I've spent a lazy morning catching up on yesterday's paper, answering emails, including a lovely newsy one from Natalie, and generally drifting about. The afternoon brings a rush of energy, and I'm in the middle of tidying Hazel's room – I am not allowed to touch Caitlin's if she isn't present, and Kitty's is definitely a no-entry zone – when my phone buzzes. It's Grace. She has a free afternoon, and would I like to meet her for coffee in the park café?

I bundle the clothes I'm holding into the laundry basket on the landing – some of them might be clean, but it's hard to tell – pull a sweatshirt over my vest top and chinos, and head out into the blue-skied morning.

I'm glad of the sweatshirt. The sun dazzles but deceives in terms of temperature, and Grace is sitting at one of the few outside tables on the decked area in front of the café. As it's afternoon and we are creatures of habit, we forgo coffee in favour of a pot of tea for two and the café's speciality – rock cakes.

'Is everything okay?' I ask, wondering if there's any particular reason we're here.

'Yes, fine. I fancied a break and I remembered you were off.' Grace bites into her rock cake and makes big eyes over the top of it. 'Oh God, these are *scrummy*!'

'Yep. There is something, though, I can always tell. And by the way, you've got crumbs on your chin.'

Grace swipes her chin with a flimsy paper napkin. 'A bit of gossip you might be interested in, that's all.'

'Just what I need. Go on, then.'

Grace's job in the property world means she has sophisticated 'local knowledge', as she puts it. The juiciest segments she unpeels for me with unbridled glee while holding up a virtual Holy Bible, swearing me to silence. I've not let her down yet, at least, not knowingly.

'I wouldn't be telling you this,' Grace begins, leaning into the table, 'if you were bosom buddies with Tessa Grammaticus. Tell me you're not, only you did go to dinner at hers, didn't you?'

'We did, and no, we aren't bosom buddies, or any sort of

buddy. I don't know why she invited us really.' In my sombre moments I still wonder if there was something other than neighbourliness behind Tessa's invitation. 'Is this about her, then?'

'Not *as such*.' Grace purses her mouth, as if she might not, after all, share this gossip. I nod encouragingly. Grace continues.

'Did you know they lived in Brighton before they came to Oakheart?'

'Yes, Ben— they did mention it. Why?'

'Did you ever wonder why they moved? They had a gorgeous house, Edwardian or something, in a nice street, good schools and everything. And he, Ben, commutes to London, which is a darn sight easier from Brighton than it is from here.'

I'm not sure about that, but Ben's commute is irrelevant, and I don't contest the point. 'They wanted to live somewhere rural, and to move while Zoe was still young enough for the change of school not to be a disruption. They looked around the villages in Sussex, Tessa saw Rose Cottage, and that was it. Nothing strange about that. Rose Cottage is beautiful, inside as well as out.'

'I don't doubt it.' Grace pulls a face. 'Tessa would never live anywhere that wasn't picture-perfect.'

'She's worked hard to make it so,' I say, for some reason feeling defensive of Tessa while wishing Grace would get to the kernel of the story.

'When they lived in Brighton, they had a woman working for them, domestic help. Goodness knows why they needed her, except it was a big house, so...' Grace notes my impatience. 'I *heard* – and I don't know if this is true, but it sounded credible – I heard that Ben and the domestic help became very *close*.' Grace taps the side of her nose.

My stomach quakes and I don't say anything.

'He was screwing her; you see what I'm saying?' Grace adds.

Of course I see what she's saying! It couldn't be plainer if she drew me a diagram.

'He had an affair with her, or he might have done. I get it. Grace, who told you this?'

'I was chatting to a colleague of mine, Tony. You might have heard me mention him. He's an agent based in Brighton. It's a small world, property selling. He sold the Grammaticuses' house, and the agent who sold them Rose Cottage is a mate of his. I don't know exactly how they worked it out, or what they heard or saw, but as I say, it's a small world. As is Oakheart, of course.'

I wish she wouldn't remind me of that, not on top of what I've just heard about Ben.

'Yes, but how did it come up in conversation, about this so-called affair? It seems a bit random to me.'

'We were talking about the variety of situations you come across when you're selling somebody's house. The personal stuff isn't always as hidden as they'd like it to be. The clues are there. And people talk, neighbours and so forth. A new For Sale board going up unleashes tongues.' Grace nods at me. 'I've told you a few tales in the past, haven't I?'

'Are you saying they moved house because of the affair? What happened? Did Tessa find out?'

'Ah, now that we don't know. But what we *do* know is that she – the woman – did no more than up sticks and follow them here. The agency in the high street, the one that handled the sale of Rose Cottage, put her in touch with the housing association which owns the new development near Tesco's. Pretty places but tiny, more like rabbit hutches than houses.' Grace chuckles. 'The rents are reasonable, which I imagine was the attraction. Apart from Ben, of course.'

Oh God. My recent suspicion that I may not have been Ben's only illicit lover joins hands with the possibility that his former lover lives in Oakheart, and a lugubrious, circular dance begins. Have I met this woman? Do I know her? I'm not aware of knowing anyone who lives in that part of the village, but that doesn't mean a thing.

Was he seeing her at the same time as he was seeing me?

Is he still seeing her? And if so, why do I care?

I recall the slight atmosphere Hector and I noticed when we went to dinner. If that was connected to this other affair of Ben's, what else does Tessa know? I swallow in an attempt to relieve the dryness in my throat. Grace reads my mind – or rather, she thinks she does.

'I know. Poor Tessa. Whether she knew or not – I imagine she must have done and that's why they moved – it's still abominable, isn't it? And when there are children involved...'

I think back to Ben and me. Children. *My* children. 'One child. Zoe. Not that it makes it any better.'

'She had a child as well, a little boy. No husband that we know of. She lived in Brighton with her sister, until she struck out and followed her heart.' Grace tuts, shakes her head. 'I'm being judgemental. Who knows what goes on behind closed doors? What lies in other people's hearts and minds? I don't condemn anyone, because you just don't know. It is interesting, though, isn't it?'

I remain silent.

'You just don't know,' Grace repeats. Her eyes are sad. 'She came to a tragic end. Maybe it did have something to do with the affair. Tony seemed to think there must have been a link, but again...' Grace shrugs. My heart dives.

'Tragic end?' My voice is hardly above a whisper. 'What happened?'

'Funnily enough, you already know what happened.'

'Do I? Grace, stop talking in riddles!'

'Do you remember that woman who killed herself by jumping off the cliff at High Heaven? When would it have been? Two, three years back?'

My brain forages for the memory, which doesn't come. I shake my head slowly, my eyes on Grace's.

'It was in the papers, and on the local news. We saw the police cordons up around the bottom of High Heaven, don't you remember?' Grace frowns. 'Actually, that might just have been me. Anyway, she was Italian, or of Italian descent. Dark, petite, attractive, you know the type.'

'Italian, yes...' Something triggers in my mind. 'I do remember reading about her, now I think about it. That was her, the woman Ben was seeing? She committed *suicide*?'

'Yep, that was the verdict. Nobody falls off High Heaven by accident.'

'It's not impossible. That fence has been broken down for years. If it was dark, or raining and slippery, it could happen.'

'Could, yes. Not likely, though. Why would you go up there in the dark?'

I cast Grace a meaningful look.

'Yes, all right, but no witnesses came forward – which I suppose they wouldn't if they were up to no good – but the sister gave evidence that she'd been feeling low and that was it, case closed.' Grace lets a beat of silence fall. 'Poor woman.'

'What was her name?' I ask.

'Maria. Maria Capelli.'

I feel quite shaky as I walk home from the café. Grace believed she was providing a harmless afternoon's entertainment with her shock revelation about Tessa's husband. I didn't step up to the mark by joining in her theorising with theories of my own. My mind was too busy paging through the short history of my liaison with Ben, looking for something I might have missed.

Over the coming days, the story Grace told me haunts my thinking. I'm ashamed to say that Maria's tragedy is not uppermost. I'm feeling aggrieved that he lied to me about not having any other lovers – if indeed the story is true. I can't rule it out, though; I'd be even more of a fool if I did. Ben may have spun me a white lie so I wouldn't see him as a serial adulterer, hardly an appealing quality. He wanted to make me feel special, and in that he certainly excelled. It might be simply that, or the gossip that came Grace's way might be completely unfounded. I doubt I will ever know, and why would I want to?

And yet somebody died. A woman called Maria who may or may not have been Ben's lover at some point, but whom it seems certain worked for the family, ended up dead at the bottom of a chalk pit.

Supposing the gossip is based on fact and Maria was having an affair, fling, whatever, with Ben? How did he react to the news of her death? Was he still seeing her at that time, or had it ended back in Brighton? Surely, if he'd been forced to move away because of the situation – Grace's theory – he wouldn't have carried on seeing her? Or was he pleased she'd moved to the same village, been flattered – and foolhardy – enough to resume the relationship? Enough to risk his marriage? Ben is a risk-taker. He wanted us to carry on seeing one another, despite my insistence that we stop. He reacted badly when I told him it was over. I guess he gets off on the danger.

None of this introspection and second-guessing is helping. My peace of mind shatters into even smaller pieces than before. I had hoped that after our family visit to Rose Cottage, Ben and Tessa would be relegated in my mind to just another Oakheart couple who we know quite well through our children and are friendly with when we happen to come into contact. No more than that. No surprises, nothing to set my nerves on edge.

It isn't happening. It's my fault, I know. Nobody forced me to have an affair, nobody held a gun to my head and made me betray my husband and children. I did that all by myself. The mess I'm in is all of my own making. And now Maria is factored into the equation and I can't get her out of my head. I have to know what happened, or at least take a few steps nearer the truth, even if what I find is disturbing.

The good news is that nothing weird has happened to me lately; there have been no odd gifts, funny phone calls, expired wildlife on the doorstep, nothing. I no longer have that eerie sensation of being watched when I walk through the wood, something which continued after the first occasion, although I would never give my voyeur the satisfaction of changing my route.

So, it looks as if Mirabelle Hayward has either forgiven me for my non-crime – doubtful – or she got tired of playing games. Small mercies.

TWENTY

TESSA

I haven't seen Mirabelle Hayward since the badger episode – at least, not to speak to, thank goodness. I was using the self-service checkout in the local supermarket when I saw her waylay some innocent passer-by outside. The shop door was open, and I caught the words 'ignorant lorry drivers' and 'humps in the road' accompanied by much arm waving, and I gathered she was back on her traffic-calming hobby-horse, presumably having forgotten about revenge tactics on Fran Oliver.

That's quite a relief. Mirabelle came in useful but nobody in their right mind would want to spend more time in her company than strictly necessary. Besides, I've passed the stage where poking around in Fran's head, causing her brief dips of anxiety that I can only visualise, is enough. It was a start; an oblique way of offloading some of my animosity towards her.

When she brought Caitlin to my art club – which went wonderfully well, by the way – she was all bright smiles, and clearly in control of her perfect little world. I didn't go over and chat because I was busy setting out objects and photos for the children to use as inspiration, as well as doing a million and one other things. But Cleo booked Fran's daughter in, so she would not have thought I was being unfriendly. Not that I care what she thought.

A little later, I was presented with a bonus, quite unexpectedly. One of the children decided to sharpen all his coloured pencils, holding the sharpener over the floor instead of the bin. I went to fetch a dustpan and brush from the storeroom where the cleaning things are kept; it's at the front of the building and has a small window. I happened to glance out in time to see Fran and my husband entering the Pot and Kettle on the other side of the street. The storeroom window was grubby, the view of the café partly obscured by traffic, but the snapshot gave me enough to realise it was no coincidence that they were going in at the same time. He held the door open for her, and she performed a coy little bob as she ducked beneath the arch of his raised arm. There's no doubt in my mind that they were together.

Had their little rendezvous been prearranged? It's possible, in theory. Anything is possible. But I'd only asked Ben the night before if he could spare ten minutes to help me set out the tables, it being the first meeting of the art club, so my guess is that it was a spur-of-the-moment thing when they ran into one another outside the hall.

Honestly, I don't know why I trouble my brain with the technicalities. Ben and Fran went for coffee together, and yes, you could say that's a normal enough thing to do. What is *not* normal is the fact that he didn't tell me about it later. Considering who his companion was, there's no way in this world he forgot.

She could have mentioned it herself when she came to collect Caitlin, but she said nothing. I knew she hadn't spent the whole two hours with Ben because he'd had to be home to take Zoe to her swimming lesson, so I imagine she'd gone home after they'd had coffee. This time, I made a point of singling her out for a chat, using the child as a buffer – it's not that easy, pretending to be somebody's friend; you have to be super-cool about it. Fran, I'm sorry to say, didn't falter. There's an art to that. When it comes down to it, we're all acting a part. Life is just a series of scenes in which we take on one role or another. We are all players; some are better at it than others.

Maria took her part well. The dutiful domestic help, all smiles, nothing too much trouble. Showing fondness for my cute daughter, leaving little posies in her bedroom, and once, a book about a family of frogs she'd found in a charity shop because Zoe liked frogs. Before long, it was Ben's study she took more than a friendly interest in. My meticulous eye for detail picked up the extra shine on the antique wooden surfaces, the regularly damp-wiped picture-frames, the pens bunched in pots, the levelling of the books on the shelves. She even replaced one of the castors on the vintage rotating office chair, arriving one day with a bagful of screwdrivers and a cry of 'It's no trouble. I will fix it!'

I should have been warned then, casting my mind back to Suzanna Henderson. Our house in Brighton was large, with a lot of rooms to keep in order. I took on Maria for three sessions of two and a half hours a week because I was working at the time as charity fund-raiser for our local hospice, but I did most of the housework myself. Maria was only expected to keep the bathrooms, kitchen and utility room spotless and drive the vacuum around the rest. She should not have had time for personal touches, but make time she did.

Maria lived a few streets away from us, in a scruffy terraced house with her sister and family, and her own son, two years or so younger than Zoe. I saw the advert she placed on a postcard in the newsagent's window, offering her services. When I found out she was fucking my husband, I wondered why she didn't put the card in the phone box and have done with it.

How did I find out? I sometimes think I've been blessed

with some kind of second sight, an enhanced instinct for the truth. Or perhaps that is not a quality I was born with but have subconsciously learned through being with Ben. I came home early one day – such a cliché! – and didn't exactly catch them at it, but I walked in on the aftermath.

Ben was working from home that day, and it was one of Maria's days, which as it transpired was no coincidence. It was two twenty-five when I arrived. Envisaging that Ben would not have bothered to make himself lunch, I'd picked up the makings of a mackerel salad on the way home. Lunch in the orangery, a summer treat. That was in my mind when I entered the hall and saw that Ben's study door was open and he wasn't there. The vacuum cleaner stood on the first landing, one flight up. No sign of Maria.

Moments later, she appeared, hastening down from the further flight of stairs that led to the attic room we used for storage, black hair springing out of the combs she wore to keep it in place, her face a fast-moving film of expressions until, finally, it settled on smiling with mild surprise.

'You're back! I was just off,' she said. It was then that I noticed the belt she wore around her denim dress was all askew, the end missing its loop as if she'd fastened it in a rush.

'Where is Ben?' I remember asking. Or, actually, I think I said, 'Where is my husband?' thus driving the point home.

'Mr Grammaticus is...' Maria hesitated, looking flustered for the first time since I'd come in. She never called us Mr and Mrs. It was always Ben and Tessa, as instructed by me at the beginning.

Ben strolled down from above, looking perfectly calm and put together, neat shirt tucked into neat jeans, welcoming smile in place. The only incongruity was the strand of cobweb in his hair, and that was explained away in an instant.

'We were looking in the attic. You know I've been thinking of turning out all the junk for ages. We could make better use of the space, perhaps as a den for Zoe. Maria said she'd help clear it out.' He glanced at Maria for confirmation. She nodded, seemingly incapable of anything else.

'A den for Zoe? Oh, Ben, she's got a huge bedroom as it is, and other rooms to play in if she wants to.'

I thought that was clever of me, extending the topic, forcing Ben into a conversation, trapping him there, on the stairs, in his post-coital state. You won't run away from me, I was thinking.

He rubbed the top of his head, spiking his short hair and sending the cobweb floating into space. 'Yeah, good point. But there's so much stuff up there, my college stuff, things from our old flat we'll never use. What's the point of hanging on to it all?'

'None at all,' I said, smiling beatifically. I was no more interested in the contents of our attic than Ben was, but I was enjoying my moment of power. 'Maria, if you really have time to help Ben in his attic-clearing, that would be great. You'd have to wear an overall, though. It's dreadfully dusty up there.'

I was rewarded by Maria's automatic glance downwards at her dress. I managed to smother a smile. Yes, I was shocked and upset and suffused with rage, my emotions bowling like tumbleweed – although in some corner of my brain this all made sense, as if I'd known all along – but I held it all back. Feelings of that sort need time to settle. But as I looked at the two of them standing helplessly on the stairs, my hatred of Maria began to take hold. I felt it in my shoulders, an iron-like tension.

'Well,' Maria said eventually. 'I'll just put the vacuum in the cupboard, then I'll be on my way.' She looked up at Ben, then down at me. 'I will leave you to enjoy your afternoon.'

'How long?' I asked Ben. This was much later, after I'd made him sit through a mostly silent lunch, during which he must have been wondering if I'd realised what he'd been up to.

We'd had a glass of wine each – I used to drink then, moderately. Ben, I could tell, wanted a second glass, the rest of the bottle, probably, but he'd obviously thought better of it and put the bottle back in the fridge. I'd made coffee and taken it to the orangery where Ben still sat inert, the daily paper, virginally folded, on the floor beside his chair.

He visibly started at my question, although he must have expected it.

'How long what?'

'Oh, come on.' I almost laughed. 'You know what, or rather, who. Miss Butter-wouldn't-melt Capelli.'

And yes, there followed the standard hollow protestations that he didn't know what I was talking about, the look on his face identical to the one I saw when I challenged him about Suzanna.

'No.' His eyes were alight with fury at my allegation. '*No*, Tessa. There's nothing going on between me and Maria. As if I would do that...'

'"Under my own roof".' I looked at Ben. 'That's what you were going to say, wasn't it?'

The words were superfluous really. I knew. He knew I knew. Maria knew I knew. The only question was, what was I going to do about it?

I put our mugs of coffee down on the glass table. Ben stared at them, then at me. Why was I giving him lunch and coffee while accusing him at the same time of having an affair with the domestic help? But he should have known me by then. My life until I met Ben was one of uncertainty, disruption and loss – all outside my control. But I will never let that happen again. I will take what comes face on and deal with it. I won't crawl away and hide from life like my mother did.

It may seem strange, but I didn't sack Maria immediately, and she had no choice but to continue working for us. If she'd left of her own accord, it would have seemed like admitting her sin. I had to keep Maria Capelli close, where I could see her, while I planned my next move, and in that waiting, she would suffer. It is the anticipation of what is to come that causes the most pain, don't you think?

Maria waited for me to move in for the kill, and I waited for the right time to take the right action, the one that would have the biggest impact. The only person not waiting was Ben. Like a naughty little boy who'd been caught opening his Christmas presents early, he adopted a 'so-what?' attitude, flinging himself around the house in a strop as if it was my fault.

Then, as suddenly as if a switch had been thrown, he went into full-blown remorseful mode and became very loving and considerate towards me, cooking special dinners, being extra helpful with Zoe, making sure I had everything I needed, basically. When Maria was in the house, Ben stayed out of it, whether he was at work or not. He even went so far as to make scathing remarks about her. *Too much, Ben!* Playing a part, you see? We all do it.

Meanwhile, Maria's housework took on new impetus. She rubbed and scrubbed and polished and shone, while keeping out of my way. When she couldn't manage to avoid me because I made it impossible, her dark eyes became even darker with fear, and something else – loathing probably, jealousy, too – and she would dash off to some other part of the house. One day I caught her standing in the doorway of our bedroom, just standing and looking, and I wondered if she and Ben had ever done it in our bed. I decided not. I also decided she wished they had done.

Then, in early September, the day Zoe returned to school after the summer holidays, Ben rang the plumber and arranged for the boiler to be serviced for winter – something he had never done before and has never done since. I reminded him of our plan to leave town and set up home in a more rural part of

Sussex. Somewhere cleaner, leafier, healthier for our daughter. A more pleasant way of life for us, in a small community.

'We should move now if we're going to. Zoe starts secondary school next year. Less of an upheaval to do it now,' I said.

The way he agreed so readily made me understand that he felt trapped, caught between Maria and me. The Devil and the deep blue sea. Though which of us was which I couldn't say. I may have forgiven Ben for his weakness in letting himself be seduced by that tramp, but he wasn't getting off that lightly. As for Maria, she was obsessed with Ben, I could tell. The ultimate punishment for her, the thing that would hurt her most, was that he should be removed from her world completely.

So that is what I did. The For Sale board was up within a week, and Ben and I toured our favoured area in search of the Holy Grail which, in the event, turned out to be Rose Cottage in Oakheart.

But that wasn't, as it happened, the last we saw of Maria.

And Fran? I've only just begun.

TWENTY-ONE

FRAN

Caitlin looks up from her colouring. 'Are we going to see Granddad Oliver when we go to Cornwall?'

Sunday afternoon. It's rainy and dull and we've stayed in all day, just chilling out. The lazy day suits me; I feel tired, which is in part due to the low-level anxiety that follows me about like a faithful spaniel.

'I don't know,' I say. 'I suppose we could.'

Hector puts my tea down on the footstool near the sofa. 'Yes, we are calling in on Dad. We've already decided?' There's a question in his voice, a frown on his face. 'We had that conversation.'

'Oh, yes, so we did.' I pick up my tea and cradle the mug as if I'm cold, but it's actually quite stuffy in here. 'Sorry, I forgot.'

Hector's father lives in North Somerset; it's a diversion we usually make either on the way to Cornwall or on the way home. We would have him to stay here with us like a shot, but these days he prefers to be in his own home. Despite a lack of mobility and poor eyesight, he's very independent, but that doesn't stop a bevy of neighbours, mostly female, calling in to make sure he has everything he needs.

'Good. I like Granddad Oliver. He's funny.' Caitlin sits back on her heels on the rug in front of the fireplace, carefully puts the cap back on a coloured pen, and uncaps another.

'Fran, I don't know where your head is but it's not here, that's for sure.' Hector laughs, but there's an impatience about it which fills me with guilt.

'I'm sorry,' I say, smiling across as he sits down. 'I know we decided that, I remember now. My mind's full of other stuff.' Hector waits for me to elaborate. 'Oh, you know. End of the school year, arrangements for our holiday, the usual.' I shrug vaguely.

End of term events are already marked on the calendar: sports day at Oakheart; concert at Honeybee Hall; meeting with Kitty's form tutor – she goes into her GCSE year in September. All defined, nothing to think about. I keep a running list of what to take with us to our Cornish cottage, so not much to trouble me there, either, although some new summer clothes will be needed, especially for Caitlin and Hazel who are still growing. But I can hardly tell Hector that what really fills my head is an image of the broken body of a complete stranger.

'Sorry, Hec,' I repeat.

Hector smiles. 'Stop apologising. I wondered if you were okay, that's all?' Again, the questioning intonation, requiring a reply.

'I'm fine,' I say with deliberate emphasis, and turn my attention to my tea. 'A bit tired, but you are too, I expect.'

'Who will look after Miss T when we go away?' Caitlin's blue eyes are wide as she looks up at us.

'Evelyn, the lady who works with me at the vets'. She'll come in twice a day and feed her. She does it every year. Why?'

'Oh. Well, I only wondered if the lady in the old house, the one with the funny hair, might like to have her, because if she's got so many cats she must really, *really* love them, mustn't she, Mum?'

The mention of Mirabelle causes me a spike of anxiety – typical, when I'd managed to put her out of my mind. Not Caitlin's fault, of course.

'I'm sure she loves cats,' I say, 'but we don't know Mirabelle very well, do we? And neither does Miss T. She'll be much happier in her own home with Evelyn calling in.'

Caitlin looks doubtful. 'Has Evelyn got cats, too?'

'No. But she works at the vets', remember, so she knows exactly how to look after them. She looks forward to seeing to Miss T.'

Oh, do stop, Caitlin!

She obeys my unspoken command and returns to her colouring, sticking her bottom up in the air, the way all the girls used to sleep in their cots. Thinking of the girls as babies brings a warm rush of love for them, and I go upstairs to see what Hazel and Kitty are doing. They're both in Kitty's room, Kitty lolling on the bed, Hazel cross-legged on the floor. They're watching a boxset of an American teen soap, and my mind registers that it's the same one they watched, briefly, with Zoe when we went to Rose Cottage. Not for the first time, I wonder if there are unseen forces at work, ensuring that the Grammaticus family, and Mirabelle Hayward, are for ever sewn into the tapestry of my life.

Hazel, bless her, brings me back to Earth. 'Is it teatime? Can I have peanut butter and banana sandwiches?'

'Ooh, yeah.' Kitty sits upright on the bed. 'Is there any of that apple pie left from dinner?'

I laugh. 'You two have got hollow legs. Yes, I'll get on with the tea. Come down in ten minutes, right?'

'Right,' Kitty says, as two pairs of eyes whisk past me, back to the TV screen.

Summarily dismissed, I drop a curtsy, maid-style, and back out of the room. But I'm smiling.

.   .   .

That evening, while I'm reading a bedtime story to Caitlin and she's all pink-faced from her bath and snuggled in her dressing gown, I spot a message come through on my phone.

'Message, Mum,' my daughter says helpfully.

'I'll look in a minute, darling. Let's finish this chapter and get you up to bed first.'

'My hair is still quite wet.'

'Not wet, only damp at the ends. It'll be dry in a minute.'

'Or we could get the hairdryer?' Hopeful eyes look at me, delaying the inevitable.

I don't reply but carry on reading. I saw who the message was from: Tessa. I have no idea what she wants, but console myself with the belief that it's something to do with art club. Perhaps it's cancelled next week and she's contacting everyone to let them know. We have an email group set up for that, but I can't think what else she can want with me. If she's hoping to rope me in for another charity thing, she would probably ring rather than text.

But this is Tessa we're talking about, so who knows?

Once Caitlin's in bed, reading another book – one about frogs that Zoe gave her because she's too old for it – and under instruction to switch her light out in fifteen minutes, I deliberately take time to go and check on the others. Kitty is in her room, thumbing at her phone. She looks up at me with a distinct expression of impatience. Kitty has a sweet temperament – usually – but she also makes it known she doesn't like to be disturbed when she's 'chatting' to her mates. I smile and leave her to it. Hazel is downstairs with Hector. They're in the kitchen, matily making hot chocolate together. I watch them for a moment from the doorway, treasuring the snapshot of family life.

'Ah, want some?' Hector turns.

'No, thanks. I'm going to have a glass of that Shiraz if there's any left.' I cast my eyes to the wine rack. 'Purely for medicinal purposes, of course. I need the boost.'

Hazel raises her eyes at me. 'Mum...'

'Yes, Hazel?'

'Oh, nothing,' she says airily, making an exaggerated face at her father. 'Hot chocolate would be much healthier for you.'

I watch my middle daughter reach for the squirty cream, load it onto her drink, and top it with two marshmallows. 'I'm watching my cholesterol,' I say, and Hector grins at me.

It's not until Hector and Hazel have taken their chocolate through to the living room and I've poured myself some wine – a small glass, just enough to take the edge off – that I bring myself to read Tessa's message. *I need to speak to you. Meet me at the cut-through behind the indoor market. Tomorrow 2.45.* She makes it sound like a royal command.

Damn cheek! My first reaction. Swiftly moving on to wondering what it is that can't wait until we next happen to meet, say, next Saturday at art club. Or, for that matter, what is so important that she needs to see me face to face? None of which makes me want to leap to reply. So, I leave it a while, quite a long while.

Hazel wants some advice over her English homework which she has completed, but is now having doubts about whether she's done it right. Hector is already handling this, but I sit down and put in my two-pennyworth because it's what I do, and Tessa Grammaticus is shunted from my mind for a few moments longer.

Let her wait.

And wait she has to, until my curiosity rushes to the surface and has me texting back to ask her what it is she wants to see me about.

Hazel leans over my chair and taps me on the shoulder. 'Mum, you do think that's what Mr Hall meant, don't you? The way I've answered the question?'

'Yes, I think you've tackled it the right way. I'm with your dad on that. *Plus*, Hazel, there's no time to change it anyway, so go on up and I'll come and see you when you're in bed.'

Hazel pulls an unconvinced face but trots off anyway. Hector goes to the kitchen to start on tomorrow's packed lunches. Meanwhile, the phone in my hand has buzzed again. *You'll find out when we meet. Please be there,* Tessa writes.

A swift and nervy *OK* is all I can manage in reply, while my mind grows as heavy as a thunderstorm as the awful possibilities roll in.

TWENTY-TWO

FRAN

The next day, the surgery is towering busy all morning, as it often is on a Monday, owners being unable to bring their animals in for minor problems at the weekend; we are open on Saturday mornings but only for emergencies. I'm on duty with Sally; she's about my age and has two teenagers at Oakheart Academy, which gives us plenty to talk about, when we have time to talk, that is. This morning there's little opportunity, and for once I'm glad of the stream of clients clutching baskets and pet carriers or holding dogs on leads.

But after a while, the buzz of the waiting room begins to increase my anxiety rather than helping it, so I go round the back to the cages and comfort a sweet little black-and-white cat called Freddie. Far from being sleepy after his neutering op earlier, he is making an unholy squalling noise which carries through the surgery. I take him out of his cage and cradle him, letting his velvety warmth soothe me as much, I hope, as my petting is soothing him.

David comes through. 'Ring the owner, get her to come and fetch him, Fran. I'll give him the once-over, but he seems fine.'

'He's certainly letting us know he's ready to go,' I say, handing the cat to David.

Before I go back to reception, I check on the other animals: a poorly dog with a bandaged leg; a rabbit who is having a cyst removed later; and two more cats, either awaiting procedures or waiting to be collected. It's a part of the job I enjoy, perhaps even more than meeting the people, and I've learned a whole lot about animal care from the vets since I started.

Do you hear that, Mirabelle?

Eventually, time has winged on. It's early afternoon and I can no longer put the impending meeting with Tessa out of my mind. Most of my packed lunch ends up in the bin as nerves pilfer my appetite. This is stupid, I tell myself, as I put on my jacket and take an age unlocking my bag from the cupboard where we keep our personal belongings. Whatever Tessa wants to see me about, it won't be anything like I'm imagining. How could it be? Not after all this time.

Halfway along the village's main street, a twitten cuts between the shops, snaking past fenced back yards, skirting flint walls, before it emerges into a cobbled square in which there is a jumble of shops of the kind that look temporary, with corrugated tin roofs, bright-painted wooden walls, and a haphazard arrangement of doors and windows. It's a sort of indoor market, designed with tourists in mind. There's an antiques and curio shop, one selling flowers and plants, another with gifts and cards, a couple with pottery, wooden and hand-knitted items, and a kiosk selling drinks and ice cream. There are no visitors today, as there often aren't, and as I pass through, smiling at the shopkeepers who make eye contact, I wonder how the place keeps going. This thought is by way of a diversion, and all too soon I'm through the market, ducking along a continuation of the twitten, and reaching the part where it widens out again.

No shops here, nothing except high flint walls on two sides, over which ivy trails and tree branches hang. It's a hidden place, a little-known cut-through to the oldest, quietest part of the village, a place of shade. It seems a strange place for a meeting, of whatever purpose, and I can't think why I agreed to come in the first place. Now I'm here, I can't think at all. About anything.

Tessa is standing to one side, appearing to be examining the flints in the wall. She turns at my approach. 'Fran.'

'Hello, Tessa.' I don't smile, but neither does she.

She is dressed all in black: narrow black jeans and black cotton sweater, throwing her pale face and blonde hair into sharp relief against the dark flints. I feel suddenly annoyed with her for bringing me here, and this annoyance hoists me out of my trance-like state, and I face her, head on.

'Tessa, what's this about? Why are we here? I haven't got long. I have to go home and fetch my car, then collect Caitlin.'

Tessa looks at her watch. 'I know.'

She knows? Tessa knows what time I leave work, and what time I collect Caitlin, that's obvious, and extremely disconcerting. My legs feel weak and I glance at the narrow wooden bench against one of the walls. The wood is blackened with damp from yesterday's rain, which is probably why Tessa is standing, although I have the feeling this is not a womanly sit-and-chat kind of thing. The spectre of Ben appears across my mental vision.

Oh God.

'How did you do it, Fran?'

The question shoots across the space. I don't answer.

Tessa takes one step closer to me. I stand my ground, with difficulty. 'How did you do it? How did you lure my husband into an affair?'

My mouth dries. My brain atrophies. I can't speak.

The one thing I've been so afraid of is finally happening. She even said 'affair'. She knows it wasn't a one-time mistake. Now the real nightmare begins, right here, right now.

'Easy, was it, beguiling a man like Ben? Seducing him while his defences were down?' Tessa says.

Defences? Ben? I would laugh if it wasn't so tragic.

I have to stay on top of this, stay in control. She has no proof. She can't have. If Ben had told her, or she'd found out some other way, he would have let me know. I've always believed he would do that.

I have no choice but to brazen it out. I find my voice, keeping it even, emotionless. 'Tessa, I don't know where this is coming from, but you're talking nonsense. You're accusing me of something I didn't do.'

'Fran, Fran.' Tessa's expression softens. She's acting, trying to force a confession out of me. 'I know what went on between you and Ben, the summer before last. There's no point in you denying it, so please don't waste my time.'

I give a short, violent shake of my head. 'No. You've got this wrong.'

I have to keep up the pretence. What else can I do?

A silence stretches between us, blossoms like mist between the dank walls. Tessa breaks it.

'High Heaven – does that mean anything to you?'

The moment she mentions High Heaven, I know I'm lost. We went there three, four times at most? Including the first time. And the last. Somehow, Tessa has picked up on that. But wait. High Heaven is a known spot for lovers, illicit or otherwise, as well as for suicides. She could be guessing. One look at her face tells me she's doing no such thing, and I can no longer deny it with any credibility.

I swallow, trying to disperse the mesh of fear that closes my throat. 'Okay, yes.'

'Finally, she tells the truth.' Tessa throws up her hands and addresses the space around us.

I continue. 'It was a mistake, a really bad mistake, and I'm so very sorry, Tessa. I was at a low point, which is totally no excuse, and I should never have let it happen. But I did, *we* did, and I know there's nothing I can do about it now. It happened, and I'm so sorry for the pain we've caused you. Ben loves you, that's clear. There was never anything of that kind between us.'

This speech steals the last of my breath, my energy. I sink onto the bench, damp or not. Tessa remains standing. She starts a slow handclap, just four times.

'Very good, Fran. I could have written the script.'

I gather myself. 'Well, what did you want me to say? I have nothing else to offer except my apologies, and to say again that I'm so sorry for hurting you. But, Tessa, what is the point of this? Okay, I'm guilty, and believe me, I'll regret what I did to you, and to my family, as long as I live. But Ben isn't exactly innocent either. Is it not hurting you even more to bring it up now, after all this time?'

'*Hurting* me?' Tessa shakes her head. 'My God, Fran, you have *no* idea. No idea at all. You with your perfect life and your sheltered middle-class upbringing.'

That's an odd thing to say. 'You don't know anything about my life.'

Tessa doesn't speak. She looks at the ground. For a moment, I'm on top. It doesn't last. She tosses her head, eyes glittering.

'Understand this, Francesca Oliver. Nobody who seduces my husband gets away with it. *Ever.*'

My mind switches to Maria. I swallow painfully. My resolve to find out more about that poor woman strengthens.

'I haven't got away with it. Not one day goes by when I haven't regretted what I did. If you think I haven't suffered enough, you're probably right. But again, what do you expect me to say? What do you want from me, Tessa? I can't turn back time.'

She turns on her heel, then turns back again, just as swiftly. 'Are you still seeing him?'

I stand up again. '*What?* No, of *course* not!' Is this what's it's really about?

'You went to the café with him, while your daughter was in my art club.'

How does she know that? Ben must have told her, obviously. I gather up the little bit of sense I have left.

I sigh. 'We bumped into each other outside the hall. Ben asked me if I'd like a coffee and I said yes. Half the village was in there, too. If Ben told you, does that not show how innocent it was?'

'Oh, Ben didn't tell me. I saw, with my own eyes. That's how I know.'

'I expect he forgot. It was nothing. A friendly coffee, that's all. I have no feelings for Ben whatsoever, not in the way you seem to be implying, and he has none for me.'

'How do you know that, Fran? How do you *know* how Ben feels about you?'

The question hits me like a bullet. I feel my face heating. I remind myself that whatever Ben has said, or done, recently, it's a game he plays. I have never encouraged him, nor taken any part in that.

Guilt creeps in as I realise I should not have gone for that coffee, not when it was just the two of us. He might have taken it as a sign that I still liked him in that way. I pray that I'm wrong. But this has come from somewhere, this hellish conversation with Ben's wife. Has she caught some kind of vibe from him, concerning me? She knows him, I don't, not really. Is this what it's all about, Tessa thinking Ben still wants me?

I let the question go. I have no answer to it.

'Two of your girls go to Oakheart Academy, don't they?' Tessa says, throwing out a topic at random, it seems. Her voice changes, lowering in tone to something approaching conversational. If these twists and turns are meant to mess with my head, she's doing a fair job. I haven't got the inclination to talk about our children, or school. It couldn't be a more inappropriate topic for this moment.

'You know full well they do. Why?'

'Are they safe while they're there, do you think? I mean, who is watching, making sure they don't do themselves a nasty injury? At break, for instance.'

I freeze. Tessa is fixing me with a meaningful stare.

'Oh my God, it was you! You pretended to be the lunch assistant. You rang me, telling me Hazel had cut herself. *Why*, Tessa?'

'Now you're just being stupid. Why do you think? To make you panic, to make you uncomfortable.' She gives a humourless chuckle. 'I made quite a fist of the voice, don't you think?'

I shake my head in wondrous disbelief.

'Okay,' Tessa says, taking a step nearer to me. 'Let's play a game. Here's a word for you, a couple of words: "chilli pepper". What comes into your head?'

'The cupcake. That was you, too.'

'Ha. Now she gets it.'

My nerves are in tatters, my heart won't stay in my chest. It's loud, thumping, somewhere near the base of my throat. Now I have the answer to one of my questions: Tessa has not just found out about me and Ben, she's known for a long time. Possibly, the whole time.

'Plus,' Tessa points a finger at me, 'I know somebody else who has cause to wreak havoc on your cosy little life.' She nods firmly. 'Want to know who it is?'

I nod weakly. I am done for, beaten, and Tessa knows it.

'The poor old dear whose cat you seem to have accidentally killed. Or was it an accident? She certainly doesn't think so.'

Mirabelle again. 'Is that all? We had that conversation before, Tessa, if you remember, and I told you at the time it was nonsense.'

Tessa shrugs. 'Whatever. Dead animals seem to be your forte.'

'Dead... the badger! That was you as well.'

'Nope, wrong. That was actually Mirabelle, and great pleasure it gave her, even if she couldn't be there to see the result.'

'But you put her up to it.' My understanding dawns.

'She had, shall we say, a little bit of help. It was heavy, that thing. And it stunk.'

'I suppose you sent me flowers as well, to the surgery. A basket of roses and gypsophila, no name of sender.'

'Anonymous flowers, huh?' Tessa pretends to be thinking. 'Yes, I can see how that might seem weird, a little bit sinister, as if there's someone out there watching you.'

'Exactly.'

She laughs. 'Good one, but it wasn't me. I would tell you if it was, since we're into the truth here.'

I don't know whether I believe her or not. But actually, I do believe her. I cast the matter of the flowers aside and open my mouth to speak again, whilst not knowing exactly what I'm going to say, but Tessa holds up a hand, the palm facing me.

'And now, I shall come to the point of this discussion. No.' She stops me again with a look. 'As I said, nobody who so much as looks at my husband gets away with it. I will stop this, and I will stop *you*. So, you will go home, and you will tell Hector all about your sordid little affair with Ben... or I will.'

'Tessa, please, you can't...' I feel faint. I move to the wall and place one hand on it to steady myself.

'Oh, I can, and I will.' She looks at her watch. 'You'd better get going. I wouldn't want you to be late picking up Caitlin.'

TWENTY-THREE

TESSA

I stay where I am after Fran has left. Zoe won't be home yet; I'm in no hurry. I sit down on the bench, less damp now that the sun has moved and cast a little warmth and light into the walled space. I need a moment to gather my senses, allow my breathing to regulate, my heartbeat to normalise.

In the last ten minutes, Fran has discovered just how far I will go to wreck the lives of people who threaten to wreck mine. I have discovered something, too, or rather, had confirmation: Hector doesn't know about the affair. There was always the slight chance that she'd already confessed and I was wasting my time. Clearly, that isn't the case. It did once cross my mind that Hector has always known and chose to do nothing about it, but he'd hardly have been able to sit around my table playing happy families, unless he's one hell of a lot more devious than I've given him credit for.

It's the children I feel sorry for, the pretty trio of Oliver girls. But they'll survive whatever is heading their way. Kids do. I did, and I came through all the stronger for it. It was the thought of those girls that almost stopped me from taking the conversation to its extreme, even though that's what I had planned. But then I thought about Zoe and how I need to protect her – and Ben, too, because, as I have said before, Ben needs saving from himself – and I did what I had to do.

I don't at this point know whether I will carry out my threat and go to Fran's husband if she doesn't tell him. Maybe I will, maybe I won't. It will be the not knowing that will floor her, turn her days to a black, quaking mess of wondering and waiting – and if she does confess, she won't do it right away.

How will I know if she's told him? She might tell me she has, but I'll know if she's lying. If she does what I ask, that will be apparent, too, especially to me. Our families see enough of one another to recognise that something has gone badly wrong. However she tries to hide it, it will show. Ben will know something's happened, but not what. Even if he works it out – or Fran tells him – what can he do? He's hardly in a position to complain that I've finally taken revenge. He would probably cheer the fact that it is Fran who has paid the price, not him.

Yes, I have considered the possibility of Hector storming Rose Cottage and punching seven bells out of Ben, but I don't believe that's his style. And anyway, if it looks like happening, I'll find a way to forestall it.

I check my watch. I have fifteen minutes before I need to be home for Zoe. It's peaceful here, in this hidden backwater of the village. Very few people pass through; visitors to the little shops arrive and leave the way they came, back to the high street. A woman came through just now from the houses at the back, walking a small terrier. The dog pulled to be allowed to sniff at the weeds growing at the base of the wall but was soon hurried on. I gaze up to the sky which is almost clear now, the blue brighter than before, and into my mind comes Suzanna.

My private name for her was Simpering Suzanna, because that's how she behaved, simpering around Ben, fetching him drinks from the cafeteria in the office building where they both worked, handling his emails and phone calls to save him time.

Acting like his personal assistant, and more, even though that was not her role. It wasn't anybody's role; Ben had not been with the advertising company for very long and hardly qualified for an assistant.

There was a purpose to it all, of course, that was as plain as day. She wanted to flounce around the city with a tall, dark, strikingly handsome man on her arm, being the envy of all. I know the type; I came across enough of them when I worked in London. Most of all, she wanted him in her bed. She could hardly keep her hands off him in the workplace, let alone in private.

We were living in our first flat at the time, not married but talking about it, in a vague one-day kind of way. I was working in an art gallery near the British Museum. The hours were flexible, and I was left to my own devices much of the time. It was easy to call in on Ben at work, ten minutes' walk away. I would arrive in time to meet him for lunch, often when he wasn't expecting it. A couple of times, he'd been in meetings and I'd had to wait a while, but it was never a problem. The atmosphere in the office was creative, arty, laid back; people seemed to come and go all the time. I was just one of a number.

It didn't take me long to sum up Suzanna. If she'd been in a meeting with him, she'd be practically hanging onto his arm as they came through the door, fixing me with a supercilious stare when she saw me. 'If looks could kill.' That's the saying, isn't it? If she'd been at her desk when I arrived, she would immediately rush over to Ben and engage him in an apparently urgent and meaningful conversation, shuffling bits of paper in his direction, jotting down notes, brushing close to him and keeping her back to me as I stood at the edge of the open-plan room. Eventually, she would have to release him, and I would patently ignore her as Ben greeted me and we went off to lunch.

'She fancies you,' I said one day. 'What's more, she's

expecting you to do something about it. If you haven't already.' I had not learned to bide my time then.

The way he responded, with a gruff, pointless denial and a protestation of innocence, confirmed that the feeling was mutual. Not that I needed confirmation. Suzanna was beautiful, I couldn't deny that. But her beauty didn't reach her eyes, which had a marble hardness about them. That would not have worried Ben, had he even noticed.

I never did know whether he'd screwed her or not. What I did know was that he was more than capable of doing so while telling me I was the love of his life and planning our future together. It didn't put me off him. Perhaps it should have done, but I believe in fighting for what you want. I don't give in.

As I sat quietly in the back office of the mostly empty gallery, I spent my time wisely, using the computer to do a spot of digging into Suzanna Henderson. I hit on a result fairly early on: a newspaper report, a court case concerning the diversion of large amounts of cash from an account at her last company, a suspended prison sentence, a sacking.

I enjoyed composing that letter, almost wished I could have signed it. I sent a copy to every name on the staff list at Ben's workplace, every name except Suzanna's. She left very quickly after that, without working out her notice. And Ben never said a word about it.

I narrowly miss mowing down the crossing patrol man as I drive Caitlin away from Honeybee Hall, causing her to gasp and exclaim at my idiocy from the back seat.

'Mummy! The lollipop man held up Stop just then, and you didn't.'

I meet her wide-eyed gaze in the mirror. 'It was fine, darling. If I'd stopped just then, the van behind would have run into us.'

Caitlin twists round and looks at the van which has stopped obediently at the crossing, knowing as well as I do that it had been some distance behind us. She sinks into her seat, her face a crease of puzzlement and concern.

'Sorry,' I say. 'I didn't mean to frighten you. Or the lollipop man. The children were on the pavement, everyone was quite safe.'

'I wasn't frightened.' Caitlin's bottom lip protrudes.

'Okay. Let's just get home, shall we?'

And we do, but now we're at the house, I've already forgotten how we got here. All I can see is the willowy figure of Tessa Grammaticus, all in black, delivering my death sentence.

How do I live with this? Do I assume she's serious and tell

Hector about the affair, throwing myself on his mercy? Or do I hope and pray that Tessa said what she said to scare me, and has no intention of carrying out her threat? Even without the ultimatum, the idea that Tessa knows about me and Ben is terrifying. Is it a recent discovery, or has she been playing me for a fool, making out she's my friend, and all the while repulsed by me? If so, to what end? Why string it out before she confronted me? And what about Ben himself? How much does he know? Why has he not warned me?

It's only been an hour since my meeting with Tessa, and already the questions are dividing and multiplying, attacking every cell of my brain, like a mutant monster. My overriding feeling is one of pure dread, which caps everything I've felt before: the permanent state of unease, the guilt that is sewn into my days, and is no more than I deserve. But I'm not thinking about myself now. I'm thinking of Hector, and the girls, and how their worlds could be ripped apart by a few words from Tessa.

Or from me.

Once we're indoors, I'm swept into my motherly, domestic role, providing drinks and snacks – Kitty and Hazel arrive home soon after Caitlin and me – refereeing a tussle over the last piece of chocolate cake in the tin, collecting up shoes and discarded bits of school uniform from the floor and stairs as the rush to pull on jeggings or shorts, T-shirts and animal-print trainers begins.

Hector comes home at just after five thirty, complaining mildly about being stuck behind a tractor for half a mile. I can't look at him. I disappear to the bathroom and lock myself in. Perched on the edge of the bath, I steeple my hands to my face. The longing to share this pain is overwhelming. But who with? Grace? Should I call her, ask her to meet me in the pub later and spill the whole story? She won't judge. But Grace lives in Oakheart. She knows Tessa and Ben, she knows everybody. She probably thinks she knows me. Can I really disillusion her? She would keep the secret, no doubt about that, but it wouldn't be fair to burden her with this, expect her to come up with a plan, an answer to my dilemma, when there is none.

Never have I needed my mother as much as I do now. I want to throw myself into her arms, be five years old again, feel her soft hands stroking my forehead, comforting me with kindness and understanding. *Mum, why aren't you here? Why are you so far away?*

A single knock lands on the door. Kitty's voice filters through the wood panel. 'Mum? Dad says what's for dinner and shall he start cooking it?'

I haven't given our evening meal a single thought. I stand up on woolly legs, open the door and come out onto the landing.

'Shall we have fish and chips for a change? I'll go to the shop.' I smile at Kitty, as best I can.

'Cool.' Kitty goes downstairs to relay this news.

'Are you okay, Fran?' Hector says from the bottom of the stairs, as I follow her down.

'What? Yes, just a bit of a headache that's all. Tricky day.' *You could say.*

I glance in the hall mirror. A mess of red face, smudged mascara and tangled hair looks back at me.

Hector gives me a brief hug, then holds me away from him, inspecting. I struggle to meet his gaze. 'You do look a bit off-colour. Go and sit down, put the telly on. I'll fetch the fish and chips.'

And so my lovely, kind, wonderful husband brings me a cup of tea, goes to the village to collect our dinner, pays the girls plenty of attention during the meal, and doesn't even let me clear away after we've eaten.

These are the important things. Love and kindness make a marriage work. It doesn't have to be all fireworks. Yes, I felt sidelined when Caitlin's autism became apparent. Hector disappeared inside himself, and left it to me to cope. That was how it felt at the time. But I've come to realise that was his way of coping – his way, not mine – and I respect him for that. Okay, he didn't pay me as much attention as I needed at the time, and with my parents missing from the scene, I felt as if I had nobody. Again, I don't hold this up as an excuse for what I did. It's just the facts, as I see them.

But the distance between us gradually lessened, the atmosphere warmed, and Hector, in his own time, came back to me.

We're good, the two of us. I don't deserve it to be so, but we are. How can I break his heart? How can I?

TWENTY-FIVE

TESSA

The day our father packed all his belongings into the car and left home for ever, my sister Amelia and I walked around the streets of Plymouth, hand in hand. We didn't usually hold hands; my sister being nearly fourteen and me only twelve meant she felt a lot more grown up than I was. I was tolerated by her, no more. But that day, we joined hands by unspoken agreement and we walked along our terrace in our green gingham school dresses, round the corner where the pub was – the pub that Mum said was Dad's second home – past the bookies' and the sweet shop, turning left into the street that backed onto ours.

When we reached the end of that street, we turned right into the next street, walking and turning, walking and turning, until my legs ached. It was after school; the day had been tiring enough.

'Will he be there when we get back?' I asked, puffing slightly from the walking.

'That's the idea,' Amelia said. 'We just need to give him time to come back and talk to Mum. In private.'

'Is that why we're walking?'

'Well, *obviously*.' Amelia's voice was sarcastic, her eyes lifted to the sky at my lack of understanding.

But as we turned one more corner and headed homewards, our ears tuned for the hopeful sound of the clapped-out Volkswagen, I felt my sister's hand tighten around mine and I realised she was taking comfort from me as well as giving it. She didn't believe any more than I did that our father had changed his mind and returned home.

'What will we do?' I asked Mum, when we got home and found her, feet up on the worn settee, hugging a cushion on her lap.

'Do?' She looked at me as if I was a stranger who had appeared in her living room. 'What is there to do? He's gone, and good riddance.' She rose from the settee, went upstairs, and shut herself in her bedroom. We didn't see her again until morning.

Our days went on much as before, but with our mother growing ever more distant until she seemed like a tiny figure, silhouetted against the skyline as she vanished over the horizon. She never spoke about Dad again.

After a month, Amelia and I each received a letter from him. He was sorry, he said, but his life had been intolerable and although he missed us both, and loved us, it would only cause trouble if he stayed at home and we were better off without him. The letters were almost identical. Neither of us knew what his words really meant. There was no address, so we couldn't write back.

'I think,' Amelia said, as we sat on my bedroom floor, our backs to the door, 'he means he doesn't love Mum any more, and that's why he went.'

I thought about this. 'What's wrong with Mum? Why doesn't he love her? Does he love those other women, the ones he went out with?'

'I don't know,' my sister said. 'But people stop loving other people all the time, even if they once did. It's one of the facts of life.'

To me, the facts of life were all about what people did to get babies. I was young for my age, confused, sad. But I realised that if Mum didn't have Dad to look after her, then all she had was me, and Amelia. It gave us something to think about, something to focus on, keeping a watchful eye on our mother in case she did anything stupid.

We prepared simple meals like beans on toast, eggs on toast, and more or less anything on toast, until, by trial and error, we extended our repertoire to things like sausages, and roast chicken. It turned out that roasting a chicken was easy, providing you got it safely out of the oven without burning yourself on the hot fat in the tin. The potatoes and cabbage were usually cold by the time the meat was ready, but Mum didn't seem to notice.

Amelia and I fed ourselves – and our mother when she would let us – we bathed, went to school, did our homework, passed our exams. We survived, and somehow, eventually, we grew up.

And then Amelia left to go and live with Dad – she was always his favourite. So I was completely alone, if not physically then certainly in every other way. I think it was then that I vowed never to lose anything, or anyone, who was precious to me ever again.

TWENTY-SIX

FRAN

Two weeks pass – don't ask me how, they just do – and nothing happens. By which I mean that Tessa hasn't been in touch with me, nor has she contacted Hector. I feel as if I'm constantly underwater, holding my breath, not daring to believe that Tessa has relented, or never intended to see the ultimatum through in the first place. Every time I look at Hector, the words form in my brain, words Tessa commanded me to speak. Unspoken, impossible words.

The school year draws to a close, and still nothing. I can't avoid the village – I work there, for goodness' sake – and the risk of running into Tessa, or Ben, is ever-present. Two days before the end of term at Oakheart Academy, Hector and I go to sports day. Caitlin has already broken up and is at Maisie's house. We watch a game of netball, cheering on Hazel's team, then attend a gymnastics display in which Kitty shows a surprising, almost balletic, prowess, despite her declared absolute hatred of anything to do with PE.

It's not until we gather on the playing fields for the lower school athletics events that I spot Tessa and Ben among the crowd of spectators, on the opposite side of the running track from us. I glance warily at Hector, wondering if he's seen them too, and whether he'll think it rude not to go over and chat. But he says nothing, and I assume he hasn't noticed.

Tessa is animated, her pale blonde head bobbing as she talks to other parents nearby. Ben stands facing the track, hands in pockets, looking as if he'd rather be anywhere other than here. Silently, I admonish him for not entering into the spirit of the day. He is a good dad to Zoe, though, I know that, and it panics me slightly as I wonder if he has other things on his mind. Namely me. And Hector.

I decide I'm giving my imagination too much freedom. I can't second-guess this situation and it's pointless to try. Relieved that neither Tessa nor Ben seem to have seen us, I give all my attention to Hazel as she crosses the finishing line in fifth place in her race. She looks over at us, throws up her hands and grins. Hazel doesn't need to win. Hector says she lacks competitive drive, but I think she's all the happier for it. It is all I want – for my daughters, as well as my husband, to be happy.

Please God let me keep them that way.

I shed tears of relief when holiday time comes around and we head for the West Country, every spare inch of the car stuffed full of essentials, and in the case of the girls, a number of non-essentials – according to Hector, anyway. We don't use the roof-rack any more, not since the time the whole lot slid off on a tricky bend, leaving us scrabbling around on the grass verge picking up clothes and beach gear.

Nothing awful can happen while we're out of Tessa's range; as far as I know she doesn't have Hector's mobile number. The prospect of a fortnight of relative safety helps soothe my frayed nerves; relative because the problem is still there, just postponed.

We leave home at eight on Saturday morning, only half an

hour later than scheduled, which is a miracle in itself. Kitty's hair is wet, and Hazel complains she keeps flicking it in her direction on purpose. Caitlin moans that she's squashed and can't lift her elbows to do her colouring. Hector and I shut our ears as best we can, and I pass into the back a stash of sweets I've been saving for the journey.

My benign expression falters as we drive past Rose Cottage and my stomach swerves. But a little later, some studiously casual questioning of Hazel reveals that the Grammaticus family are going to Positano for a fortnight, leaving at the end of next week. This fortunate overlap means I have almost three weeks' grace instead of two, and by the time we hit the motorway, I've resolved to enjoy this holiday, and worry about Tessa when we're all back in Oakheart. If I have to.

Hector's father, George, lives in a neat 1930s semi in a quiet, leafy crescent on the outskirts of Taunton. We decide to make the diversion on the way down rather than on the return journey, when all we want to do then is get home.

The first thing George says to me is that I look pasty.

'That's what I keep saying,' Hector says, smiling fondly at me.

Does he? Clearly, I've not been paying attention. Unsurprisingly. Something else I must do: focus on my husband, and not let the troubles I brought upon myself take precedence over my marriage. Ironic, of course, given the nature of those troubles.

'I'm fine,' I say, kissing George on the cheek. 'I just need my holiday, that's all.'

George has had warning of our visit and a mountain of triangular sandwiches teeters on an old blue-and-white meat platter in the middle of his dining room table. Lettuce leaves

TWENTY-SEVEN

FRAN

Monday morning. We came back from Cornwall on Saturday, and since then my mind has dwelt, not on Tessa and her ultimatum, as you would expect, but on Maria Capelli. And I suppose it isn't surprising that I'm drawn to High Heaven, despite its dubious connotations.

The magnetic tug of the place has me on my feet and ready to leave the house by nine thirty, safe in the knowledge that the girls are taken care of. Kitty, to her credit – and our surprise – has found herself a holiday job at the Pot and Kettle; Hazel is at a friend's house in Oakheart, along with a group of other girls including Zoe's friend Tayler, whom she apparently now likes – we all raise our eyes at this news; and Caitlin has gone with Hector to work. We're all linked by mobile phones, and for a few hours at least, I am free.

I have the week off from the surgery and plan to use the time to solve my dilemma. There has to be a solution; I won't be beaten by this. First, I need to clear my head and do a little thinking, on my own, without Hector present to distort any logic I still possess.

The grass at High Heaven is crisp and fawn-coloured in

places from lack of rain. The meadow where the sheep graze and the fields below are turning from emerald to olive for the same reason. The sun today is accompanied by a stiff, drying breeze, brisker up here than down below. It whips the ends of my hair across my face, and I find an elasticated band in the pocket of my jeans and gather it into a ponytail.

Despite the early hour, I'm not the only visitor to High Heaven. A dog-walker's van was in the car park, and two young women wearing cropped combats are walking away from the crest of the hill, following the dip of the escarpment, with three dogs apiece on leads. A grey-haired man and woman in sturdy footwear take youthful strides in the opposite direction, and a young man with sunglasses on his head sits cross-legged in the grass, sketching the view on a large, white paper drawing block.

I sit down on the bench. It's set between bushes, which act as a windbreak. The wash of warmth on my face brings a welcome feeling of well-being, and for a while I let my mind drift back to Cornwall, imagining I'm back in the old deck-chair in the cottage garden, the girls happily occupied, Hector half-asleep next to me. A bird wheels overhead, cutting easily across the blue-and-white sky, the motion bringing me back to the present. I need to stay focused, and not let my mind drift.

So, Maria. It doesn't seem morbid that I've come to the place where she spent her last living moments – I can't say the other word inside my head, not right now. The more I've thought about the story Grace told me, the more believable it has become. Maria is inextricably linked to Ben, and therefore to Tessa, and now, by circumstances beyond my control, to me.

Did she sit on this bench in silent contemplation before she... did what she did? Was there a period of doubt when things could have gone either way? I shudder involuntarily. She must have had other reasons, other than her liaison, if it existed, with Ben, however badly wrong it went. Whatever tortures she suffered, whether they were anything to do with Ben or not, how could she have deprived that little boy of his mother in the most devastating way possible? It's beyond my comprehension.

But I have no way of knowing what went on in Maria's mind, what sadness she endured, or the extent of her psychological problems, any more than I could know how Ben was thinking and acting at the time. He told me he hadn't had any other lovers, and I believed him, probably because it suited me to. He's certainly not behaving well now, with his obvious remarks and his invitation to coffee. Ben has broken the unspoken contract between us, perhaps in more ways than I realise. It is with a dash of depression and regret that I conclude I didn't know Ben as well as I thought I did. In fact, I hardly knew him at all.

This is getting me nowhere. I feel no more connected to Maria in this tragic place than anywhere else, nor any closer to the truth about her death. If by some mystical trickery, her final scene was to play itself out in front of me, right now, I would still be no nearer to knowing what to do about Tessa's ultimatum. No nearer to stopping this awful threat to my husband and our marriage than on the day she delivered it.

I get up from the bench and cross the turf to stand on the slight incline that leads upwards to the precipice. I try not to think about the drop itself, and what has occurred there, nor do I think about the times when I came to High Heaven to meet Ben. Instead, I run through the script, the one where I say to Hector, 'I've got something important to tell you, and I'd like you not to say anything until I've finished.' That is how it begins, in my head. How it continues, or ends, I haven't the foggiest idea.

I'm aware of somebody approaching, and I glance round. A woman is walking up from the car park. As she reaches the top, she stops and looks around. She seems tentative, as if she might have come to the wrong place. She's small, about five foot four, slim, but with a rounded softness to her figure. Her short-cut hair is black, sprinkled with silver, and although her complexion is pale, her face speaks of a Mediterranean heritage. She's wearing a plain grey shift dress and carrying a bouquet of flowers.

Aware that I'm staring, I tear my gaze back to the landscape. But when I glance round again, I realise she hasn't noticed. She doesn't look at me, nor at the artist who is hurrying his pencil along as if his time is running out. The woman starts towards the edge, and I'm thinking I should warn her about the drop. Then she stops, looks round again, and treads over the bumpy turf to the bench. Next to the bench, the grass grows long among the trunks of the gorse and other shrubs. At some time, a bush has been sheared off a foot above the ground, either by a storm or the hatchet of a long-ago council worker.

The woman looks round once more, then stoops and places the bouquet so that it leans against the stump, then takes a few steps backwards and stands with head bowed, looking at the flowers.

The artist unfolds long limbs, stands up and walks away towards the car park, his art equipment in a rough bundle under his arm. No one else is here now, just me and the woman. I'm about to head off myself, let her have her private time alone, when she turns and gives me a half-smile. So, I walk across, slowly, giving her time to leave if she wants to. Instead, she waits.

'Hello.' I smile as I reach her, nodding towards the flowers. 'They're beautiful. I hope the wind doesn't spoil them. It can get wild up here when the wind's up.'

She shrugs. 'It is no matter. I have brought them for her, that's the important thing.'

'For...?' I wouldn't ask, only I sense she wants to tell me.

'My little sister. It's her birthday. She would have been forty-five today.'

The bouquet contains flame-orange roses, deep red antir-

rhinums, pink carnations and lime-green miniature chrysanthe-
mums. Bold, vibrant, clashing.

'They're very colourful,' I say.

'I chose them for the colours. They're just like her. She was
bright, too, and she had a fiery temperament.' She gives a little
laugh. 'It got her into trouble, a number of times.'

The question is on my lips; I daren't let it out. The woman
must have sensed it from my silence.

'You are wondering,' she says, with a small smile. 'You are
wondering what happened to her.'

'Well...'

'It is okay. I would be curious, too. You see the tributes all
the time, the bunches of flowers, mainly at the side of the road,
the places where the bad thing happened. You don't usually see
the person who left them.'

'That's true,' I say. There's something about this woman that
draws me in, makes me stay when I should be walking away.
Beneath the sadness that melts her dark eyes is a quiet fortitude
that reminds me of my own shortcomings. I indicate the bench.
'Do you want to talk about your sister? Please say if you don't
and I'll scuttle off right now and leave you in peace.'

She smiles in reply, sits down on the bench and pats the
space next to her. 'My name is Giada.'

'Fran. Francesca, really.'

Giada inclines her head and looks at me. 'You are not
Italian?'

'Ah, no. My mother just liked the name.'

Giada nods and rests her hands loosely in her lap. 'It is a
while ago now, since it happened. Three years come October.
They said she took her own life, jumped to her death, from this
place. High Heaven it is known as, right?'

'Yes, that's what we call it. You aren't from around here,
then?'

'No, I drove from Brighton, early. I went first to where she lived, just to look, you know? There have been two birthdays since she died. I took flowers to her grave, both times. But today...' She shrugs. 'I don't know. I think I should be brave and come and see this place for myself. I haven't before. I think I must walk in her footsteps, here... not over there.' She points towards the grassy rise, beyond which is the unfathomable drop. 'There, I just imagine.'

'I'm so sorry,' I say, feeling worse than useless. 'It's not an image you want in your head.'

Giada smiles, but her eyes are clear, her chin determined. 'It is fine. I am tough. There is no other way to be, is there?'

I don't reply. I let Giada talk, and as she talks about her sister, a picture is forming in my mind, outlines at first, pencil marks, like the artist made on his pad, and gradually the lines strengthen and the colours wash in, the shapes fitting snugly against one another, explaining the spaces, making sense.

And I know why I have come here today.

'My sister fell in love. He was married, and she thought he would leave his wife for her. What she did was against her beliefs, against everything she stood for, but she couldn't help herself. She worked for him, in the family house. She had no man in her life, but she had a child of her own, a beautiful little boy, Luca. He lives with me and my family now. We take care of him.'

My eyelids are hot with gathering tears. One escapes. Giada sees before I have the chance to wipe it away.

'I have made you sad,' she says.

'Yes, but not as sad as you.'

Giada straightens her shoulders, stares straight ahead. 'This is why I do not believe, you see. Because she had Luca.'

'Believe what, Giada?'

'That my sister took her own life. She was desperate for this man. He captured her heart, and he broke it. When he and his family moved here, to Oakheart, she moved, too. I did not realise at first that she was following him. She said she liked the village and it was time she made a home for her and Luca. I agreed. I missed her, but she needed her independence, and I thought it would be good for both of them.'

'That's a pretty drastic step, moving house to be near him.'

Giada nods ruefully. 'She said he was the love of her life, but she was never happy. How could she be when he belonged to somebody else? He made her promises, promises he had no intention of keeping. That is the impression I had. She did not tell me his name, or anything about him. But I knew she could see nothing but him. Except for Luca. Her son was always in her mind, in her heart.' Giada turns back to me. 'But there, that is what they say. That she must have jumped, from the edge. I tell them she was unhappy in love but still she would not do such a thing. I tell them over and over. But there was nobody to say anything else. It is different now, there does not have to be complete proof, only that suicide was probable. I do not blame the court for labelling her death that way, but it does not help.'

I let a silence fall between us before I ask the question, even though I already know the answer.

'What was her name, your sister?'

'Her name was Maria.'

Giada leaves before me. She has to drive back to Brighton to be home for her family, which I now know includes Maria Capelli's son, Luca. Before she goes, we share a hug, and she thanks me for letting her talk about her sister. As the sound of her car dies away, I sit on the bench, watching the vivid petals of the bouquet fluttering in the breeze, and feel like an absolute fraud. Giada opened her heart to me, and I didn't admit that I knew of the tragedy, and that Maria was constantly on my mind. How could I? But if Giada took some comfort from having a willing listener, my visit to High Heaven has been fruitful, just not in the way I had planned.

As I trudge down the path to the cindered car park, I start to imagine the circumstances of Maria's death in a way I have not dared to imagine before. Did Tessa deal with her in the same way she dealt with me? Did she issue the same kind of ultimatum, which drove the poor woman to despair? But Maria didn't have a husband or partner, so how would that have worked? Perhaps Tessa threatened to tell Giada and bring shame on the family, or to spread the gossip among people in the community where they lived at the time. The church may have been a factor: Giada implied that Maria had beliefs, which I took to be religious.

It wouldn't have been the same, though, without a husband involved. The impact of the ultimatum would surely not have been enough to force Maria into committing suicide, especially as she was a mother, as Giada said.

My thoughts wind on inconclusively. Was Maria clinically depressed? Was it her mental state which sent her on that fateful mission to High Heaven, the hopeless situation with Ben a contributory factor to her tragic end, but not the actual cause of it?

I can't get my head around this at all. By the time I've bumped the car down the lane and reached the hamlet of Lower Hovington, my grief for Maria has started up afresh, and I'm grieving for myself, too, for the dreadful mess I've made of everything. I may never know the truth about Maria, and I will always be sad for her. But I do have my life, and it is up to me to take control of it.

TWENTY-EIGHT

FRAN

Three days later, around eleven in the morning, I ring the doorbell at Rose Cottage, having dropped Caitlin off at Maisie's, as arranged. For the first time, I have reason to be thankful for the friendship between Hazel and Zoe, providing me with the information that the Grammaticus family returned home from holiday yesterday. I also know that Hazel texted Zoe this morning, suggesting they meet up today, and received by return a selfie of her on the train, on the way to London with her mother to do some shopping.

What I do not know is whether Ben has the rest of the week off. And I could be about to find out.

Having resolved to make some decisions this week and to return to work on Monday lighter and happier and ready to face the world again – a tad over-optimistic, but still – I have failed spectacularly on that front, and now I am acting more or less on impulse. Apart from Tessa, Ben is the last person I've wanted to set eyes on. But I can't just sit and think. My thoughts rotate like a hula-hoop, getting me nowhere except back where I started. Time is running out; I need to *do* something, even if that something turns out to be disastrous. I reason – if reason comes into it – that I can't be any worse off than I already am.

Even as my finger leaves the bell, I've convinced myself that Ben is not home, and I'm backing away, ready to fly down the path, having narrowly missed making a huge mistake – another one. But no, here he is, opening the door as fast as if he's been waiting behind it, and I am bathed in the familiar expression of pleasure and surprise as surely as if somebody turned a spotlight on me.

My stupid heart responds with a little jump, and an electrical tingle reaches the base of my spine. The feeling lasts only for as long as it takes me to snap it off and discard it, like a dead twig.

'Fran! Come in!' Ben holds the door wide for me to enter.

'No, thank you.' If I never set foot in Rose Cottage again, it will be too soon. 'I just came to ask if we could talk. Not now, not here, just...'

Ben's smile doesn't falter. He's got this all wrong, I can see that. Ben has trouble with reading people's faces and body language, I've noticed that. This will take careful handling.

He takes a step forward onto the doorstep, causing me to take a step back. 'What's wrong with now? I'm on my own, I've got all day. Come in, Fran.' He makes it sound like an order, but then he always did.

'No, I don't want to come in. It's not appropriate. I only want to talk to you about what's going on, that's all.'

Arrogant man that he is, Ben is still thinking I've come here for an entirely different purpose. I can't help that and I don't care. He'll find out soon enough. Now he's here in front of me, though, my doubts about coming here have fled and I do need to talk to him. I need to know if he is aware of Tessa's threat, for one thing.

'Okay.' He stretches the word out. 'How about I meet you in

the Pot and Kettle, where we had coffee before? In, say, half an hour?'

'God no. My daughter works there.'

'Well, if we're going under the radar...' He grins and widens his eyes a little. 'High Heaven?'

I almost shriek a 'No'. Ben's enjoying this, I can tell. I'm glad somebody's finding amusement in my misery.

Eventually, we settle on a small pub called the Black Sheep. It's in Lower Hovington, along one of the back roads. It has no garden, so doesn't attract families with children, and doesn't sell food other than crisps. It's a scruffy little place, the décor untouched for decades, the star attraction a dartboard that is more hole than board. We arrange to meet in forty minutes.

Ben is there before me. I almost turn round and go back home when I see his car, wedged half on the strip of road and half on the pavement – there is no car park – but instead I pull in in front of it and take a moment to gather myself after all the rushing around.

I join Ben on a squashed leather L-shaped banquette in the corner and accept a half of cider. I need something to steady my nerves. Ben has a pint of one of the only three keg beers they serve. There are two elderly men nursing pints at a table on the far side of the small bar, nobody else apart from the lugubrious landlord polishing glasses in slow motion.

'I wonder how this place keeps going,' Ben muses. 'Maybe it's a front for some sort of dodgy dealings.' He looks at me, expecting me to smile. I don't.

'I didn't want to do this,' I begin, 'but I'm in a quandary and you might be able to shed some light.'

'Quandary? What kind?'

'The kind that involves your wife holding me to ransom. She's threatened to tell Hector about us if I don't tell him first.'

'That's it?'

'What do you mean, "That's it"? Isn't that enough? When did she find out about us? How long has she known?'

'Some while, I imagine. You know Tessa. Nothing stays secret from her for long.'

I see red. I bang my glass down so forcefully I'm surprised it doesn't break. 'You *imagine*? Does your marriage mean so little to you that you don't know when your wife discovered you were unfaithful? It must have been a memorable event, surely! If you knew she'd found out, did you not think to warn me?'

'Does Hector not know already, then?' Ben says, turning the tables on me. 'Well, well, for a man of his intelligence I'd have thought he'd have worked it out long ago.'

'Right, so you think Hector would have blithely gone along to your house for dinner, knowing you and I had... well, you know? That he'd have associated with you at all? That my family would still be in one piece, for that matter?'

I can't believe this man.

'Well, Tessa invited him, all of you, to ours, didn't she?' Ben shrugs. 'Stranger things have happened.'

At this moment I'm hard pressed to think of anything stranger. Tessa obviously knew about me and Ben when she invited us to dinner, and had known for some time beforehand, hence the chilli-laced cake and the fake phone call – and the dead badger, aided and abetted by Mirabelle Hayward. My mind rewinds as I begin to view the past months through different eyes.

'Ben, has she always known about us, right from the start?'

'I don't know about *always*. We never had that conversation, not about you, anyway.'

Not about me. But about somebody else. Maria?

'No accusations, no scene, no drama? Is that even normal?'

'All marriages are different, Fran. I'm a man with needs; Tessa's always understood that. Don't make this into something it's not. Something it doesn't need to be.'

I drink some cider, put the glass down again, and bite my lower lip. I bite it so hard I feel the sting of pain. A maelstrom of emotion swirls inside me. How could Ben care so little about Tessa, let alone about me? And we haven't even got to the main purpose of this meeting yet.

I have a thought. 'You didn't tell her about us, did you?'

'Of course not.' Ben dismisses this with a wave of his hand.

'So how did she find out?'

'No idea.'

'Don't you care how she found out?'

He looks at me as if he's genuinely puzzled, and a little irritated with me for pursuing this. 'No, why should I? It doesn't matter now, does it?'

I blow out air. 'No, I don't suppose it does. That ship has well and truly sailed. Look, Ben, I don't know how you and Tessa operate, but my marriage is conventional – or it was until I met you, and how I wish I hadn't. Hector must *never* know, never, and I'd be grateful if you'd take this seriously.'

'You don't mean that. You don't wish we hadn't met.' Ben ignores my plea and latches onto the few words that are directly about him. 'Don't say you regret it. Remember how we were together, how wonderful it was? I would never have ended it if you hadn't insisted. I wish we were together now. I wish I could love you, like before.'

'It was lust, Ben, not love, you know that. Okay, there was a time when... look, I'm not going to analyse our relationship. That's not why we're here. I made a massive mistake, I jeopardised my marriage, and I take full responsibility for that. I could have said no, walked away, but I didn't. Now it's payback time, and it's my fault as much as yours. So, tell me what to do, tell me what happens next, because I'm damned if I know.'

'I still care about you, Fran. I've made it plain enough recently.'

I let out a big sigh. This conversation is so disjointed I wonder if Ben's taken in anything I've said at all.

'I hoped I'd imagined that,' I say.

He smiles, aiming it at my eyes. I quickly avert them. 'Remember, Fran?' he says softly. 'How lovely it was when we were together? How romantic, and exciting?'

And I do. I *do* remember, soured though the memory is. He doesn't have to keep reminding me.

We fall silent for a minute. Then Ben says, 'Did you like the flowers?'

Flowers? The basket of roses that came to the surgery with no card?

'Oh my God, Ben. They were from you?'

He gives a little laugh. 'Yes. Who did you think sent them? I didn't think I needed to spell it out. They were my way of telling you I still had feelings for you, still *have* feelings, and I think you do, too.'

'No. *No*, Ben.' My voice is stuck in my throat. Nothing else comes out.

'You came to me today.'

I swallow, shake my head to clear it. 'I came to you not because I wanted to but because I had nobody else to turn to. Tessa's your wife, I thought you might understand. I need to find a way out of this mess.' My voice sounds needy to my own ears. It shouldn't have to be like this. I shouldn't have to plead for help, not if I ever meant anything to him at all.

Ben moves along the seat, closing much of the space between us. If I could lean my head on his shoulder, take comfort from him, I would. He has no idea how strongly I'm fighting the urge to do that. I win the fight, shuffle away, fix him with as cold a look as I can summon.

'Well, what do you think I should do? Go on. You're the one with all the answers, apparently.'

'That's easy,' Ben says. 'Do nothing. Tessa won't tell Hector.

Call her bluff and carry on as normal. It'll go away of its own accord.'

This, now, is exactly what I want to hear. If only I could be sure...

'Do you really, truly think that, or are you just saying it to placate me?'

'I wouldn't do that, Fran. Believe me.'

Somehow, this time, I do believe him. I don't know why, given how the rest of this off-the-wall conversation has played out, but I do.

'Think about it,' he continues. 'If Tessa went to Hector and spilled it all out, the first thing he'd do would be to confront me, have it out, man-to-man, Tessa and I would have to talk about it, bring it all out into the open, and there you have it. One fan. One shedload of crap. Not gonna happen.'

'I had thought about that,' I say. 'If Tessa was going to split with you over me, she'd have done it long ago.'

And over Maria, too.

'Precisely. Tessa needs me. She's playing you, Fran. Don't let her have the upper hand.'

I fall silent, thinking. Ben is right about one thing; all marriages are different. The dynamics that work for some don't work for others.

I stand up. 'I'm going now. I would appreciate it if you would stay behind for ten minutes. I don't want to see you on the road behind me. If I had my way, I wouldn't clap eyes on you ever again. And while we're about it, don't even think about playing any more games. No loaded remarks, no looks, and definitely no gifts. Got that?'

'Got that.' Ben drops his gaze to the table. His penitence is plainly fake, in fact I can sense a smile behind it, but I have done my best.

I sit in the car for a few minutes, hoping Ben will do what I ask and hang back. I think about what just happened, and I'm already wondering if I wasn't too harsh with him. After all, it is true what I said. I could have said no. I could have let myself out of his car when he dropped us home after the ballet class and refused to accept his mobile number, adding a few stern words to allay any future misunderstandings. I could have exercised self-restraint. But I didn't, and that is my fault, not his. He had strayed before, with Maria, and heaven knows who else. Ben was a past master at infidelity; I was the rookie.

I got what I came for today – Ben's advice on the ultimatum, which seems genuine enough. And rightly or wrongly, I have to run with that. I have nothing else. I take out my phone and scroll to Tessa's last text message. No time like the present.

TWENTY-NINE

TESSA

Italy was wonderful, as I knew it would be. We have been before – to Rome and Florence, before Zoe was born – but never stayed on the Amalfi coast, and Positano was poster-perfect. It's a small price to pay that my calf muscles are still aching from climbing all those hills; it isn't called the vertical town for nothing.

We had thought about Italy for our holiday last year, and I think the year before – I can't remember whose idea it was originally, Ben's or mine – but somehow it didn't happen so I'm glad we made it this year. Zoe adored the hotel with its roof-top pool and has come home golden-brown; she has darkish blonde hair, not so fair as mine, and her skin is fortunately less delicate. She made friends with a girl her age and a boy a year older, both French, and had fun hanging out with them, which was good to see.

I loved our holiday, but I loved coming home as much. The house welcomed me in, and my first job was to check on the garden to make sure the gardener has watered sufficiently. He's usually reliable, but I trust him only as much as I trust anyone. The weather in our part of England has been almost as sunny and hot as it was in the Med. I was pleased to find the lawn and borders had been taken good care of, the flower-heads ripe and full, and giving off a heady sweetness. The charm of Rose Cottage goes some way towards making up for the shortfalls in my life.

By some miracle, Zoe has holiday money left, and is keen to pick up some new clothes to show off her tan – money to be topped up by her parents, of course, but that's fine. We decide to go all-out for our shopping trip and go to London, the day after our return from Italy. Ben, I sense, is keen for us to go and leave him in peace for a day. That's fine by me; there is a limit to the amount of togetherness one couple can accommodate. At least, I have always found it so.

Zoe is on her fourth circuit of Topshop in Oxford Street while I stand dutifully near the changing rooms, holding a bundle of items she's already chosen, when I hear my phone beep. I can't help smiling when I see her name come up. It's about time.

> You can go on waiting. I will not tell Hector. I won't dance to your tune.

I guess I'm not that surprised at her reply. It's not as if she hasn't taken risks before, is it?

Well, okay, Fran. You take your chances if you want to.

I do wonder, though, why she has replied after all this time. I'd decided she wasn't going to – when I'd thought about her at all. Francesca Oliver is a first-class bitch, not the sort of person I want haunting my mind for long, wrecking a perfectly lovely holiday. Anyway, I'm bored with it now, bored with her, fed up with the whole thing.

Which doesn't mean I'm giving up, letting go. Oh no, she will get what she deserves. I will pursue her until she breaks.

Zoe's back, snipping off the thread of my thoughts. She joins the queue for the changing rooms and tries on an armful of garments, of which we buy around a quarter before we head off for a late lunch.

It is not until we're on the train home that I allow that woman more space inside my head. But soon I find myself thinking about Maria Capelli instead.

I had no idea Maria had moved to Oakheart until one day Ben and I passed her in the car as she came out of a shop in the high street. Ben was driving and we were heading for a place on the outskirts of the village to look at wood-burning stoves, as I remember. Ben didn't seem to notice her, or if he did, he didn't say, but my heart thumped as I instantly recognised her.

I said nothing to Ben – I needed to find out more first. Was she just visiting the village, passing through, with no thought as to who lived there? Unlikely. Or had she come looking for Ben, hoping to bump into him? That would have meant her risking bumping into me, of course. As it turned out, Maria apparently had no compunctions about seeing me again, since she'd actually moved to our village. It didn't take me long to establish that; I sometimes think I'd have made a good detective.

The shop I'd seen her come out of is half deli, half greengrocer's, selling organic fruit and vegetables, speciality meats and cheeses, artisan breads, pots of olives, that kind of thing. Select, expensive. I would have thought the supermarket was more in Maria's line. I'm quite a regular and I called into the shop the day after. As I paid for my purchases, I asked Marcus, the owner, if he remembered a petite Italian woman coming in the day before. I'd seen her as I drove past, I said, and recognised her as a friend from way back.

He did, as it happened. She had asked for a particular Italian cheese, one they didn't stock. He'd promised to try and get some in for her.

I smiled. 'That sounds like her. She liked to have things that reminded her of home.'

I don't even know if Maria was born in Italy or was second generation, but it prompted Marcus to say more.

'Did you want me to pass on a message when she comes in again? Mind you, knowing what Oakheart's like, you're bound to run into your friend before long.'

'She's local then?' I asked.

'Not long moved here, so I gathered. Taken one of those housing association places, down by Tesco's.'

'Well then, that's where I shall find her,' I'd said. 'I'd like to surprise her, so don't tell her I was asking if she comes in.'

Marcus tapped the side of his nose. 'Mum's the word.'

Armed with my new information, I tackled Ben that evening, after Zoe had gone to bed. Not my usual style, no, but I needed to find out how much he knew, and what I could expect in the future.

'*What?* Maria Capelli is in *Oakheart?*'

His eyebrows shot up as his mouth fell open. The fake expression of shock was almost comical. *Nice try, Ben.*

I waited. Eventually, he let out a big sigh and rubbed the top of his head. 'Okay, okay, I knew she'd moved here. I hold my hands up to that.'

'You didn't think to mention it.' It wasn't a question.

'I didn't want to upset you. I know how you felt about her and what you decided went on between the two of us. Which, by the way, was all in your head. And in hers, as it goes.'

That was a new twist. Ben acting the victim, making out his fling with Maria was conjured out of her vivid imagination and misplaced lustful longing. Ben was playing me for a fool, but I decided to ignore it; the history wasn't relevant. It was the future I was interested in. Maria's in particular.

'Has she contacted you?'

'What?'

'It's a simple enough question.'

Ben had begun to pace the room. He had his back to me when eventually he answered.

'Yes, once, and I told her I wanted nothing to do with her. End of story.'

It could have been true, that Maria was obsessed with Ben and was, in effect, stalking him. Could have been. But my gut instinct told me it wasn't.

'You haven't been seeing her since she moved to the village?'

He spun round on his heel. 'Tessa, I told you. *No.* Why would I, since I was never "seeing her", as you put it, in the first place? Yes, she wanted to meet up with me, but she'll get over it. It's not all about me, you know. She could have many reasons for moving to the village. The environment, the schools, the... God, Tessa, stop this or you'll make me angry.'

His face had coloured up – with guilt, frustration and, yes, anger, directed at me for daring to doubt him; almost causing him to lose control, which for Ben was never an option.

'I think it's a little late for that,' I said coolly.

I walked away, leaving Ben to calm down, which he very soon did. Nothing is allowed to ruffle him for long.

We were quiet that evening, not speaking much, but the near-silence became charged with the unmistakable frisson of sexual tension. We made love that night by the soft, rosy light of the Tiffany bedside lamp. And, as usual, Ben was present, yet not present.

THIRTY

FRAN

Having had no response to my message to Tessa, I'm sensing a return to my old self – if I haven't forgotten what that was. The wariness, anxiety and fear are all still there, like a lumpy cluster of frogspawn lurking beneath the still surface of a pond, waiting for its moment to arrive, but I've trained myself to ignore them. First and foremost, I am a wife and mother. I have responsibilities, I have a life. I can't afford to cave in at the first sign of trouble.

I don't have quite enough flexi-time credit for another day off work, but Evelyn understands I want to spend time with the girls while they're on school holidays and we make a private arrangement between ourselves.

Taking Hector's car, which is bigger than mine, I drive my daughters to Brighton for the day. We stroll along the lower promenade among the August crowd, like proper day-trippers, as Kitty puts it, playing the machines in the arcades, shuffling through the racks of souvenirs, darting onto the beach every now and then to watch windsurfers, laughing at Caitlin as she goes into hysterics whenever one of them falls off and hurtles into the waves. We traipse up and down the pier, eating pink candyfloss that threatens to fly off the stick as the breeze picks up. Then, under pressure from the girls, I shell out for us all to go on the i360, in which we are raised up a pole inside a glass doughnut-shaped capsule to gaze in awe at the coastline spread beneath us.

Caitlin complains that the i360 is not as exciting as the London Eye because you can't see Buckingham Palace, and the others tease her by quoting my mother's favourite saying: 'Well, you can't have everything' – all the funnier when said totally out of context. I promise we will Skype Nan and Granddad tonight, and Caitlin can stay up late for the purpose.

It's a good day, quality mother-and-daughters' time, and I have a smile on my face as I drive us all home, stuffed to the gills with pizza we ate in a restaurant in town.

It is while I'm quietly tidying Caitlin's room – it's so late she fell fast asleep as soon as her head touched the pillow – that I discover a long white envelope beneath a pile of discarded clothes on the chair. It's addressed to the parents or guardian of Caitlin Oliver, and I remember it came home with her from art club last Saturday. Embroiled in the usual distractions, I forgot about it, and obviously so did she.

Art club has not so far been a problem. I would never stop Caitlin from attending – it would be impossible, anyway – but now she's used to it, all one of us needs to do is drop her off and collect her. Therefore, I'm not bothered if it's me who takes her rather than Hector or Kitty. I have other parents to chat to, including Maisie's mum, Afia, and I feel effectively barricaded against Tessa (and Ben if he happens to be around).

Tiptoeing out of the room, I slit open the envelope as I go downstairs.

'What's that?' Hector looks up from his chair.

'From art club. They're having an exhibition.'

'Already? It's only been going five minutes. Anyway, I thought the painting was just for fun.'

'It is. It's not an exhibition *as such*. Tessa is putting on a display of the kids' work and charging to get in, for charity.'

'Wow.' Hector chuckles. 'That woman'll be charging people to watch her having a wee soon.'

I laugh too, although the contents of the letter fill me with dread. I drop the piece of paper onto the arm of Hector's chair as if it's red hot. He picks it up and reads it.

'A raffle, lucky dip for kids, sale of books and art equipment, refreshments – pricey, no doubt – Cleo drawing portraits to order... well, I suppose all of that, added to the entry money, means she'll net a fair few pounds. Did you see what charity it was?'

'I didn't get that far.' I was already plotting what could possibly prevent us from being available on the day in question, a Saturday in just under three weeks' time.

'The donkey sanctuary, near Henfield. Crafty move. What kid doesn't want to save a poor old donkey from the knackers' yard? They'll all be clamouring to take part and dragging their families along.'

'Caitlin included,' I say, forgetting to restrain the grimness in my voice.

'Why not? She'll love having her paintings pinned up. I bet she's one of the best in that group, better than some of the older ones.'

This is true. Caitlin uses her time in art club wisely, and prolifically. She has a bundle of work ready to display. Three pieces maximum per child, the letter says. Her only problem will be choosing. *Whereas mine...*

The letter asks for adult volunteers to help set up the hall, and to run things on the day. Tessa can go whistle for that.

The paranoid part of my mind explores the idea that Tessa has arranged this event purely for my benefit, or rather, for hers, and I'm not talking about glory for herself here. Tessa knows full well that Caitlin will want to show her pictures, and that she will want her parents there. Both of us, a captive audience. My previous mood of almost-calm is showing cracks on the surface, cracks that will surely widen into deep, black chasms. And there isn't a damn thing I can do about it.

My feeling of helplessness burgeons when, the following day after work, I receive a phone call from Afia. Maisie, it seems, is keen for her mother to get involved on the day, so would I like to join forces and the two of us run the book and art stall? What can I say? I have no logical reason for refusing, especially as Afia has found out we would not be responsible for acquiring the stuff for sale – Tessa has that under control already.

Those two words 'Tessa' and 'control' uttered in the same sentence shoot ice through my veins. Okay, being on the stall would keep me busy, and not easily accessible, but would also leave Hector to move freely around the hall, innocent and unguarded.

I can't second-guess any of this. Tessa has proved how unpredictable she is, as well as downright vicious. Anything could happen on the day, and I await it with a prevailing sense of doom.

As it happens, the art club charity morning goes remarkably smoothly and without drama, unless you count my frequent visits to the ladies' due to nerves each time I see Tessa so much as glance in my direction. This is after the necessary interaction before the doors open, when Tessa makes sure Afia and I have all we need and know what we're doing – and reminds us to stow away our handbags and phones in a lockable cupboard in the kitchen area. 'You can't be too careful.'

Between bouts of sales activity, I am watching her, tracking her movements to see if she makes a beeline for Hector. As far as I can tell, she doesn't go near him, and after a couple of hours, Hec comes to say that if I don't mind, he'll head off home. It's with a hefty dose of relief I tell him that of course I don't mind, and yes, I will ring him if Caitlin wants to go home before I'm ready. I doubt she will; she's been with Maisie the whole time, plus some of the other children from art club, and is obviously enjoying herself. This is not such a big event that she feels over-whelmed, and she isn't amongst too many people she doesn't know, which can also cause her anxiety. I'm glad I didn't find an excuse to duck out, for Caitlin's sake.

Finally, it's over. Half the village turned out to support the event, the children have had a whale of a time, the donkeys will be eternally grateful, and Tessa can add another gold star to her personal success chart, which I wouldn't be surprised to learn existed in physical reality rather than as a product of mine and Grace's imagination.

There has been no sign of Ben the whole morning, and again paranoia kicks in as I wonder if he's stayed away to avoid me or, more likely, to avoid getting involved in any trouble. Until I remind myself that not everything involving the Gram-maticus family is about me, even if it feels like it is.

But drama or no drama, Tessa has again manipulated me and corkscrewed my brain. I expect she's crowing inside at the thought of that.

The following day, Sunday, I discover that messing with my head again isn't enough for Tessa. I'm sitting alone at the table on the patio with my coffee, the girls occupied in the house, when Hector comes out and hands me his mobile phone. 'Tes-sa,' he mouths.

My heart stops. I mime a questioning face at Hector, at the same time as muttering 'Hi, Tessa,' into the phone, which I can hardly keep a grip on since my hand is shaking.

'Sorry about that, Fran,' Tessa trills. 'I must have mixed up your two numbers and called Hector instead of you. I'm glad you're there, though.' A silence follows, a deliberate pause on her part, during which my fear escalates. Hector is still standing beside me. I glance up at him.

'What can I do for you?' My voice is light and friendly, for Hector's benefit.

'I wanted to thank you for running the stall yesterday. You made eighty-seven pounds! Isn't that marvellous? I've already called Afia and told her.'

'That's great,' I say breathlessly. 'I was pleased to help. I'm glad it went well.'

'It certainly did. I'd say it went very well indeed. Right, I'll let you get on with your day. Say "hi" to Hector for me.' She laughs. I hear it as a witch's cackle. 'Actually, I've already done that. Goodbye, Fran.'

I click the call to end it, and pass Hector's phone back to him.

'That was nice of her,' he says, having heard my end of the conversation. 'She rang to thank you for yesterday, I take it.'

I nod. Something gives way inside me. 'How come she rang you instead of me?'

'What? Oh, I don't know. Numbers next to one another on the list, I suppose.'

I feign a casualness I don't feel. 'I didn't know Tessa had your mobile number. She usually uses the landline if she calls here. She's only had my number a little while.'

'Search me,' Hector says, and heads for the back door.

'Hec?'

He stops and turns. 'What?'

'Nothing, doesn't matter.'

Hector shrugs and smiles, and goes indoors, leaving me to gasp inwardly at what almost happened there. I was going to say it, I really was, because the truth is, I don't think I can stand much more. I was about to tell Hector about me and Ben, and

Tessa's threat, spew the whole thing out, and then, possibly, fall on my knees and beg his forgiveness, and understanding. One nightmare would be over, the new one beginning no easier to handle.

I couldn't do it, though. I *can't* do it. It would destroy Hector, and destroy our family. I may deserve punishment – I know I do – but they don't, they really don't. I have to protect my husband and daughters, and the only way I can do that is to keep quiet, even though my secret is ripping me apart inside, piece by painful piece.

And so, Nightmare Number One continues.

THIRTY-ONE

FRAN

Tessa has Hector's mobile number. Unless I steal his phone and block her – the risk of getting caught in the act is too high, I decide – she can call or message him any time she chooses, wherever he is. It has crossed my mind that she could have gained access to him in any case by phoning his workshop, but Hector rarely answers the landline there if he's working, and half the time it is unplugged to allow some bit of electrical kit to be plugged in. This has never made much business sense to me but, as Hector points out, his primary links to the public are his website and business email, and the rest of his commissions come in on personal recommendation.

I have come up with a theory as to how Tessa obtained Hector's number – as if it matters now, but I have to do something to pass the sleepless nights away. Tessa was most insistent that Afia and I lock our personal belongings away during the art club charity morning. I had no reason to object to such a sensible arrangement. Why would I? But, of course, Tessa herself had access to the cupboard and my phone was in my bag, unprotected by a password as I never saw the need. It's the only answer I can think of, and now I know what kind of a person Tessa is, I know she wouldn't hesitate to 'steal' my phone for a few minutes.

As the days pass, I find myself leaning more and more on Ben's 'advice': *Do nothing... it'll go away.* All very well, but at what point will Tessa decide she's punished me enough and let it go? I have to draw on all my reserves, forage for every crumb of inner strength to stop me doing something stupid, like confessing all to Hector and threatening not only my marriage but my relationship with my daughters, who would surely be horrified if they knew what their mother had been up to. They may understand in years to come, when they've done a lot more growing up, but it would be too late by then, the damage done.

I try to imagine what my sister Natalie would make of it all. She's only two years younger than me and we've always been close. I shouldn't have to imagine, I should know. It depresses me slightly that I don't. She wouldn't judge my behaviour, not outwardly, and she'd be incensed on my behalf that I was being blackmailed. But inside, where the truth lies, would she be able to stop herself from being even a tiny bit shocked that her sister had been unfaithful? Would the idea that I have got what I deserved cross her mind, even for a second? I couldn't put her in that position; it wouldn't be fair. If I had any thoughts of confiding in my sister, enlisting her support, they're already gone.

I'm still thinking about Natalie as I stand at the kitchen window on Monday morning, watching Caitlin and Hazel setting up camp on the lawn with the old tepee we've had since Kitty was a toddler. Kitty herself is at work, at the Pot and Kettle. I'm home until two, when Hector will take over, then I'll be at the surgery until five thirty, making up the rest of my hours as and when I can. It's a cack-handed arrangement, but it works.

The tepee has acquired a few holes and rips in the fabric over the years, and is decorated with cowboys and Indians, which have faded into the buff background. Caitlin squeals with laughter as, for the third time, the wonky canes forming the ribs of the tepee collapse inwards. They're using our old tartan picnic rug, and, I notice, three of the best cushions, if any of our cushions could in any way be described as 'best'. Hazel rights the canes again and fetches Miss T, dumping her in Caitlin's lap. The cat immediately jumps off and stalks back to her original spot behind the hydrangeas.

I smile at the sight of the two sisters, sitting cross-legged on the rug, heads together in a moment of shared secrets. Natalie and I made camps; it was our favourite pastime in the long summer holidays. Our garden in Harlow was long and thin, and well-tended up until the last six feet or so, at which point our parents gave up and left the rest to turn into a jungle of black-berry thorns, dandelions and nettles. The advantage of this was that nobody inside the house could see what went on at the end of the garden, and so our camps, made out of old sheets slung over branches, were 'top secret'.

As we grew older and no longer bothered with the sheets, we still sat at the end of the garden in the long grass, appreci-ating our separateness from the house and Mum and Dad. When I was fourteen and Natalie twelve, we tried our first ciga-rettes there – I'd been given two by a boy at school, in fair exchange for a chaste kiss behind the canteen block. We didn't much enjoy our first attempt at smoking, although I think I told Natalie I did. My father saw the smoke rising, came marching up the garden, confiscated the cigarettes and matches, and hustled us indoors to face a lecture on the dangers of smoking – especially amongst dry grass.

Fun times, happy memories. I must talk to Natalie about that when we next speak.

While I'm in this nostalgic mood, which feels more melan-choly than it should because of everything else that's going on in my head, another memory comes to me. The scent of lemons filling our small kitchen. I thought of it back then as the scent of summer. As soon as the weather turned hot, Mum went into production, turning lemons and sugar into refreshing lemonade which she served from a green glass pitcher into matching glasses.

I can see her now, an apron over her summer dress, washing the lemons, peeling the rind thinly, then boiling it up in a big old saucepan with the sugar before adding the juice of the lemons – the same method her own mother used. The recipe said to strain the liquid through a sieve, but Mum usually didn't bother, fishing out the bits of rind with a slotted spoon instead. As long as it tasted good, we didn't mind a pip or two. Once we had wind of the citrussy fragrance, Natalie and I could hardly wait for the drink to cool sufficiently to be decanted into the jug.

I open the kitchen window and stick my head out. 'I'm popping to the village. Don't answer the door to anybody. I won't be long.'

'What for?' Caitlin says.

'Lemons.'

'Why do we need...?'

I close the window and go and find my purse before Caitlin can suggest she comes with me. I just want to get to the shop and back as fast as possible and brew up some old-fashioned lemonade for my girls, as Mum did for me and my sister.

It's as I'm passing the oak tree in the square, clutching a paper bag containing four lemons, that I hear my name. I don't recognise him at first – on this bright day the oak casts charcoal shadows beneath the spread of sturdy branches. I squint into the gloom and realise it's Ben, sitting alone, a newspaper folded virginally on the seat beside him. I give a slight nod towards him, slowing my pace but not stopping.

'Fran, here. Come and sit down.'

I wander across with a sigh. 'I can't stop. The girls are at home on their own.'

'They'll be fine.' He smiles.

'Why aren't you at work?' I say, standing a few feet away from him.

'Dentist.'

'Good luck with that then.'

'I've already been. Filling.' He aims a finger at the side of his cheek, which I can now see is a bit swollen. I also notice a slight slur in his voice. 'I'm waiting for the anaesthetic to wear off.'

'It's as good a place as any,' I say, cursing myself for allowing this conversation – any conversation – with Ben.

'That's what I thought. Fran, please sit down. I want to say something.'

I glance anxiously around the square. 'Where's Tessa?'

'At home, busy doing something or other. You're quite safe.' He flashes his eyes.

'That isn't funny,' I say, but I sit down anyway, at the other end of the bench.

'I'm sorry,' he says. 'About the other day. I wasn't fair to you. You were worried and I dismissed it. I'm very sorry.'

I wasn't expecting an apology. It doesn't sit easily with my view of Ben, and it takes me a second or two to regroup. 'It's okay. I suppose.'

'I'm sorry for the things I said about my feelings for you, and for sending the flowers. In fact, I'm sorry for anything I've said or done that has upset you. I really don't want that. I think too much of you, Fran.' Ben reaches out to me, then he pulls his hand back, obviously thinking better of it.

This is getting heavy now, but I don't get up and leave because, after our prickly conversation in the Black Sheep, I'm intrigued, as well as confused, to be shown this glimpse of the charming, thoughtful man I once knew. Or thought I did.

'Like I said, it's fine.'

A leaf drifts from above, curling out of the shadow to land in a wedge of sunlight between our feet. We watch it in silence. Then Ben speaks again, his voice modulated, pliant.

'Nothing's happened, I take it.'

'If you mean with Tessa and Hector, no, nothing's happened. Nothing's changed.'

'But it will, Fran, it will change. After a while, you'll see I'm right, that Tessa has no intention of telling tales to Hector, and the whole thing will vanish into the mists of time.'

'I sincerely hope that's true.' I allow myself a little smile at Ben's use of the mists' cliché. This, from such a pragmatic man, is as novel as his apologies.

I update him on the Hector/mobile phone number issue. Strangely, as I relate the brief story, it doesn't seem nearly as important now, nor as frightening. Ben certainly doesn't think it's anything to fret about, and reacts to the news with polite disinterest. I'm beginning to believe I can handle the Tessa situation after all, that some benign invisible force is handing me part of the control that was exclusively hers.

The church clock chimes eleven. I've been out longer than I intended; Hazel and Caitlin are home alone, and the lemonade-making awaits. I stand up. 'I have to go.'

Ben doesn't try to stop me. He smiles up at me, reaches for my hand, brushing it with his fingers before I have time to retract it. 'Don't be a stranger,' he says.

I don't feel I can leave without saying anything. 'I hope the tooth doesn't give you any trouble, when it comes to.'

Ben nods, and with that small gesture, releases me. At least, that's how it feels as I walk away.

'Why didn't you just bung the lemons in the processor?' Kitty puts her empty glass down on the kitchen table.

'Because I wanted to make it the proper way, like Nan did,

and your great-gran. No "bunging" involved. Anyway, if you include the pith it makes the drink bitter.'

It does taste good, if I say so myself. I was lucky there was half a glass left for me by the time I got home from work.

'Okay.' Kitty smiles absently and takes the biscuit tin down off the shelf.

The front door bangs. Hazel thumps along the hall and arrives in the kitchen with a squeal of rubber soles.

'Ooh, is there none left?' She eyes the empty plastic jug.

'Sorry, no. I've got two more lemons, though. I'll make some more tomorrow. Or the next day.'

'It tasted wicked,' Hazel says. 'I had some before I went.'

'Went where? Where have you been?'

'To Zoe's house. Didn't Dad say?'

I haven't had time to talk to Hector since I got home, but my stomach's knotting up for an entirely different reason.

'You've been at Rose Cottage?'

'Yes, I said. At Zoe's.' Hazel raises her eyes. 'We watched films in her room.'

'Films? On a lovely day like this?' Do I sound like a casually interested mother? *Do I?*

'She's got some new ones. She's been saving them until we could watch them together. Don't worry, Mother, they were suitable for my age group.'

That hadn't crossed my mind, which is fully occupied elsewhere. Mainly on the seat beneath the oak tree, with Ben, who seems to have inveigled his way back into my sympathies. I don't know how he does it, I really don't.

Hazel helps herself to a can of cola from the fridge. 'Zoe's mum always asks me how you are when I go there, but you never ask Zoe how *her* mum is when she comes here.'

I'm trying my hardest to hang onto my earlier placid mood in which the classic nightmare elements of pursuer and pursued have paled to almost nothing and the simple pleasures of life once more have a place. I have a feeling it's a battle already lost.

'What about it?'

'Nothing, I just thought of it, that's all,' Hazel says, frowning at my unduly curt response. 'I'm not saying you should ask her. It was just an observation.'

'What is an observation?' Caitlin wanders in from the living room where she's been watching TV.

Nobody answers her.

'Mum doesn't like Zoe's mum,' Kitty says.

'I never said I didn't like Tessa,' I say rather too quickly, as a sense of *déjà vu* sucks me deeper into the mire. 'It never occurs to me to ask Zoe how her mother is, that's all.'

'It doesn't *matter*. I was only *saying*, that's all.' Hazel flounces her shoulders, as if she hadn't kicked off the subject in the first place.

I escape the madness that my daughters so easily conjure up and go upstairs to shower in peace. But as the water cascades over my overheated skin, all I can think of is Tessa asking my daughter how her mother is, for what reason I can only imagine.

Later that evening, all of us except Caitlin, who is in bed, gather in front of the laptop and chat to my family in New Zealand. It was my idea; I hoped to recapture something of this morning's reminiscences. Natalie remembers even more about our garden camping escapades, including the smoking incident, and Dad chuckles over her shoulder in the background. Kitty relays my forays into lemonade-brewing, to my mother's delight.

'What happened to the set we used? The green jug and glasses?' I ask.

A pixellated chuckle twists from Mum's lips. 'Your father dropped the jug and smashed it. Don't ask me what happened to the glasses. They just went, I expect, one after the other. Nothing lasts for ever.'

THIRTY-TWO

TESSA

It's been a strange, unsettling sort of day. I'm not sure why, except Ben was home because he had a dental appointment, which meant my routine was interrupted. And he seemed a bit off when he came back. Not with me, necessarily, but quiet, quieter than usual, his face set as if he had something on his mind. I know that expression, and I know not to ask questions.

Zoe asked if she could invite Hazel to ours. My immediate reaction was to say no and dream up some activity that would not include a friend. But then I thought, it's not the child's fault her mother has no shame, and I don't feel like going out today anyway, so I told Zoe it was fine. They spent most of the time in Zoe's room, watching films, and I only saw Hazel in passing, just enough time to say hello and ask how her mother was, which is a habit I've developed and can't seem to get out of, not because I need an answer.

If anybody knows how Francesca Oliver is these days, it's me.

Dinner was a silent affair, and I felt I was the only one of us present at the table. Ben spent the whole meal looking past me at the television news – I've always meant to get rid of the smaller set in the dining room but somehow never got round to it. Zoe had her phone out on the table. I didn't tell her to put it away or stop responding every time it beeped; there didn't seem much point.

I came upstairs a while ago, and nobody seems to have missed me or come to see where I've got to. Normally it wouldn't bother me but sometimes, like now, it would be good to have somebody to talk to, somebody who is there just for me. Somebody I can tell my darkest secrets to. Not my family, obviously, but somebody.

My hand automatically reaches for the drawer in the bedside cabinet, and I find myself holding Caitlin's pink notebook. After my discovery about her mother's claustrophobic tendencies, I didn't find much else of interest. I don't know why I kept it really. Sitting on the bed, I thumb quickly through the pages. From the middle onwards, the pages are empty, but I flick through to the end anyway. And that's when I find the drawing – a pencil sketch filling the whole of one page, drawn with care, style and skill. Young Caitlin is the star of my art club. She demonstrates real talent for drawing and painting, and I have found myself wishing she didn't have such a bitch of a mother.

But there it is, nothing will change that.

The drawing is of a house, their house – I recognise its uncompromising squareness – and there is a tiny face at each window. Five smiling faces. The Oliver family. It's a smug little image of domestic bliss. Even the cat sitting on the doorstep looks happy.

Something shifts and buckles inside me, a softening, melting sensation, like marshmallow. My brain resists, just in time, reshaping, hardening the shell against signs of weakness. I take a firm grip on the notebook and rip out the pages until all that is left is a ragged bunch of paper, and then I go to the en suite and drop the lot, including the ravaged pink cover, into the waste bin. Nobody will notice and wonder what it is. Ben certainly won't.

Back on the bed, I fumble inside the still open drawer, idly sifting the contents while knowing exactly what I'm looking for. The envelope emerges as pristine as the day I put it there. I open the loose flap and ease out the cutting from the local paper. *Coroner's court issues suicide verdict on Oakheart woman* reads the heading. The report is a clipped precis of the proceedings, concentrating on the name and age of the deceased – Maria Capelli, 43 – the fact that she was new to the area, and where she died. If anything, High Heaven gets more wordage than Maria does, as if the junior reporter decided its common name and the chalk pit closure with its link to Sussex's industrial past was of more interest than the woman herself.

Rereading the article, I feel nothing. These are the facts, in black and white. There's no disputing them.

Ben calls up the stairs. He's about to watch a murder-mystery we recorded, and do I want to watch it with him? I call back that I'll be down in a minute. Zoe is in her room but not in bed when I pop my head in. Her attention is split three ways, between the TV, her phone and a magazine draped over a cushion on her bed. I add a fourth diversion when I go over and kiss her, telling her not to stay up too late.

Then I go downstairs to spend the rest of the evening with my husband.

THIRTY-THREE

FRAN

I'm at work when I hear a faint ping indicating a text message. My phone is in my bag, and that's where it stays for twenty minutes or more. The surgery is hectic this morning, with end-to-end appointments and two emergencies. We're one vet down, too. David should have been back from his holiday in Madeira last night, but his flight was cancelled for some reason and he won't get another until later today.

I peer inside the blue knitted blanket that cocoons a beautiful grey Persian cat. His owner, a girl about Hazel's age, holds him close, tears pouring down her face while her mother tries to pacify her.

'He's going to be fine, darling,' she says, then looks up at me. 'His paw got crushed under a child's scooter wheel. He will lie across the pavement in everybody's way. Not the child's fault, of course, although she could have looked where she was going.'

At this explanation, the girl's tears increase. 'Will the vet see him soon? *Please?*'

The cat doesn't seem too bothered by his injury and wriggles his upper half out of the blanket in a bid for freedom. The girl clutches him tighter. 'Oh, look at his little foot – it's bleeding again!'

'Wait there. I'll see what I can do.' I trot through to the side room off one of the consulting rooms, where Rowena stoops over the scales, weighing a Pekinese dog which looks grossly overfed to me. Yes, Rowena will see the cat next. I return to reception and relay the welcome news. Mother, daughter and cat subside onto the plastic chairs at the side.

Evelyn has found time to make coffee, and I take advantage of what will surely be merely a brief lull to sit down at my desk. Remembering the text, I retrieve my phone and click on the message with one hand whilst holding the mug in the other. I'm fully expecting it to be Caitlin, reminding me yet again that we are going shoe shopping in Worthing this afternoon. If she's gone up another size, which I suspect she has, she'll be ecstatic at the prospect of more summer sandals as well as the promised new trainers, and won't be easily coerced into making do. My thoughts dwell hopefully on summer sales as I look at the screen.

It is not Caitlin's name I read there.

'You're going to spill that if you don't watch out,' Evelyn observes.

I hurriedly right my coffee mug that I've let tip perilously sideways, and set it down on the desk with a shaky hand.

'Everything hunky-dory?' Evelyn inclines her head towards my phone. She wants to peep but doesn't quite have the nerve.

'What? Oh, yes. It's nothing.' I click away from the message; the words are already branded across my brain with a red-hot poker.

> Fran, I don't think you understand the situation so I will make it clearer for you. Let's make the deadline the end of the month, 31st August. Tell Hector by then or you know what will happen. TG.

I'm beaten, well and truly. And I'm at breaking point. There is no convenient exit, no waking from this nightmare.

I can hardly put one foot in front of the other as I walk home after my morning shift. I stop off on the way to collect Caitlin from Maisie's house, turning down Afia's offer of coffee or a glass of wine and hurrying my daughter away as fast as is decently possible. Caitlin is puzzled and not very happy about this, but for once I don't try to appease her or divert her with chat. I walk silently home, my daughter trailing behind.

Kitty isn't working at the café today and has promised to stay with Hazel while I'm at work. I'm expecting to find my two eldest girls at home, but the house is silent. There's a note in Kitty's writing on the kitchen table, telling me she and Hazel have gone by bus to the swimming pool, and Kitty promises 'on her absolute life' to stay with her sister 'at all times'. They expect to be home by four and Kitty hopes I have had a nice morning at work.

Although I'd rather they'd have texted to check with me first, it's fine. They are responsible girls when they have to be, and actually I'm relieved it's just me and Caitlin at home. She will soon settle down to some colouring or something, leaving me to engage my brain on what is to happen later – or rather, what I must make happen. But God knows how. Do I talk to Hector here at home, where the girls, even if they don't over-hear, will catch the fall-out pretty quickly? Do I take him out, talk to him on neutral territory, with the added complication of leaving our daughters at home? Should I not attempt to talk at all but write him a letter instead? There is no manual on this, no set of instructions, no map to guide me, no rules.

How in hell's name am I supposed to do this?

I hear a thump from above that makes me jump as if I've touched a live wire.

'Hec? Is that you?'

'Yep. Up here.'

I tread upstairs, my heart heavy in my chest. Hector has our small case open on the bed and is layering clothes into it. For one crazy, panicky moment, I think I must have already delivered my shocking news – or Tessa has – and Hector is leaving me. For a second, I stand frozen in the doorway, staring at the case, and then an influx of adrenalin lifts me back into the real present.

'Where are you going?' My voice is high to the point of shrillness.

Hector immediately drops the washbag he's holding, comes over and wraps his arms around me. His touch brings a surge of emotion and I can hardly breathe.

'It's okay. Well, it's not completely okay but there's nothing for you to worry about. I'm going to Dad's. His neighbour rang me – Carol, that nice woman who keeps an eye on him. She's worried Dad's not coping too well, and the stubborn old fool won't go to the doctor. I'm popping down to see what's what. You don't mind, do you?' Still with his arms loosely around my waist, he looks into my face. 'Hey, what's up?'

I struggle to rearrange my expression. 'Nothing, I wondered what you were doing, that's all.'

'Ah.' My poor innocent husband releases me and returns to his packing. 'Right then.' He is distracted, probably more worried about his father than he's admitting to.

It's my turn to offer some comfort, as if I have the nerve to even try. 'George seemed really well when we were there. Hopefully it's just a little dip, a temporary thing. They do go up and down, the elderly. The same as kids.'

'Yes. I expect he'll be as right as ninepence by the time I get there. You'll be okay, you and the girls?' Hector halts his packing again and looks at me. 'Will you be able to manage with work? I'll try not to be more than a couple of days.'

I assure Hector we'll be fine. I can't at this moment force my brain to consider childcare – it seems such a tiny inconvenience compared with the bigger, technicolour picture – but I will sort out something. To my shame, I wish it was the start of term next week and the girls safely back at school.

'What about your work?' I harness my concentration and focus on my husband.

'Dillon will keep the workshop ticking over. I trust him, he's a bright boy.'

'That's all right then.' I sink onto the bed. I'm not sure my legs will hold me up much longer. 'There are some clean T-shirts downstairs, on the airing rack. Not ironed but still...'

Hector smiles. 'I'm all right with these.' He hesitates, narrowing his eyes at me. 'Are you sure you're okay, Fran?'

I summon a laugh. 'Of course! Shall I make you some sandwiches to have on the way? Have you got George's door key? It'll be late by the time you get there. He might be in bed. You won't drive too fast, will you?'

'No, I'll stop off on the road, grab something to eat. Yes, I've got his key. And no, I won't drive like a bat out of hell. Stop worrying.' He grins. 'But thank you for worrying, all the same.'

He sweeps me into his arms for a kiss. It takes superhuman effort to calm my racing heart as Hector presses me to him.

So, I am granted a reprieve, ironically by the very man whose life I am about to wreck. As I lie in bed alone, I consider the wildly ridiculous possibility that Fate – whoever or whatever that is – has intervened, a radical change will take place in the time Hector is absent, and the action I dread won't be necessary after all.

Little hope of that.

My mind switches to Ben and I wonder if I should make him aware of the latest development, show him he was wrong about Tessa, and that she was – is – totally serious in her quest to destroy me. But what purpose would it serve? Even if he was being kind to me when we met in the village, and that kindness was genuine, he's hardly likely to confront Tessa and ask her to back down, is he? He will stick to his view that I should call her bluff and wait for the whole thing to blow itself out; I know him well enough to predict that.

No, I can't tell Ben, nor enlist his help. It's his marriage, too, that's at stake, however unfair it is that the punishment should fall squarely on me and my family. But life isn't fair, is it?

THIRTY-FOUR

FRAN

Hector came home a few days ago. During the time he spent in Somerset with George he managed to persuade the old man to let the doctor check him out. He hasn't, as Hector had feared, succumbed to any form of dementia, but a few physical problems including high blood pressure have contributed to his weakening condition and made him a little confused.

Hector is setting up a care package, somebody to call in once a day to add professional backup to the kind neighbourliness George already has.

He makes phone calls and sends emails to the various people involved in the care package, as well as increasing the frequency of his phone calls to George. And I can't help feeling a little thankful this has happened, even though it's very wrong of me because it seems as if I'm glad my father-in-law is not in such good form as he was. I'm not, of course I'm not, but while my husband is busy with the important business of making arrangements for his dad, I know it's right to hold onto my secret a little longer.

But not much longer. I have just eight days left until the thirty-first. The clock ticks louder as it counts down the hours.

Meanwhile, my energy is focused on being one step ahead all the time in order to avoid running into Tessa. When Hazel says she plans to see Zoe, I get in first and tell her to invite her friend to our house. More often than not, the café in the park is their eventual destination to which there is a shortcut from Woodside Villas, so it's not unreasonable for them to set out from here. I can't prevent Hazel from spending time with Zoe, much as I would like to, but at least I can try to keep her away from Rose Cottage.

I don't have to pass the house on my way to and from the surgery, but the high street makes me nervous, and I use the footpath through the woods instead. When I need to go to the shops, I take Caitlin and sometimes Hazel with me as a barrier. I can be shameless in my use of my daughters if I have to be.

My heart performs a drum-roll every time Hector's mobile rings or beeps, and then, as he accepts a perfectly innocuous call or text, my legs almost buckle beneath me with relief until the whole 'will-she-won't-she?' cycle starts up again.

It's an exhausting way to live, being on the alert every waking moment. I stumble through the days in a miasma of guilt, regret and terror. All this for an ego trip; the potent, addictive sensation of feeling desired, and desiring. All this for a string of cheap thrills.

All this.

Then, with three days to go before the deadline, something happens which should throw my mind into even deeper chaos. Except it doesn't because, subconsciously, I have never lost hope that there will be a way out.

We need to talk, reads Tessa's text message. *Meet me at High Heaven. Tonight, 8pm. Do not under any circumstances reply to this message. I shall expect you there.*

On this occasion, she hasn't added her initials, which is

always pointless anyway. I take a moment to wonder why I am instructed not to reply and can only imagine it's because she refuses to enter into a conversational dance with me. Tessa's control must be absolute, and uncompromised.

The time, eight p.m., could not be more inconvenient. The place – well, the same really. Why she couldn't have made it daytime, in the hidden square with the ivy-draped walls where we met before, I have no idea. Nobody disturbed us there, and I didn't have to make up an excuse to be out of the house.

I set the logistics aside in a flash as one word flames up in my mind: *rescue*. Tessa has not exactly come to her senses, but realised the price she's asking me to pay is way too high. She has something else in mind, something I can perhaps comply with. I'm not in such a dreamworld as to believe she will let me off completely, and truthfully I don't care. If I don't have to spill all to my husband, that's enough for me.

THIRTY-FIVE

TESSA

I wish I hadn't reread the newspaper report on Maria Capelli's death – I don't even know why I kept it now. She's been on my mind ever since, and that is not a pleasant experience.

Looking backwards is not something I do readily, and yet I find myself constantly drawn back to my discovery of Ben's infidelity with Maria, recalling with agonising clarity the eruption of rage, spewing white-hot lava to fill every cell of my body while on the surface I exhibited a tranquillity that seems impossible now. In that moment of recognition, I could easily have taken the cord of the vacuum cleaner, wrapped it round her dainty neck, and tightened and tightened, until... A lesser woman might have done just that. A crime of passion, they'd have said. If such a thing exists these days.

I don't want to think about that day, but I can't seem to stop. Neither do I want to think about the day I saw Maria in Oakheart and knew she had followed Ben, much as he denied it. Much as my husband denies anything that spoils the illusion, anything which detracts from Ben the charismatic charmer, the carer, provider and lover.

Lover.

Ben doesn't love me; has never loved me, except maybe at the beginning of our relationship. He needs me, which is not the same thing at all. Scarred by his tragic home life – the suicide of his mother, his father's coldness and eventual death in a car crash – he saw something in me that signalled safety and stability. The fact that he chose to ignore my own troubled background, has never once alluded to it in all the time we have been together, points to a self-centredness as glittering and hard as a diamond chip.

Yet, for all his faults, I love him. Unconditionally, the way a mother loves a child. Is this how it's meant to be? I don't know. I'm not sure I know anything any more, apart from this: I have lost my mother, my father, my sister. I almost lost myself in the process. I cannot lose anyone else.

I sit among yellow cushions on the turquoise sofa in my beautiful living room. Beyond the window, a song thrush gives its final, bittersweet performance of the day. Otherwise, all is silent. Zoe is at a sleepover at Tayler's house; I dropped her off there earlier and when I came back, I was surprised to find Ben's car missing and no sign of the man himself. There was no note or message.

It took me a while to establish that he hadn't texted or called, because I couldn't immediately locate my mobile phone. I knew I didn't have it with me when I took Zoe to Tayler's, and I hadn't used it all day. When I did rouse myself to go in search, I found it on the window sill of the upstairs landing, somewhere I never leave it. I expect either Zoe or Ben found it in the bathroom or somewhere, and put it on the sill in passing.

Where Ben is now, I haven't a clue. I'm not surprised he forgot to mention where he was going – he's had an air of distraction about him these past few days – and I'm not worried either. I don't suppose he's gone anywhere in particular, just for a drive about, probably, as he does occasionally. As I do myself, when I want some thinking time.

Maria once more invades my thoughts. I sit a while longer, mulling this over, wondering why I'm caught up in the past. Maria has gone; I have no need to think about her any more, and yet I do. I try to stop the train of thought from taking over completely and ruining the rest of my evening, but it leads me on, unrelenting, until High Heaven comes into my mind's eye, and my mental meanderings set me on a different path.

The antique long-case clock in the hall ticks on. Where *is* Ben?

My phone sits on the arm of the sofa. I bring it to life and scroll the messages again, this time for Fran's name, and find a new message, sent to her today. But not by me.

And I know where Ben has gone.

THIRTY-SIX

FRAN

I have no choice but to line up Grace as my alibi and pray she won't be called upon to corroborate it. Picking up on my tone, she asks me if everything is okay. With fingers crossed, I assure her everything's fine and promise I will explain later. Reluctantly, she lets me go, and the question hangs in the air long after the call ends.

My second problem is the car. I've said I'm going to Grace's house because she wants to talk to me about something – I couldn't go full out and say it was a girls' night as I don't expect I'll be gone for long. But Grace's house is near enough to walk to, and Hector knows – or thinks he does – that there'll be a glass or two of wine involved.

It's said that if you must lie, keep it as close to the truth as you can. I'm thinking about this as I pull on a grey hoodie over my jeans and T-shirt. Should I have said I was meeting Grace at High Heaven? It would sound so unlikely that Hector would be sure to question it. And even if he did believe it, he would be worried about me going there in failing light with the danger of the unfenced drop. I haven't got the strength, nor the time, to counter this and assure him I'll be perfectly safe; it's already twenty to eight. Besides, it's too late to change my story now.

I'm held up further when I'm called upon to referee an argument between Kitty and Hazel over the ownership of a pair of earrings, and then Caitlin demands to be told exactly where I am going, why, and what time I will be back.

'To see Grace. I won't be long,' is all she gets, before I bolt out of the front door.

My nerve-endings are already ripped to shreds by the time I jump into my car and dash off, past caring whether Hector has noticed I'm driving. The only thing now, I tell myself as I make it out of Woodside Villas, is to focus on Tessa and what could be the most important meeting of my life.

By the time I bump the car up the uneven track towards the car park, I'm almost calm. My mind projects forwards, past this meeting, to the future: a future in which my secret remains under lock and key, Hector still loves and believes in me, and I have nothing to fear from Tessa Grammaticus. I even go so far as to imagine my guilt over the affair assuaged – if not totally, then diminished to a tolerable level. Whether I deserve that luxury is not an issue, not at the moment.

On the way up the track, I pass a man with two dogs walking down. He yanks on the dogs' leads and stands to the side to let me pass safely, and we wave and smile politely at one another. No one else seems to be about, and there are no cars in the car park. If this is another of Tessa's little tricks, I'll be furious. I hadn't considered that possibility, but at six minutes past eight, it seems all too real. I park neatly in one corner of the cinder patch, even though there's plenty of space. I sit and wait, but at ten past eight, there's still no sign of my adversary.

I decide to give her until twenty past, and then leave. It'll be a nuisance having to drive around until it's a reasonable time to reappear at home. Even more of a nuisance – no, a disaster – to end the evening with nothing resolved, and the sword above my head swinging even closer.

I take a deep breath, snap down the mirror above the windscreen, and fiddle pointlessly with my hair. And that's when I see it – the car I hadn't heard approach, its tyres crunching as it turns off the track into the parking area.

It isn't Tessa's car. Hers is white and this one is metallic grey, like Ben's. I push back rising panic. Perhaps Tessa is using Ben's car; I expect she does sometimes, as I use Hector's. I'm still staring into the mirror at this point. Now I take courage, snap it back into position and turn round in my seat.

The car is definitely Ben's. The driver is not Tessa, but Ben himself.

Our gazes meet midway; mine, I'm sure, confused, Ben's inscrutable. He stops his car behind mine and gets out. I'm tempted to drive off, but for one thing he's parked in such a way that it would take me a few minutes to negotiate my exit, and for another, I want to know what he's doing here, and what the hell is going on. So I get out of my own car as he walks towards me.

'Fran, you came.' He smiles. 'Thank you.'

'No, Ben. I didn't come to meet you. I came to—'

'Meet Tessa. I know.' He drops his gaze. 'I had to make you think you were meeting her. If you'd known it was me, you might not have come.' He stands, hands in pockets, looking pensive for a moment. Pensive but not uncertain. Not Ben. I can't speak. My head is all over the place. He smiles. 'You would have come anyway, though, wouldn't you, Fran.'

It's not a question. But I have plenty of my own.

'Why have you tricked me into coming here? Ben, what's this all about?'

'I had to see you,' he says, as if it's obvious. He turns and walks the short way to the car park exit, then stops and holds out a hand towards me. 'Let's go up on top. We can watch the sunset.'

'For God's sake, Ben! I'm not here for the view! I thought I was coming here to talk, to sort things out with Tessa.' Even as I say this, my treacherous feet carry me forward, following Ben.

He waits for me to catch up, then goes ahead, up the path and across the turf where he stands and waits again. I march forwards, facing him, adrenalin pumping. 'Where is Tessa? Does she know you're here, with me?'

'I sincerely hope not. Although...' he shrugs. 'No, she doesn't. I saw the text she sent you, though. Four days until she drops her bombshell on Hector? So she says.'

'Ben, you might be in denial over this but I'm not. Yes, the thirty-first is the deadline. I told you she was serious, and you did nothing to help. You just let me get on with it. Okay, maybe I deserve that, but this is not fair. Tricking me into meeting you, manipulating me. It just isn't fair, not on me and, as it goes, not on Tessa either. Much as I dislike her for what she's doing to me, it wasn't her fault what we did, and she shouldn't have had to suffer. Have you got no shame at all?'

'Fran, my lovely, I thought we were okay, you and me? When we met in the village and had that little chat, I thought we'd reached an understanding.'

Understanding? What planet is he on? But this is Ben. He hears what he wants to hear. Puts his own spin on everything. He speaks again before I can form my next sentence.

'This is our special place, remember?' He smiles into my eyes. 'Of course you remember. You are all I think about whenever I come here.'

I step backwards, away from him, shaking my head. 'High Heaven was never our special place, Ben. Okay, we met here the first time, and a couple of times afterwards. We never had a "special" place, just hideouts, shameful places where we thought we were safe. You're romanticising the whole thing –

fantasising. In fact, if *you* remember, this is where it ended. Where I told you we had to stop.'

'And we did stop,' Ben says. 'Except I came back here, many times, to think about you, feel close to you.' He gives a self-deprecating smile.

After all this time I can't believe he hasn't let this go – the comments he made on Worthing pier, the pointed looks, floral offerings notwithstanding. This is different. I want to tell him to grow up, get over what was a massive mistake in the first place, think about his wife and child, if not about me and my family. I want to take him by the shoulders and shake some sense into him. I don't. Arguing will only delay things, and I can't wait to leave. But there's one thing I need to know.

'Ben, what did you hope to achieve by getting me up here on false pretences? You must have known I'd be angry about it.'

He flinches, and I realise he can't tolerate anger directed at him. He quickly recovers.

'I want you back, Fran. That's why we're here. Remember how good it was between us? How we couldn't wait to be together, couldn't keep our hands off each other?' My turn to flinch. 'It's still there, Fran, what we had. I will leave Tessa, if that's what it takes.'

The hope in his eyes is painful to see. He's delusional. He really believes this nonsense.

I soften my voice, moving nearer to him, although I'd rather run a mile in the opposite direction. 'Ben, there is no going back, not to how we were before, or anything else. I thought you understood that. We can't be together. I never wanted that, and neither did you. I don't love you; I love Hector. Besides, it was so long ago, more than two years now since we... started that foolish affair.'

He smiles sadly. 'As if it was yesterday.'

The light is fading now. There are clouds overhead, but there is enough clear sky to show colour above the horizon where the sun dips low. Gold, pink, apricot, cobalt, melt into one another. Shadow-shapes form and reform, smoke-like, across the darkening landscape.

Ben walks towards the cliff edge, where bone-white chalk falls away to the blackened hollow. He stands, gazing out.

'See the sunset? Glorious, isn't it?'

'Ben...'

My voice tails off. I'm thinking of that September evening when I asked him to meet me here, and I ended the affair – or I thought I had. Reluctantly, painfully, I recall his desperation, his talk of suicide pacts. Wild talk. Melodramatic. He apologised afterwards, but what is said cannot be unsaid.

Seeing him standing on the edge of the precipice, I fear for him more than I fear for myself. I say his name again, but he doesn't seem to hear. I move to stand next to him, linking my arm with his. He looks at me in surprise, as if he'd forgotten I was there.

'Ben, I'm sorry if I've not made it clear how I feel, although deep down I think you know. There's no point in continuing this. Come on, let's go home. It's time.' I smile, as I might smile at a child I'm trying to cajole.

I tug gently on his arm to get us away from the edge. He holds firm, his muscles tensing to hardness.

'No! I won't let you do this again, Fran. I won't let you walk away. That is *not* how it works.' His eyes bore into mine, glittering with intensity. '*I* say what happens, not you.'

My stomach quakes. I pull my arm from him, move a few feet away and turn sideways, but when an irresistible magnetism draws my gaze back, Ben's steely outline is furred with a kind of defeat, his arms hang loosely by his sides.

'Come on, let's go.' I hold out my hand to him. It will be all right. I could walk away now and chance he won't follow me. But I can't leave him, not like this.

'It's always the same,' Ben says, in a voice so quiet I hardly hear. 'Love me. Leave me. You never learn. You're all the same.'

All? My mind swings to Maria, a lead weight, landing the truth at my feet.

'Were you here with Maria, when she...?' I have to know, whatever the outcome, however dangerous the conversation.

'*Maria?* What do you know about *her?*' His voice is scathing, but somehow I'm no longer afraid.

'Maria Capelli. You had an affair with her, before me.'

'Who told you that?'

'Never mind who told me. It's true, isn't it?'

'So what if it is?'

'So nothing. It doesn't matter, it's all in the past.'

I have Ben's full attention now, and as I'm speaking, I'm moving slowly backwards across the grass, away from the point of potential danger. To my relief, Ben moves with me.

We're among the bushes now, almost at the bench, and I feel able to continue this enquiry. I think of Giada leaving her lonely bunch of flowers in this very spot, the blackened stalks of which still lie on the ground beside the gorse stump, and my heart puckers. I need to know the truth, and it has to come from Ben himself.

'I asked if you were up here with Maria, the night she committed suicide. Tell me, Ben. Tell me what happened.'

Silence.

The sun has sunk below the distant hills. Inky darkness heralds the birth of night. A sudden breeze rustles the scrub of bushes. A minute passes, the longest minute, and still Ben doesn't speak. And in that silence, I begin to understand.

Maria came to High Heaven to end her affair with Ben, just as I did, not to plead with him to be with her. She'd followed him to Oakheart, as Giada said, and Ben, unable to resist, took up with her again. Then everything changed, Maria realised how hopeless the situation was, and decided to end the affair once and for all. Perhaps Tessa had a hand in things, perhaps she didn't. But Maria took the only course of action possible; she did the sensible thing and told Ben it was over.

Only he couldn't accept it. He couldn't let her go. Ben has to be in complete control. Everything on his terms.

Giada didn't trust the suicide verdict. She was the person who knew Maria better than anyone. Maria may have found it hard to end the affair, but surely that wouldn't have driven her to kill herself.

I scan Ben's face forensically for clues, clues I desperately need. I can almost see the cogs of his mind working away behind his eyes.

My hands are clenched, the nails spiking into my palms. My voice comes as hardly more than a whisper. 'Maria didn't commit suicide, did she? That isn't how she died.'

Ben springs back to life. 'Of course it was suicide! Don't ask me why she did that, it was nothing to do with me. Fran, I don't know why you think I was here with her at the time. I wasn't. I was nowhere near. If I had been, don't you think I'd have stopped her?'

My turn for silence. He's wrong-footed me, made me doubt the version of the story my mind has put together using the available evidence, some of which is, admittedly, dubious. But still...

'If you're really that interested,' Ben continues, 'we did meet here, Maria and me. She told me it was over, and she walked away. But that was well before she did what she did.' A belligerence had crept into his tone, softened before he spoke again. 'I don't know what you're accusing me of here, Fran. Maria's death was nothing to do with me. Look, we haven't come here to talk about her. I want to talk about *us*, where we go from here. Let's not waste any more time, eh?' He smiles.

I'm so confused now, I don't know what to believe any more. Have I got this so wrong? Is Ben as innocent as he's making out?

I take a long breath, releasing it slowly to calm myself. 'I'm sorry, Ben, but I don't want to talk about us. There is no *us*. Go home now. Go home to Tessa.'

Ben opens his mouth as if to speak but no sound comes out. His shoulders are rigid; his eyes as he stares at me are hard, cold, and I need to be out of here. Now.

But before I can move, he whirls round on the spot, round and back. And before I can duck out of his way, he grabs me by my upper arms, and my legs are forced to move away from the relative safety of the shrubs, towards the edge of the cliff.

THIRTY-SEVEN

TESSA

Hector plumps into the passenger seat of my car and slams the door shut. The downstairs window of his house frames three anxious faces.

'They'll be okay,' Hector says. 'I called Grace to come and sit with them. She'll be here shortly. What's going on, Tessa?'

I repeat what I'd said on the phone, a rapid account, no details, giving him just enough to form the impression that his wife may be in danger. I'm taking a risk here; if I'm wrong and there's no sign of either Ben or Fran at High Heaven, Hector will think I've lost the plot. But since Fran has gone out somewhere and lied about it – which Hector knows as he's already spoken to Grace – it's a very small risk.

Hector shakes his head in denial. 'This can't be right. Fran wouldn't be at High Heaven at this time of night, it's not safe. She wouldn't put herself at risk.'

'Not knowingly, she wouldn't.'

'Why is she with Ben?' Hector says, as we fly through Lower Hovington. 'What's he got to do with Fran? I don't get it.'

I cast him a look and watch his face change. Inside me, a tiny fist punches the air.

'You're telling me that Fran and Ben... *He* was the one she was seeing?'

'Yes, that is what I'm saying. Sorry, Hector.'

'I knew it was somebody, at the time.' Hector looks stricken.

'You knew?'

'It didn't take a genius. I had no idea it was Ben, though. My God...' Hector slaps his forehead. 'Of course it was Ben. It all makes sense now. But surely he wouldn't let Fran come to harm? Anyway, it was over between them, long ago. The whole thing only lasted a matter of weeks, as far as I could judge.' He shakes his head in disbelief. 'Tessa, are you telling me they're still seeing each other?'

I don't reply. I just let Hector process the scant information he has, making goodness-knows-what of it. I just need to get him there. The rest will follow.

We hurtle up the track.

'Fran's car,' Hector says quietly, as if to confirm it to himself. 'And that's Ben's, right?'

'Yes.' I'd half-expected to find them together in one of the cars, which would have speeded things up nicely, but no. Both are empty. I feel a twinge of panic.

I stop the car, the wheels spewing up cinders, and we pile out. Hector gets a head-start on me, racing up the hill on light, fast feet. I catch up, and I realise with a jolt that my suggestion of impending danger was actually close to the truth.

It's almost dark. The sky is heavy with clouds, no moon or stars. Ben and Fran are silhouettes on the cliff edge. They appear to be locked together, but their embrace is not of the amorous kind. At the sound of our voices, their heads turn towards us.

Fran shrieks, an unnerving spurt of sound which reverberates around the chasm below. Ben stares at Hector and me before he faces Fran again.

We're within ten feet of them, and for once I have no idea

how to act, how to deal with this. Fran's voice reaches us as she addresses Ben. The words are lost but the pleading tone is unmistakable. Indicating to me to stay back, Hector inches forwards.

Hector the hero. I said he might yet surprise me, didn't I?

'Ben, let her go. Let her come to me.' Hector holds out his arms.

I move alongside Hector and call out, keeping my voice even. 'Ben, come on. You know you don't want to do this.'

'Don't I? *Don't I?*' Ben's voice splits the night air. *'There's nothing left!'*

In that nanosecond I know for certain what is really happening here, and I think, Why not? It's his life, he has the right to end it if he chooses. Then instinct kicks in and I rush forwards, stopping a few feet from him.

Hector is with me, and at the same time, Fran breaks from Ben and throws herself into Hector's arms. My eyes are fixed on Ben, but I sense Hector leading Fran away from the precipice.

'Ben?' I step carefully towards my husband. He's facing outwards, into the blackness of the sky. We're so close to the edge; the chalk beneath our feet could crumble and give way at any moment.

Hector is back, urging me to come away. His voice is all breath and hardly any sound. My heart leaps and bangs against my chest wall like an animal trying to escape from a cage. I take no notice of Hector.

'Ben?' He turns to look at me and I see the gleam of tears on his cheeks. I stretch out my hand. 'It's all right, it's going to be all right. Just come away from there, please.' With a silent gesture, I instruct Hector to move back and leave us. 'Ben, it's me, Tessa. Only me. Come on, love.'

Another long pause before, eventually, Ben takes my hand and lets me lead him down from the crest of the cliff and across the grass. Hector and Fran materialise out of the darkness, Fran a few steps behind her husband. I nod to Hector, giving him the message that I am all right, that the danger is past.

I hear the soft sound of an engine, maybe more than one, and we all turn to see headlights approaching as the police vehicles move slowly up the track. Ben wrenches himself from my grasp, half runs, half staggers, to the cliff edge.

Seconds later, he's gone from sight.

THIRTY-EIGHT

FRAN

Tessa's mouth forms an 'O' shape, but no sound emerges. I run to her, putting my arm around her shoulders, but she shakes me off. For a second I think she's going to follow Ben, and then her legs buckle, and she subsides onto the grass. I drop down beside her, and now she lets me hold her while her body rocks with silent sobs.

I'm aware of Hector talking to the police. I hadn't realised he'd already called them, but of course he would have. Tessa and I are left alone for a while, then Hector comes over to us with two police officers. I scramble to my feet, not wanting any help, not wanting to be touched, and tell them that I'm all right and it's Tessa they need to focus on.

For several endless minutes I was sure Ben was going to push me off the top of High Heaven, the same as he did Maria. The dismissive way he spoke about her, his obvious annoyance that I brought her up in the first place, fuelled my conviction that Ben killed her. I don't know why I ever doubted it.

As he forced me to the edge, he began talking very fast, the words tripping over themselves in their hurry to be released. None of it made any sense. I remember begging him not to kill me, over and over, but I couldn't stem the flow of his speech, which grew more intense and garbled as it continued. And then he fell quiet, while he still had hold of me, while we still had hold of each other. I didn't dare move. I didn't dare speak, in case I said the wrong thing, the thing that would trigger disaster.

After a while, he looked up to the sky, murmuring words I couldn't make out, as if sending up a prayer. When he looked back at me, it was as if he couldn't see me.

His next words were clear enough: 'It has to stop, all of it. I can't do this any more.'

I realised he no longer held me in a firm grip. His hands were on my forearms, but loosely, and I knew I could break away at any time, but I didn't let go of him. I began talking to him, quietly, calmly – I don't remember my actual words. I was so focused on trying to prevent him from leaping to his death that I swept aside any danger to myself. I wasn't being heroic, nor especially brave. My brain could only deal with one crisis at a time.

When Hector and Tessa arrived, I panicked, pleading with Ben to stay with me, while at the same time I could have prostrated myself with gratitude and relief at the sight of them. I might have screamed, but I can't be sure. It felt like hours before I felt able to let go of Ben and go to Hector, but it could only have been a matter of minutes. Had I held onto him, refused to leave his side, he might be here now. But I had no fight left in me, and Tessa was there.

We failed, the three of us. We failed to save Ben; me, mostly. In retrospect, there seemed to be an inevitability about the way it ended, as if Ben's fate was sealed from the moment he set foot on High Heaven tonight.

Sirens now, piercing the night air: police, ambulance, on the road below. A helicopter circling over the valley, lights pulsating. The thought of Ben's crushed body lying among the trees in the desolate chalk pit has me fighting back waves of nausea. The police activity around us seems to have increased. Tessa is sitting in the back of a police car, a female officer at her side. Her face is a moon-pale mask of shock. She is beyond tears. I find myself being led to a second car.

I turn to see where Hector is. He's standing by, watching, as if he's afraid to come near me. And then he does. And as we reach the police car, he gathers me into his arms and presses his lips to the top of my head.

'I thought I'd lost you.' His voice breaks. 'I thought you were going to be taken from me.'

I look up at him, and I know he isn't only talking about tonight.

THIRTY-NINE

FRAN, ONE MONTH LATER

It wasn't until we had given statements and answered all the questions the police had for us – a process which took place over several days following that catastrophic night – that Hector and I talked properly. Grace, by then being fully aware of what had been going on, sat with the girls one evening while Hector and I drove out of Oakheart and had a quiet drink at a familiar country pub. There, by unspoken mutual assent, we began the slow process of reconnection through general chat.

The days leading up to that had been chilly and difficult; I had no right to expect anything different. We acted our parts in front of the girls, but in private we used averted gazes and studious politeness as barriers. I longed to reach out to Hector but knew I must not deprive him of the virtual distance he needed.

I knew something else, too. I'd been incredibly stupid to believe that my unfaithfulness had gone undetected. There must have been moments when I'd looked a certain way, used a particular tone of voice, over-compensated to cover my guilt... tiny nuances that only the person closest to me, in every sense, would notice. After all, Tessa had known about Ben, which did not mean he'd been less than meticulous in covering his tracks.

I wonder why I'm not grieving for Ben; it would be natural to do so, in spite of what he did – what he was. Perhaps that feeling will arrive one day, come crashing in when I least expect it. For the moment, he is out of sight, a blind spot on my retina.

Hector was angry. Still is, I'm sure. Discovering it was Ben I'd been seeing must have invoked a paler version of his original reaction. There have been moments when I've caught him looking at me with something close to disgust, and at those times, when my heart turned inside out, I believed this was the end of us, and nothing I could do or say would change that.

After we left the pub, we sat in the car at the entrance to a shadow-swept field of wheat and carefully opened the metaphorical box containing our deepest thoughts and feelings.

It's not a conversation I want to revisit. Suffice to say we talked for a long time, afraid we might forget or leave something out which might in time reappear and fester. Ben's name came into it, of course. Hector banged the steering wheel with both hands as he said it.

'Ben, of all people! Somebody that close to us!'

It transpired that Hector had been thinking more along the lines of a man I'd met at work – a locum vet, perhaps.

'I'm not a saint, Fran,' he said. 'It wasn't easy to hold it together once it hit me that you were seeing somebody. I did it for the girls' sake. Whatever you'd been doing, I wasn't prepared to disrupt their lives to that extent. Because I love you, and I hoped that if I waited, you would come back to me. Which you did, in the end. I couldn't have gone on much longer, though. If it hadn't ended when it did – I sensed that, too, from the way you were – it might have been different.'

I told him how sorry I was, of course I did. But my apology sounded woefully inadequate and pathetic to my ears, and Hector stopped me with a nod and a squeeze of my hand. Yes, he is hurt, and will carry some of that with him for as long as it takes. For my part, I am beginning to see a time when I might be able to forgive myself. It is, as they say, a work in progress.

There was something I needed to check with Hector while I had the chance, something I already knew the answer to, but I wanted to hear it from him.

'Can I take it,' I said carefully, 'that my... what I did, will remain a secret between us, and there will never be a time when the girls might get to know?'

'They won't hear it from me, ever. I can promise you that.'

'Thank you,' I said quietly.

Hector continued. 'There is always the slim chance they might find out another way.' He looked pointedly at me.

'Tessa. Yes, I know. She's unpredictable, but she'll want to protect Zoe as much as we do our girls. It's highly unlikely she'd say anything about... me and her father. Especially now.'

'Highly unlikely, I agree. That's the best we can give it.' Hector gave me a half-smile which I could tell wasn't easy for him.

We sat in silence for a while, thinking about our daughters. At least I was, and I believe Hector was, too.

'We were right to tell the girls that Ben took his own life, weren't we?' I said eventually.

'Definitely. Who knows what gossip they'll hear in the village? Bad news travels fast. Anyway, if Tessa's got any sense, she'll have told Zoe the truth.'

'Yes,' I said. 'Poor Zoe.' I was thinking how hurt the child must be, knowing her father had left her in that devastating manner. But at least she would never know he was a murderer.

Hector and I had made a mutual decision to tell our daughters what happened at High Heaven that night. They obviously needed to be told something, and the following morning, we'd sat them down, Caitlin included, and given them the news of Ben's death.

ACKNOWLEDGMENTS

My heartfelt thanks to my writerly friends for never being too busy to chat, share experiences and help unravel the knotty problems. I couldn't be doing this without you. Thanks also to the lovely people who gamely read this book in its very earliest stages, in particular, Jo Bartlett and Susan Hope, and commented so usefully, and kindly.

A big thank you to Kathryn Taussig for seeing the potential in this book and taking me on, and to the rest of the amazing team at Storm who helped make the book the best it could be.

Thanks again for being part of this amazing journey with me and I hope you'll stay in touch – I have so many more stories and ideas to entertain you with!

Deirdre

 facebook.com/deirdre.palmer.735
twitter.com/DLPalmer_Writer

A LETTER FROM THE AUTHOR

Dear reader,

Huge thanks for reading *The Wife's Revenge*. I hope you were hooked on Fran's story. Sign up for my newsletter to hear about new books.

www.stormpublishing.co/deirdre-palmer

If you enjoyed this book and could spare a few moments to leave a review that would be hugely appreciated. Even a short review can make all the difference in encouraging a reader to discover my books for the first time. Thank you so much!

My books always begin with the tiniest seed of an idea, which in this case was the setting. Chalk pits are a familiar feature of the landscape around the county of Sussex where I live, a permanent reminder of the days when chalk and lime industries were key. We even have a museum dedicated to chalk quarrying! So, looking at the dizzying height of a chalk cliff-face and the sheer drop below it, I knew it was the perfect place for something dreadful to happen, and the story idea grew from there.

Once I'd finished writing the book, I realised that it's not only about danger and disaster, it's also about forgiveness. In particular, forgiveness of oneself, which is something Fran struggles with over the course of the story. And can Tessa ever be forgiven? As a reader you'll have your own views on that!

on part as loving daughter and sister. And when she comes home to Oakheart, the scars on her marriage already fading into obscurity... I will be waiting.